dirt

Also by Susan Senator

Making Peace with Autism

Autism Mom's Survival Guide

Susan Senator

dirt

a story about gardening, mothering,
and other messy business

Stellated Books

A Word To My Readers

Dirt has been in the works for about seven years. What started out as a hot-and-heavy exposé of life in the PTO and the suburbs (the original title was *Suburban Blue*) eventually became the story of a family in trouble. In writing this novel, I aimed to create a family of five equally important characters. I drew upon the voices of my three sons, Nat, Max, and Ben to get at the personalities of the brothers Nick, Henry, and Dan. Emmy and Eric, the parents and the other two main characters are drawn from bits and parts of people I know and people I imagine. What happens with them is fiction, although some of the conversations between Emmy and her sons are close to reality.

I was especially challenged by creating Nick, Emmy's oldest son who has severe autism and is barely verbal. Nick is based on my Nat but is not Nat any more than Emmy is me. The great thing about fiction is that it allows one to bend reality and truth to suit an author's vision. And so I envisioned Nick as almost a counterpart to Christopher, the protagonist in Mark Haddon's *The Curious Incident of the Dog in the Night-Time*, but representing the other end of the Autism Spectrum. I wanted Nick to be just as whole a person as Christopher, equally complex and likable, and to come alive as a real person with thoughts and emotions— a whole inner life. I don't believe there are many novels out there with a main character from the extreme end of the Spectrum. And if a severe autistic is included at all in a story, he is usually portrayed as a savant, mystery detective or oracle of some sort. Nick, on the other hand, is just a teen with severe autism, lovely, flawed, and human.

But the story is not just Nick. This is not an Autism Novel, although autism provides much of the salt in its flavoring. The intersection of the five people is the story, along with a few outside catalysts: Dan and Henry dealing in their own ways about their father moving out; Emmy feeling stagnated by her job and life; Eric not knowing how to connect with his family anymore. I wanted this story to convey truth, a real glimpse of a family struggling not only with autism, but also divorce, sibling rivalry, loneliness, and dissatisfaction with life.

Finally, the people in this book are alive to *me* and are real, but they only exist within these pages. *Dirt* is a novel, a work of fiction and any similarities to people or towns are coincidental.

Part I

Late February

Frozen Ground

Chapter 1

"Eye, heeem," Nick said. He reached up and touched his open eyeball, then blinked at the unexpected jolt of pain. The pain spread, flashing red light everywhere. He could feel the sharpness opening outward, and he silently endured it, waiting for it to subside. There were no sounds in his throat right now, and he was glad. His noises made Mommy talk to him, and there were always too many words itching deep inside his ears.

A few moments later, there was only a soft ache behind his lid, and he opened his eyes. They were clear again. He looked skyward, and his eyes followed the rays of the sun to where they hit the porch door. He liked the way the sunlight slanted when it went behind a cloud, like an eyelid closing. He shut his eyes and rotated his head until he almost couldn't see it. The light became a tiny ribbon, shining across the back of his eyes. Happiness coursed through him at the beauty he was seeing. "Heee, light," he said quietly. Every now and then, his own words appeared to him, and he could say them. Letting them out was like bubbles popping, like the ones Dan used to blow. Nick enjoyed the tiny sound of their pops; he felt he could hear the little click each breaking bubble made. Also that was how words came out of his mouth: a sudden, round pop in the air.

"Nick!Whatswrongwithyoureye?"

It was Mommy, and her line of words flew past his ears, like a sharp, stinging wind. He shut his eyes so that she would stop looking at him.

"What. Happened. To. Your. Eye?" Mommy said this the right way, with spaces of air between the words. Nick loved air. He liked to squeeze it with his hand—open shut, open, shut.

"Nick!"

Mommy was very close now. He could smell her skin, which he loved. It made him want to sleep. He knew she was waiting for him to talk, and his stomach squeezed itself. Then he realized Mommy was saying a lot of words again. He felt them rushing up to him like water, and enjoyed the sensation, without trying to break the sound into words. He closed his eyes while she talked, rat-tat-tat, like when it rained hard:

"I know you won't like this, honey, but I have to look at your eye to see if it's okay." She approached him slowly, and Nick felt her pry open his lid. "It looks okay, just red," she said. "You must have gotten something in it and rubbed it too much. Try not to rub your eyes, Nick." Mommy let out a big gust of air and tilted her head, still looking at him. Her eyes were so big, and he could see that shadow in them. He knew the word for this: sad. He would never forget that word. He saw it pass over Mommy's eyes, like the cloud and the sun. He hated that because it always spread into him.

Once she saw that he was okay, Emmy leaned over to give Nick a kiss but then thought better of it. A kiss would feel good to her, but not to him. Nick endured kisses and hugs, but never offered them himself. She sighed, breathing extra deeply to suck in the cold air so that it might freeze the flare-up of sadness before it got any worse, then walked through the garden, back inside the house.

Although she hadn't noticed it before, it looked as if a wild animal had been let loose in there. Henry's junk was strewn everywhere. When she started gathering it into a pile for him, so that she could walk more easily through the living room into the kitchen, she found herself staring at a notice that had been stuffed into Henry's backpack. Henry, although newly fourteen, still did not mind his mother's going through his backpack, or cleaning his room; at least she thought he didn't. Her hand pushed aside a half pack of Juicy Fruit gum (were they allowed to chew gum in school these days?), a crumpled lunch bag, a rubbed-raw binder with "Green Day" written in big letters and then "sux" in Henry's handwriting right beneath it. Finally she seized on the usual small pile of flyers and sifted through. An offer for cheap tickets to several performances: Boston Ballet, Flying Karamazov Brothers, Alvin Ailey. She tossed it.

A torn note, written in smeary gray pencil. Henry's handwriting. It said, "play structure—J." The rest had been ripped away. Emmy suddenly felt a pang—guilty to be going through his stuff, she supposed, because this was obviously personal business of Henry's. His secret life. She smiled, thinking of him and his messy head of hair. She was so proud of his emerging independence, achingly proud. She embarrassed him with her overflow of love, she knew that. It was hard to control, hard to get things right with a crabby teenager.

She put the backpack away and walked over to the window to watch Nick. He was standing still in the very center of her brown, dead garden. The tendril of sadness unfurled, fully this time. She had thought she was long inured to that kind of pain by now. Nick was fifteen, after all. Why was she still susceptible to sudden waves of grief?

She shifted her focus, stretching her view outward, beyond Nick. There was not a spot of green in sight, and the soil, where it peeked out from receding snow, was mummified, wooly gray and dead.

Late February. It occurred to her that it was nearly the one-year anniversary of her husband's moving out.

Although she'd been apart from Eric for almost a year, she had not yet fully processed what had happened to them. It still made her stomach hurt and her heart sore—she now knew exactly what that cliché felt like. It also made her crazy angry at times. Her life these days felt exactly like February itself: a steppe-like stretch, dull, painfully frozen, and endless.

Emmy had never liked being alone. And she had never liked winter—hated it, in fact. And now she was alone, in the middle of winter. Not entirely alone, because she had her boys. But no partner. That was over.

She also wanted sun, hot sun, but she had always lived up here in Boston and knew she always would. To be fair, this winter had not been a particularly hard one, for Boston. There had been no snow in December, or January, the chipper snow lovers would point out. But why be fair at a time like this, when she was probably a hairbreadth away from divorce?

Clearly she needed to be gardening, and that was still at least six weeks away. Lately she had been craving the dirt, like some sort of earth-worshipping pagan, or a geophagist. The thought of the warm, baked smell of really good garden soil was driving her crazy. She almost wanted to eat it, the way she had when she was a kid—the way Nick did until recently. Everyone else had been horrified, but Emmy secretly understood her son's taste for dirt.

Emmy stepped back from the clammy glass of the window and wiped away the imprint of her forehead. "Oh yeah," she said, turning around and walking out to the living room, where she'd left her gardening books and notes. Lately she had given in to the need to talk to herself. It helped her think. It also comforted her, made her feel less lonely. "I almost forgot."

Her garden plans. She wanted to finish her latest idea so that she could place her orders with the online nursery she liked, the one that had her favorite perennials, but in unusual colors. Emmy curled up in her faded floral chair and a half reading her two gardening books, *How to Have an English Garden* and *A Year of Perennials*. She set about gathering little green cut-and-paste lawns to stick onto a piece of paper, and cut out tiny mounds of flowers, labeling everything painstakingly according to Latin name, color, and expected bloom time.

This was where she was in her element, among flowers. She even had a name for a small gardening business, if she could have gone that route, although starting your own business was way too uncertain a proposition (so Eric had said, anyway). But if she could ever do it, it would be called Gardens of Eden: Specializing in Urban Paradises. She would take postage stamp–size lots in her town and transform them to garden oases, little flower-filled havens to nurture yourself.

Sitting in her chair, she knew it was all a dream, wispy, ephemeral, but like old fireplace smoke, you could always faintly smell it. She stared at the tiny paper garden in her lap and tried to envision it in the space outside, so vast and brown, thinking of yellow versus blue, annual versus biennial—all of which kept her from thinking of the many other worries swarming thickly and damagingly in her mind, like the termites they occasionally discovered in their basement wall.

She found herself remembering when they'd bought the house. Eighteen years ago, after they'd first married, buying a gorgeous old place was all she could think about. So she chased that dream, and had her babies without thinking, one after the other. The youngest, Dan, was far more planned for, plotted for. But not Nick and Henry, of course, only fourteen months apart.

The boys were definitely the best of Eric and her. She had married him in rebellion against her parents' suburban Jewish thing. Eric Graham, tall, lean, blond Protestant from Vermont, a "Prattistant," he had joked awkwardly (his jokes were usually much better than that) when they first talked about their backgrounds—as if she couldn't guess! He was the perfect opposite to her dark, curvy, curly Jewishness. They had met in grad school at Harvard—when she was getting her master's in botany and Eric was getting an MFA and studying to be an architect.

Their families and backgrounds could not have been more different. She had brought a little color and excitement to Eric's dull, geeky life, perhaps, and he had brought order and humor to hers. And they'd had that, to be fair. It was good for a while. When the boys were little, cute, fresh smelling. But then they became more complicated, especially Nick. And Eric could not bear it. He had felt betrayed by it all. Emmy knew it, though she never said as much. *Poor guy. Schmuck.* In the end, she had told him—screamed at him—to go and take his "clueless ass" with him. Eric, for the first time she could ever remember, had not even been able to joke about that one. He'd just left. That particular bit still made her wince. And, of course, what had led up to it.

She sighed, forced her mind off such a painful memory, and studied her plans. Satisfied with this particular bit of her design, she rose from her chair after about an hour and her right knee complained with an almost-pop. *Et tu, Knee-to?* But, she thought resignedly, she was forty now, and these things were going to happen. She went back to the window. Nick had come inside. At last, the wan sunlight broke through the steely cloud cover, dragging its bleached-out rays behind it.

Maybe if she looked hard enough in the morning, in a full-sun spot, she would suddenly notice a green vulva-like bulb shoot poking up, waiting for the warmth that would coax it to open. Those green nubs always made Emmy tear up the first time she spotted one. She would then search the ground for more, toeing the mud and kicking away matted clumps of leaves, like a kid on an Easter egg hunt.

Chapter 2

It would be dark in about a half hour. Emmy had to go get Dan from soccer. By now, Nick was in the living room, sitting in the middle of the sofa with his gangly legs tucked under him, Buddha-like. His lanky blond hair nearly covered his eyes; he was long overdue for a haircut. She sighed. *Put it on the list.* The room was getting dark, and no lights were on. Would Nick ever think to turn on the lights himself? She figured he would someday, but . . . "I'm going out for a minute, sweetheart," she said quietly and slowly, flicking on the lights.

Nicky turned toward her, blinking, but not looking at her face. "Okay, yes, feeeem."

"You'll be here with Henry."

"Okay, yes." Then he whispered, "Whooooom."

Emmy pulled a few chicken breasts out of the fridge. She had picked up the chicken today on impulse, when she dropped the boys off. She would get started on dinner, just before getting Dan: Parmesan chicken and mashed potatoes.

She slipped her long hair into a scrunchie that she kept by the side of the sink for this purpose, and fingered a curl. Her split ends were getting scary. The lock of hair that clung to her finger ended in a point that looked like a spider's furry leg. It had probably been a year since she'd seen the inside of a salon, but who cared? No one was looking at her these days. Eric stared right through her whenever he came to take the boys for the weekend.

Into the bowl went the butter for melting, which she did in the microwave; the olive oil; some Dijon mustard; and chopped garlic. She rinsed the chicken, patting it dry. She half-filled the other bowl with flour and parmesan, Parmesan, equal parts. It had to be really cheesy for the boys, to disguise any hint of meat flavor. She dipped each piece of meat in the liquid, shook them gently one by one, then rolled them in the soft, pungent dry mixture. Soon her casserole had six fist-size white lumps. She then shoved it into the oven, set the timer, and turned the dial.

Emmy sponged off the counter, where some Parmesan had spilled. One thing was sure: Eric had loved her cooking, inconsistent and resentfully done though it was. Well, except recently. He had become a vegetarian in his efforts to simplify, but it only made things harder for her.

"Chicken? You know I can't eat chicken!" He was peering into the oven with a pinched expression. She remembered being taken aback—shocked, really—by his jutting chin, the hard Yankee lines of his face, the disproportionate anger she saw there.

"Jesus, chill," she'd said, mystified by his vehemence. "Since when don't you eat chicken?" She had turned her back on him, looking over the contents of the refrigerator, staring blankly at the teary gallon of milk and forgetting what she had opened the door for.

"Come on, you know I've been trying to be vegetarian," he said, softening his tone as if he, too, had been surprised by how pissed off he was.

Emmy remembered thinking, *Can't he say "a vegetarian" like anyone else—he has to make it sound more erudite?!* Out loud she said, "Right, but you had a burger with Dan last week!" They had grabbed dinner at McDonald's after soccer practice and come home full. She'd been furious because she had already made— what else?—hamburgers, which were Dan's favorite. And a huge *vegetarian* salad for Eric, which he had been unable to eat.

"Well, that was just that one time. Emmy, don't be difficult. This is important to me."

Difficult! Me? She had slammed the refrigerator drawer, startling them both. "And is my effort to make dinner not important to you? So I forgot about your *vegetarianism*!" She emphasized it with all the disgust she felt for what was surely only a momentary obtuseness. "So then I deserve to be treated as if I'd committed a felony?"

Later, Emmy wondered why she had said that, sounding like a combination of Old Jewish Fishwife and sulky teenager. Why she always reacted so strongly to Eric, with no respect. When Emmy thought back on it, she also wondered at how angry she was. As if she already knew somehow that it was coming to an end for them, so it was okay to say whatever she felt like.

Shortly after had been that horrible fight, about Nick. The one that had ended it all. She could still feel the screaming that had ripped from her throat, the no-holds-barred rush of words, saying everything, no censoring, no boundaries, at last, while Eric listened, wide-eyed, furious, hurt beyond words. "You don't love him—you don't know how to love! You're warped! Why don't you just go? It's worse having a bad father than none at all!"

And then he had just gone upstairs to pack a bag instead of fighting back.

"Yeah, go! Take your clueless ass with you!" she had shrieked after him, and then burst into tears. Henry had gone to her then. His face was terrible: red and raw, eyes like a beaten puppy. Oh God, she never wanted to see that look on his face again. And they'd all heard, of course. It was just that Henry was the only one who would think to come in and try to offer comfort. A thirteen-year-old!

Her heart cramped. as if it had just happened. She stopped her thoughts, imagining a huge *Get Smart*–like wall slamming down in her head. "You can't keep doing this to yourself," she said aloud. But it was too late: she *was* doing it to herself, and now she felt her grief all over again, as if the whole fight had just happened.

Henry was upstairs. She yelled to him to come down. Although she didn't like him in charge—she could not completely trust that he would be safe— knew she had to. He did not reply or come right away, but she knew he heard her. She waited by the stairs, picturing him, summoning him. He was tall and blond like Eric, and had a beautiful, slightly kooky smile that took up the entire lower half of his face—a smile that, come to think of it, was pretty rare these days. Well, he couldn't have been very happy about his father moving out.

Suddenly he was there, in baggy khakis and loose, smudgy white sweatshirt, swinging his long arms, waiting.

"I'm going out to get Dan in a little bit."

"Um-hum?" he said, looking blankly at her.

She sighed, still not really used to this adolescent sullenness, which had been part of their lives for a year now. "So I'm just telling you. I'm leaving you with Nick. Also, the chicken is cooking in the oven. If the timer rings before I come home, will you be able to shut the oven off?"

He blinked and seemed to be thinking about what she'd asked—at least she hoped.

"Will you try to hear it?" she asked impatiently. "I mean, you have to turn down that music!"

"I know, I *know*!" He took out his earbuds, turned, and stalked back to his room, slamming the door.

"Hey!" she said out loud, in frustration. He was not usually grouchy. She turned down the oven and shut off the timer. Never mind. She'd be back in time, anyway. Then she'd find out what was up with Henry. She hoped she'd remember, but with the three boys at home, and dinner, it was easy to forget things. She really did need a list.

Henry felt, rather than heard, the door slam shut behind his mother. He reached down and snicked off the music, which had been getting on his nerves. He felt all jumpy because of his mother. Maybe it was everything, he didn't know. He didn't want to know. He had homework, too. *Fuck that*, he thought, but his heart beat even faster at the prospect of tomorrow. He was already behind and had gotten a C in his latest math test. He had a whole book to read for English. He reached into his back pocket and felt around, pulling out a Ziploc bag full of brown pot. He had first tried pot only last month, with Jonah and Wesley, but it hadn't taken him long to get the knack. He took a rolling paper from the pocket on his knee and smoothed it out, just the way Jonah had shown him. He filled it with three pinches of the pot, breathing in the sweet aroma like a chef over his bouquet garnis. He rolled a perfect, tiny joint and flicked on his lighter, sinking back against the pillow. He figured he had a good twenty minutes before Mom got back with Dan, whom Henry sometimes liked to call Little Thing 2.

He was already stoned, and it had taken him only two deep drags to get to this point, he noticed. His friend Wesley had told him that the better you get at it, the less you need. This seemed to be true. He wondered if his dad ever wanted to do it. Once, his father had told him that he'd had tried pot in college, by way of saying that it was probably okay to *try* it but not to keep doing it. Henry's head had nearly fallen off when his dad said that, but he had not shown a thing.

He pulled again on the joint, for good measure. "This one's for you, Dad," he said out loud, remembering that old beer commercial from the he'd seen on YouTube or something. Then he laughed, then coughed.

He wondered, not for the first time, what it would be like to play World of Warcraft stoned. *Why not try it for once?* He flipped the switch on his computer and waited for the game to load. Wesley was on.

"What's up?" he said into the headset.

"Nothing. I suck!" Wesley was doing badly and would need the wizard soon. Henry could not follow his moves, nor could he pay attention to his own avatar. As Wesley kept talking, Nick found himself watching the screen and then his eyes would glaze, like when he was falling asleep, and then suddenly he would real-ize he was still watching the screen. His head felt like it was stuffed with wool, and he could not coordinate his thumbs with the fast action of the characters. He wiggled his thumbs and fin-gers faster on the keyboard, as if to wake them up, but his stupor was too strong.

Henry wondered if maybe he did not really love the feeling of being high, but he pushed the thought away. Jonah said it took practice, and that it was worth it. Henry felt like he'd been prac-ticing awhile now, just a few weeks, but still, he'd hoped it would feel better by this point. He had looked forward to getting to know the feeling of nothing in your head, hoping it would make it easier for him to be home. But it really hadn't. His mother still bugged him with her concerned looks, and Dan bugged him with his meanness.

What did feel better, though, was walking into the school bathroom, where the guys were all lighting up, and not having to skulk into a stall or keep his head down. Even though Henry was one of the tallest ones there, it did him no good among the cool kids. *The cool kids.* He felt a flicker of embarrassment about that phrase. It was such a cliché. *Cliché* was a word they'd worked on with Ms. Smith (or "Smithers" as they all called her behind her back because she was so mousy and suck-up, like the friend of Mr. Burns, the old rich guy on *The Simpsons*), so he was sure of its meaning, and he liked using it—but it was absolutely true.

The cool kids even referred to themselves as "the cool kids." Completely without *irony*, another word Henry really liked. The cool kids stopped ignoring him or bugging him once he started smoking with them. And then, suddenly, he *was* a cool kid. It was as easy as that. Instant friends, a ton of people to hang out with at recess and after school . . . if he didn't have to walk the twerp home. You just couldn't beat that.

He just wished he liked the smoking and getting-high feeling better. But it always just muddied his head and hurt his throat. Oh, well, he'd get used to it. He prided himself on what he thought of as his inner strength, his ability to withstand anything and to keep everything to himself. He was the strongest person he knew, and that, he felt, was his strongest feature. He shut off the game. Right now, though, he felt like Nick, with all the action flying around him too fast for him to even understand it, let alone control a character in a video game. *Not a good way to feel,* he thought, and, frowning, closed his eyes.

Emmy pulled up to Scolley Field and tried to pick out Dan from all the way across the field, satisfying herself with accomplishing it in ten seconds. Shoulders thrown back in eternal swagger, compact black curls floating around his head, her little son leaped up and headed the ball so that it sailed right over the goal. She could tell he was laughing, even though she couldn't hear it. Dan, her wild child, her dark boy, her handful. She watched unseen for a few minutes. Some laughter to her right caught her attention, and she looked to see a group of boys standing near the playing field, backpacks piled at their feet. Dan noticed, too. Two of them were good friends of his, but not on the soccer team. She watched him go through a pantomime of rubbing his head, howling with pain. The boys laughed harder. Then he turned his back on them and ran off with some team members, stopping momentarily to scoop up his things.

"Dan!"

He turned sharply. A half grin came to his lips as he ambled over, that same rascal Graham grin as his father and his brother. "Hey, Mom."

"How was it today?" *Dear, sweet boy.* Couldn't say it, could only think it, because Dan was now always so touchy about being the little one in the family.

"It was okay."

Getting Dan to try soccer had taken a big fight, particularly when none of his best friends wanted to play. Emmy realized that it was likely Dan would end up as nerdy as his father, but she was not ready to give up quite yet. She knew, from Henry's experience as a nonsports kid, that as they got older, it became harder to fit into the group when they didn't play on a team. So she had forced Dan to try it a few times, and if he still hated it after three practices, he could then quit. Today was the fifth practice, so she figured it would stick. "Great! Ready to come home?" She rubbed his shoulders as they walked.

"Yeah." He shrugged out from her grasp and sniffled wetly, a habit he'd had for as long as she could remember. "What's for dinner?"

"Parmesan chicken."

"Not the kind with the sauce?" Dan's voice took a whining

turn downward.

"No, the crispy kind," she reassured him.

They buckled up. She put on her radio station, Q96, and hoped he would not say anything negative. To Emmy it was the perfect combination: a few new songs, a few mellow old songs, a little white hip-hop, a little Carly Simon. Dan said nothing, but for a while, he rode with his hands over his ears.

Chapter 3

Eric was late getting up for work on Monday because he hadn't slept well the previous night and then missed his alarm. He sat down heavily at the blue-tiled breakfast bar and struggled to pull the stool just the right distance from the bar so that he could comfortably read the *Times*. He hated these breakfast bars. Why had so many people done away with kitchen tables? Weren't these nineties kitchens efficient enough already, with the countertop grills and the wall ovens, the under-the-cabinet microwaves and the stacking washer/dryers? He shook out the newspaper and scanned the columns, then looked up again, unable to concentrate.

Something was bothering him—something just off to the sides that he could not get a handle on. Something to do with work? No. That was fairly smooth right now. Well, then, it had to be Emmy or the boys. What had Emmy said the other day? Something about how she felt stuck. Christ, he was sick of her complaining. Of course he had listened politely, but then when she started wondering about changing jobs, he'd lost his patience. Changing jobs would do her no good. It was only going to complicate everything.

But since when did Emmy care about complications? When she wanted something, it generally happened, regardless of the consequences. She was like a dog with a bone that way, and she was already not that great at working with people. She just barely squeaked by as a realtor. And the thing was, he just didn't want to hear about her fantasies anymore. She had cured him of that need the day she threw him out. That memory could still ignite a flame in his chest, make his skull pound. *Uh-uh, not now*, he thought.

He poured a cup of coffee, cursing as the carafe leaked coffee along the sides, all over his hands and the counter. He walked to the dispenser and yanked off too much paper towel, then threw half of it away, frowning. What was with these extra-big cuts of paper? So wasteful.

The rest of his tiny apartment more than made up for the overly slick kitchen. Beyond the kitchen was a very elegant, eye-pleasing living room, decorated in a lot of rich reds and browns and antiques by Eric's sister Lucy. Lucy had swung into action the moment she'd heard that Eric had moved out of his house. Lucy had never really liked Emmy that much, so Eric was hardly surprised when she began decorating his new bachelor pad with such enthusiasm. "You're going to live alone, why not make it a real home?" she'd asked, trying to sound matter-of-fact, but with her pleasure leaking out all over the place.

"Try and cheer up, Luce," he'd replied, but he'd let her do her thing. Why fight it? Why fight any woman? When she'd asked him about colors, he thought his head would fall off. But he knew better than to say, "Huh?" So he'd told her to make the décor in the color of a beautiful woman's lips. "Up to you to fig-ure out what that means," he'd said, ignoring how she rolled her eyes.

It was a little difficult sometimes to actually see Lucy's artfully arranged tables—placed so that they looked casual, mindlessly yet elegantly set there (the concept still made Eric's head spin)— because Eric kept everything, every table surface, every spare sofa cushion, covered with his papers, his magazines, and his books. He was a natural slob. Not dirty, just untidy. Well, maybe a little dirty, he thought, kicking some dust under the couch and brushing crumbs off his pants. Xeroxed data sheets from the last conference at the School of Architecture were littered here and there. On what he thought was a nineteenth-century country French coffee table—wasn't that what Lucy had said?—there were piles, rather than neat, eye-catching stacks, of a year's worth of *New Yorker* magazines, dog-eared and torn. Lucy, like Emmy, had begged him to throw them away, but Eric prevailed this time. He still hadn't finished them. Why should he discard them? Even the kitchen counter had piles of worn paperback novels, as well as some crackly covered library loans.

Eric was proud of the few odd things he'd brought back from trips to various places, before his time with Emmy, in the days when he could afford to go, such as the pleasantly faded cheap throw rug from a street-corner peddler in Barcelona and the large, beat-up mahogany desk that housed his television and stereo. Each had special significance to him. Lucy had had quite a time blending in the myriad weird things he'd attached himself to. But she'd done admirably, with a place that was already beautiful to begin with.

There were even built-in floor-to-ceiling dark wooden bookshelves, which weren't antiques, but Lucy had used a particular aging technique on them so that now she was satisfied they looked old enough. Eric was pleased with the result, although he'd been happy with them for their sheer size. They were filled with his best books, some even dating from his undergraduate days. Books were stuffed into whichever shelves they fit, some even lying in horizontal stacks next to a vintage collection of *Playboys*, which he had fought with Lucy (and Emmy) to keep. A guy had to look at something truly beautiful now and then, and the old *Playboys*—well, there was nothing like the fuller-bodied women of a few decades ago. And that was something both Lucy and Emmy would never understand, not in a million years. One thing they had in common.

He thought back to the first time Emmy and his sister had met, when Lucy had Em and him over for dinner. He'd been completely shocked at how badly it went. Two women he loved—but they were like oil and water.

Something had seemed off right from the start, when Emmy had first walked through Lucy's wide front door, the night he introduced them to each other. "Everything okay?" he'd whispered as Emmy stepped next to him. She'd flashed him a bright, glass-like smile that he had never seen.

Then he was enveloped in a cloud of perfume and soft hair

and arms: Lucy. "Oh, Eric! It's such a treat to see you," Lucy had murmured in his ear, and then she had released him slowly, hanging on almost as if she were the girlfriend, not the sister. He remembered how she had turned reluctantly to Emmy, and then called her Emma. Em had not even corrected her. Neither had he. And he never knew why, either.

Eric took a sip of coffee, trying to push down the bitter taste of that memory. His living room had huge old black-lacquered windows in the front that overlooked Mass Ave., in Central Square in Cambridge. There was a working marble fireplace that actually helped keep the place warm in the bitter Boston winter, two bedrooms so that his boys had a place to stay when they were here—although he was not at all sure they enjoyed sharing a sleeping space like that, they were all three so different from one another—and good neighbors who made apartment living seem better than owning one's own house.

He'd done that already. When he and Emmy had enjoyed "playing house," as they'd called it jokingly—enjoyed it for a while, anyway. They had prepared so well for being the happy family. Researched everything, bought the best baby products for Nick. *Nick*. Pain, out of nowhere, washed over him like a rogue wave. Eyes closed, he waited for it to subside. After all these years, he could still almost drown in feelings about Nick. And they were feelings that had never become sorted neatly into words, so they could assume a place in his structured mind and fade into the background, like old clothes in a closet. No, his emotions about Nick were still a messy splatter of emotional mud—a mudslide, really.

There was only one recognizable emotion—guilt—that had the power to slice through the shit. When he could think clearly again, his thoughts raced backward, to one of the worst days.

"I can't. I just can't, Em," he had been saying to her after she had told him that she'd signed Nick up for Special Olympics basketball.

"Why can't you? I take him all the time. Just take him. You don't have to do anything. Just stand there. The coach is great, he'll—"

"I can't!"

"Why? You never do anything with him!" She had slapped her hands at her sides and started to leave the room. "Fine. I'll—"

Eric had suddenly felt himself choking. "Em, stop! Just stop—" He didn't know what he wanted her to stop. He was practically seeing red. He felt his eyes burning, his fists clenching. He had never been so angry in his life, and he sensed himself losing control. He gripped her by the shoulders, as much to steady himself as to grab onto her.

She had whirled around, looking horrible, her eyes wild and her hair crazy like Medusa. "You stop! You fucking stop!" She had actually said it that way, that harshly, he remembered. "Or better yet, go! Just go. I don't need this. I don't need you! And you know what, they don't need you, either!" In a hoarse, unfamiliar voice he'd never heard her use before, she had started yelling for Nick, who was huddled in the middle of the living room couch with his hands over his ears, to get ready for basketball.

Eric looked down at the food on his plate. It still hurt as if it had just happened. The humiliation of being banished, the snap of the cord that held her to him, like a broken rubber band in his face. He just could not go back after that. It wasn't the anger so much as the embarrassment and the shame of what she'd done to him. And that he'd somehow let her.

The bread looked butter soaked, as enticing as wet cardboard. Maybe the anti-carbivores had something, after all. Emmy eschewed carbs as if they were poison.

Why did he have to think of her so much? It was as if he still weren't over the whole thing. Did getting past the dissolution of a marriage usually take this long? He didn't know; he had no friends who were divorced. Actually, he and Emmy were not divorced, technically. They had never even discussed it. His moving out and getting this place had been so monumental they never had to. He had slipped pretty easily into the Weekend Dad routine. Just pick 'em up and say as little as possible to her. And hope that he could handle Nick each time. It was a chore, really, being with the kids, though of course he loved them. But his leaving had not changed anything. Being their dad, especially Nick's, was such hard work.

Ah, why was he thinking this way now? He had to get to work: he had a lot to do. He was a good father, damn it. Wasn't he? He always showed up; he'd always been there for them, on birthdays, at school plays, for important stuff. Well, not for Nick, but that was different. There might be a part of him that had given up on Nick; he didn't know. Maybe that's what Emmy was talking about. He sighed.

This was going nowhere fast. So what if he wasn't the let's-have-a-catch-in-the-yard kind? They weren't that kind of sons, either. Well, maybe Dan was. He played soccer now, didn't he? And of course, Nick and his Special Olympics . . .

Eric quickly tossed the toast in the garbage and folded the paper noisily. He decided to bring his winter coat, despite the projected temperature of fifty—you never knew in Boston—and hurriedly left behind his apartment and his memories.

Emmy was looking for a parking space, which would be tough this time of day. All the usual shoppers, plus the moms who were taking their kids into the McDonald's or the ice cream store for an after-school snack, were here. The three-story brick town house apartments and condos attracted couples; the ramshackle old Victorians attracted families who could afford to fix them up. The town was overcrowded, but happy and thriving. Sometimes, though, especially when she was trying to park, that was a pain in the ass.

She glimpsed a spot, just beyond the fire hydrant, between a Mercedes SUV and a Toyota Prius. This appointment was just after school pickup; she had left Dan at the house with Henry. A professional couple wanted to see some condos on their way home from work. The Pearls were in their midthirties, both lawyers (but not *that* kind of lawyer, they had stressed; they were with the ACLU), no kids, ex–New Yorkers, perfect for Belleville

Corner. She led them up to the second floor of an Edwardian condo on Saint Paul Street. "You're going to love this, if you loved the town house on Winchester. This is very Greenwich Village, without the attitude. And the prices." (Whatever that meant. Whenever she said it, however, clients nodded knowingly and usually made an offer.)

As the Pearls stroked the natural woodwork and gasped at the working marble fireplace, she thought about Nick, for some reason. *Oh yeah*, she thought. *The fireplace.* How excited she and Eric had been when they'd shown Nick his first fire in a fireplace.

But Nick had sat in front of the crackling fire and kept his eyes on the floor, not on the fire. It was almost as if he were blind and the fire were invisible to him. The roaring and the flickering light had no effect on him. "Look, Nicky, look!" Eric had practically screamed. It didn't work, of course. Fire made no sense to Nick, who'd never seen one, so he had no context for it and would simply try to block it out. But Emmy didn't know that at the time. All she knew was the panic in her husband's tone.

"Will you stop?" she had asked, irritated.

"I'm just trying to get him to look at it!" Eric had yelled back.

"Why? He doesn't care! Why should he care about it? He's just a baby, for Christ's sake!"

Eric had glared at her and stomped out of the room.

Baby Nick had just smiled at the lines in the wood grain of the floor.

Chapter 4

A warmish, bright day. Now, suddenly, it was as if winter were definitely on its way out. The kind of springlike day when the college students wore shorts even though it was really only fifty degrees. Emmy went out to inspect the yard.

Most of the dirty snow was gone, almost overnight. The grass was gray and bent low to the ground. The garden up on the rocks was brown, with stiff mounds of leftover autumn leaves looming here and there like gravestones. Emmy climbed up the stone wall and poked at a mound, moving it aside. There, like a tiny pile of emeralds, twinkled some baby green perennial leaves. She smiled and bent down to clean off some clinging dirt, then raised her smeared fingers to her nose and sniffed: the slightly fecal, wet smell of mud rather than the sweet yet salty smell of dry soil. Owing to the earliness of the season, she gently recovered them with the leaves. Raking was not far off, but not today, either. She felt gratified, just full enough, knowing that this satisfying yet still difficult task was indeed coming, but that she did not have to do it right now.

Emmy straightened and exhaled, surveying the rest of the property. Closing her eyes, she could see Henry and Dan playing T-ball together as younger boys, when the lawn was newer. Eric would coach, crouched down making a triangle of the three of them, and she would watch or read a book at the picnic table by this rock wall. Her heart hurt at the realization, yet another one, that this, too, was over. A strangled little sob broke loose, and she jumped off the wall to sit at the table and cry and maybe let it pass.

The metal was warm from the sun. She rested her elbows gingerly on the wobbly black table, which had a tendency to upend itself.

The crackle of tires on gravel startled Emmy, and she lifted her head. Recognizing the little black Mercedes, of Lucy, Eric's sister, Emmy quickly wiped her face. As always, Lucy's timing was just horrible; she had a seemingly uncanny ability to know when Emmy was at her most vulnerable.

"Hellooo," Lucy sang out from her partly open tinted window. "Look at you, so industrious! You're so good," she said, somehow making it sound like it was the most pathetic thing she'd ever seen. Lucy was a decorator, the big-ticket type who was hired by the matrons of Lincoln, Concord, and Weston, the software baronesses who needed to project a certain tasteful Old World style in their newly minted McMansions but had no idea where to begin. Lucy knew what they wanted because she was one of them, evidenced by the way she tooled around in that sporty Mercedes, barely holding the wheel with one perfectly manicured hand, her other hand pressing her iPhone to her ear.

Lucy stepped out. She wore a pale pink wool crepe skirt that skimmed her ample round hips and fluttered outward at the knees like a mermaid's tail. The pink skirt and the cream cashmere coat set off her carefully waved shoulder-length red hair in a very Susan Hayward way. Her penny-brown eyes scanned Emmy's face. "Have I come at a bad time?"

Emmy suppressed a sigh but ignored the question. "So what's up, Lucy?" Lucy had actually never visited Emmy since Eric had left, except once right after the split, when she came to pick up a few things for him that he'd been too cowardly to get himself.

"Wait till you see! I thought of you the minute I spotted these!" Lucy turned and dove into the tiny backseat of her car, grunting a little as she pulled out a pair of antique flower urns.

Could it be that for once Lucy was doing something nice? They were gorgeous! Just as Emmy started to smile, Lucy said, "Now, of course, they *are* lead, so that's the only thing. You might not want them around Nick, you know, in case he, well, touches them and maybe puts his hands in his mouth. Still sucks his thumb, right? Darling boy. But he's done with all the growing, right? I think by fifteen there's no more worry about, you know, *further* neurological damage . . ." Her voice trailed off.

Somehow, it was the word *further* that did it. Emmy felt as if she'd been punched in the belly. She had realized that Lucy was shallow and insensitive, but she'd never known her to be that way toward Nick. Okay, yes, Nick did have neurological damage. But. To talk about him as if he were some hopeless case! She took a few moments to answer, not even knowing where to begin. Should she just push Lucy down on her abundant pink ass? That would feel good—but no; she didn't want to give Lucy something that big to complain to Eric about. So she simply choked out, "You know, I don't think so," in a thick voice.

Lucy blinked as if she were having trouble understanding. "Oh?" she said, her pale cheeks darkening. "You don't think— what?" She was clearly waiting for something else, probably for Emmy to thank her, but that was not going to happen.

"The urns. No thanks," Emmy said. And then, emboldened now by Lucy's confusion, she added, "We don't keep lead around the house. I even had to find new bullets for my gun because of how toxic lead is."

Lucy's eyes widened. "You have a *gun*? Oh, Emmy, no! Do you know how dangerous they are? There could be an accident with the boys! What if Nick—?"

Emmy stepped forward and leaned in so that she was almost too close to Lucy. Eyes narrowed, she said softly, "You know, I think you'd better go." Lucy took a step backwards, turned and grabbed the lip of first one urn, then the other. She hoisted them into her car. Grunting, she reached in behind the seat, arranging them on the floor. She turned and merely looked at Emmy through hooded eyes, then swept into the dark cavern of the Mercedes. The door clicked shut and the window purred open. Lucy poked her head out and sputtered, "You know, Emmy, you shouldn't be so sensitive! Always telling people to go. Pretty soon there won't be anyone left." She floored the gas before Emmy could respond.

Emmy stood there, stunned. She had plenty of black feelings about Eric, but nothing like what she felt right then. Lucy could make her act so crazy – blurting out that nonsense about having a gun! Where had *that* come from? She shook her hair from her face to clear her mind. Back to the garden. The lead-urn-free garden.

She and Eric had put the garden in themselves. In those days, nobody had gardeners except people who lived in Belleville Farm, the estate part of town. It was unthinkable, offensive, to imagine hiring someone else to work on one's own yard. It ran counter to the Yankee way of life here. And Eric was determined, as was Emmy, that they would hack a paradise out of the wilderness, imagining themselves a little like Israeli Sabras. When they first bought the house, it was surrounded by tall blue spruce, pin oaks, and that old scourge of New England, Norway maples—a veritable forest in Belleville Point. It had been the "old Viorst place," according to some of the longtime neighbors. Emmy's jaw almost dropped the first time she heard it. Eric had felt the same way: "What are we, on Walton's Mountain?" he'd cracked later on, and they'd laughed for a long time, saying things like "Good night, John Boy. Good night, Mrs. Viorst." Mr. and Mrs. Viorst, who had lived here for much longer than they should have, did not believe in pruning trees. Mrs. Viorst worried that it actually "hurt" them to be pruned. Mr. Viorst wanted the place to look exactly as it had been intended to one hundred years ago (or how he imagined)—yet somehow he had conveniently forgotten that one hundred years ago these trees would have been saplings or even acorns. Now they were behemoths, with roots that had probably long since snaked into the sewer line.

Eric had brought in Bud-Insky Landscape and Tree a week after they had moved in. "We *have* to hire them, Em. For the name alone." Laughing, she had agreed.

"Oh, at least leave the spruces," begged a neighbor. "So pretty at Christmas. You'll have your choice of tree." Her blue eyes twinkled with such friendliness that Emmy's sharp retort—"I'm Jewish, so it doesn't matter"—died on her tongue. But they didn't leave the spruces, or the oaks or maples, for that matter. Eric even splurged for the stump grinding, which cost as much as the tree removal. "We'll never be able to dig anywhere with those things there," he said, motioning toward the twelve stumps that remained, like giant elephants' feet marching through the yard.

He was right. After the stumps were gone, the soil was like brownie mix, soft and sweet. Well, sweet after they had added plenty of lime to it. Most of the perennials Emmy liked preferred alkaline earth to the naturally acidic stuff they had (because of all the damned evergreens, oaks, and maples). Still, together they carted in bags of new loam, peat, manure, sand, and topsoil, just to have a really superior mix. Eric would dump a load in the newly marked gardens, and she would stir with her spade and then her hands. The smell was intoxicating. Working together side by side like that was positively erotic. They had often made love afterward, hot, voracious, and dirty, because sometimes they were just so worked up from the sun and the sweat that they didn't even wash it off first.

Then they would go out to the local nursery and walk up and down the aisles, choosing only their favorites for the cart: campanula, delphinium, lavender, like parents-to-be trying out names for their baby. The old names of the flowers charmed her, like the names of the valiant characters in a King Arthur story: Sir Lobelia, Lady Campion. "Arise, Sir Loin of Beef," Eric had said, in his best Bugs Bunny voice, whenever she spoke of the romance of the names.

Ha-ha. So funny. She had laughed back then, but now it didn't seem so amusing. He was such a jerk, who would never understand her passions, she thought now. If she could ever do exactly what she wanted with her life, she would have that little gardening business. She would be a gardener for others, her own secret version of "Tikkun Olam," the Jewish task of Healing the World. Build a better garden. It wasn't world peace, she thought. More like world peas, as the bumper sticker said. It was a start, anyway.

"Hey, Mom! Is Aunt Lucy here?" called Dan from the back porch, his voice cracking with disappointment. Dan was so transparent, God bless him. "Not anymore," Emmy replied.

Dan brightened, now that he would not be compelled to kiss his aunt's perfumed cheek. He came a little closer to her. "Are ya coming in for lunch or what?" More and more, he was taking after her in appearance, but Eric in personality: both were very routine oriented, orderly in mind, and yet slobs, too.

"Yeah, what'd you make?" She winked at him, brushing off her hands and going in.

Chapter 5

"Hew, hew," Nick said, and opened and shut his hand a few times in perfect rhythmic emphasis. He walked back and forth from the living room to the hallway, *creak-creak, creak-creak*, to the spots where the floor was softer and gave way just so under his feet, producing the same sound all the time. The crash overhead cut short this pleasant sensation, and he did not look toward the source of the noise, which he knew was his little brother, Dan.

Sure enough, as if thinking about him made his brother come, Dan was running down the stairs. "Out of my way, Nick," shouted Dan, bumping Nick roughly in the hip as he sailed by.

Vibrations coursed through Nick's body, making him see only a crackling white over everything for a split second; and then the familiar shapes quickly re-formed. He knew what they all were— Dan, hall table, overhead light, doorways—but he knew them only as shapes. He found that right now he could not remember their word names.

Mommy walked into view, and Nick tried to run the other way, even though it would throw off his walking pattern. Mommy always asked him things, and her face was too full of her eyes. This made Nick's insides hurt.

The thing about Mommy, though, was that Nick loved the way she felt and smelled, like hollybread, which they did not eat that much. Hollybread was shiny and yellow and was all tied up in knots. Hollybread came with candles, which he also loved because of the little fires on top. He knew that he shouldn't touch them, but he could blow them out. That bread smell was like Mommy's smell, and he loved it so much that he could put up with the way she suddenly touched him, hugged him, kissed him. Even though his skin would explode with the sensation of her hand on his arm, her body thrown against his like a stone wall, patting his back and blotting out all word-thought. But a second later, there would be the softness, and Nick loved softness. His favorite word was *ssh*.

But Mommy's face was full of lines right now, he saw as he turned away, and he knew this meant she would not be hugging him. She would be talking, which Nick hated.

"Nicksweetieareyouready?"

Nick did not know what she had said. He hoped she would repeat it. That was another good thing about Mommy: she was always willing to repeat what she had said.

"Areyoureadydarling?"

Ready. He heard it this time! "Yes," he said. *Yes* worked very often, for just about any question.

He *was* ready. Ready meant shoes on, coat zipped all the way up. Mommy said, "Good boy," and bent to tie his shoes. He studied her soft, snarly black hair. It seemed to be alive, always moving. Light jumped from piece to piece like a thousand ribbons. His fingers itched to grab a handful, but he knew that was bad. When he was little, Mommy used to let him wrap her curls around his fingers, pulling them this way and that. Each curl would coil perfectly around each finger and cling just the right amount. Nick wondered how that could happen again. He didn't think it could, and this made his throat and stomach feel too tight.

Nick stole a glance at his brother Henry, which was almost always okay to do, because Henry rarely looked right at him. Unlike Mommy's liny face, Henry's face was smooth and soft, and his eyes were easy for Nick to take in, like drinking a glass of milk or touching a lamb. Nick always wanted to touch Henry's face because he knew how it would be, how the skin would give way a little under his fingers, but he knew that this was another thing that he could not do because someone might yell. Nick hated yelling most of all. Dan yelled a lot, and at him, too. Dan was like the shiny piece of broken glass that Nick had found at the beach in the summer. Nick had almost stepped on that glass, but Henry had seen it and yelled a warning. "Nick, stop!" Henry's yell was not too loud, and just the right words, so they were able to break through the black that usually happened from yelling, and Nick had heard him in time. Then Nick had noticed the glass right next to his foot.

Henry had bent down and picked it up.

"Look, Nick," Henry then said slowly, holding it out.

Nick had looked at him, and then at the glinting piece of glass in his brother's hand.

"It's sea glass," Henry had explained in his quiet voice. Nick loved Henry's quiet voice; it was white colored.

Sea Glass, Sea glass, Nick had thought. Ssseeee—glasssss. "Heee, shh," he had said, imitating the rhythm and enjoying the color of the new words, sea glass, which were blue and green, and looking at the glass. He would have liked to lick it. Did it taste the way it looked? Nick had suddenly felt very happy, with the blue and green words, and Henry's quiet face and voice so close to him.

"Do you want to touch it?" Henry had offered.

Nick had reached out a tentative finger, also sticking out his tongue in case he got a chance to lick it.

"No, you can't taste it, Nick. And don't touch this part." Henry always knew. "Sharp," he had warned.

Nick knew *sharp*. A bad word. He would not lick it, even though it looked like candy. He had gently stroked the glass, carefully avoiding the part Henry held on to.

"You want it?" Henry had offered.

Nick had said, "No want it." It was too beautiful, and it was sharp. He had needed Henry to stop looking at him now, too. Henry had shrugged, and pocketed the glass.

"Boys! Come on," Mommy yelled, shattering Nick's recollections. It felt as if the air around him were all in pieces now, sharp and jagged. He tried to open and close his hands, to squeeze some of the air into his palm, which sometimes helped when people yelled at him.

Down the hall, Dan leaned in the doorway of the kitchen, his eyes glowing nocturnally through his black, curly bangs. He could see into the front hallway, where Mommy was tying Nick's shoes. Dan shook his head. "Man," he said, to himself, but loud enough so that everyone could hear. "Getting yer shoes tied, when yer a teenager!"

"Dan," said Emmy impatiently without looking up. "He is learning. It takes him longer, that's all."

"At least *he's* ready to go," said Henry, looking disdainfully at Dan's bare feet.

"Everyone's always on his side!" Dan yelled. His voice seemed to bounce off the very walls. The silence that followed was almost equally booming. Dan scowled, then went upstairs to find socks, fuming.

Anger was buzzing in Dan's head, and hot stingers of unfairness pricked at his eyes. *They don't see how dumb and annoying and embarrassing Nick is*, he thought. Mommy always thought she had to explain to him what Nick was doing, and why, and blah, blah, blah, blah, even though he *knew* it was because Nick was a crazy nuthead, which he was not allowed to say. And Henry acted like he knew everything, but Dan knew that Henry wasn't his boss.

"Dan, hurry!" Mommy was shouting from the other room, getting really impatient, and so he grabbed the first pair he could find: old red Bob the Builder socks. Baby stuff, still in his room. Why couldn't Mommy keep up with his size? He sighed and put them on. The heels puffed out in the middle of his feet like noses. They were way too small, but he didn't dare try to find a bigger pair. He knew when he really had to listen to Mommy, and now was it. He shuffled back downstairs.

Henry pulled on his high-tops. The lace was broken. He needed a new one, had needed it for days, but kept forgetting to tell Mom. Aw, even if he did, she'd forget. Shoelaces were not at the top of her list, that was for sure. She often forgot even really important stuff like milk or his favorite kind of OJ. Or she'd buy, like, one, not realizing he drank one a day. No, shoelaces were not going to get bought anytime soon. Maybe Dad had some? He hated asking him for anything. Dad always got that overeager, way-too-happy look on his face, and he'd practically jump to get whatever it was Henry had asked for. Dad was like a *slut*, which was another word Henry had just learned, from Jonah, who had sent a link from girlsgirlsgirls.com. Henry thought of the girl on the horse—yo. He'd better not remember that now. He knotted the broken lace a few slots down from the top. That worked. He sighed, hearing the door slam shut below, in the basement. Nick was already outside. Dan, he would bet, was still looking for his shoes. Sure he was, because there they were, under Henry's desk.

"Dan, they're in here," he called, resisting the urge to add, "you spaz." Not because of Dan, but because Mom got so pissed about that kind of thing, the disability thing, and anything like it, and he just did not want a hassle right now.

"Come on!" Mommy bellowed from below. She had to get outside, because Nick was now out in the driveway by himself, and even though he never ran off, he should not be left alone for long.

Chapter 6

At the end of school the following day, Emmy came upstairs to the third-grade wing, looking for her friend Beth, because Dan needed a playdate. It had been a while. He was so content to come home and just play with his LEGOs for what seemed like hours. When she went up there to check on him, she'd hear him using all different voices and making explosion sounds, holding up one tiny figure and then another. Spaceships, miniature boats, airplanes, trucks, and vehicles not yet invented were strewn permanently across his floor. She was forbidden to clean up his LEGO models. The best she could do was vacuum up to the edges and hope she wouldn't hear the awful rattling of a sucked-up LEGO piece. Sometimes, though, she'd feel a mild twinge of guilty satisfaction when she did vacuum one up because she was so damned sick of the mess. And more than that, she was sick of being the only adult in the house, and especially sick of being the only one who vacuumed. She wanted to be someone who had fun. She resented her solitary life, even though she was the one who had kicked Eric out in the first place. But he'd just gone without a word—so wasn't he partly responsible for their situation? She felt her anger, always there, a little lump of coal in her stomach, which would start glowing and come to life at the least provocation. She shut her eyes.

"Dreaming on the job?"

Emmy opened her eyes. Beth had arrived as if Emmy had conjured her. Just in time, too, because closing her eyes had not gotten rid of that picture of Eric, silently shutting the door behind him, not even fighting back. Since when did he clam up? How could he just give up? She'd never expected that. She had gone too far, and he had taken her at her word. He had abandoned her. He had abandoned them, his own children. Her stomach felt as if it had been punched, remembering how she'd felt: stunned beyond words, torn apart, bleeding tears, choking on her rage.

"Yeah, a nightmare," she replied.

"Oh, honey." Beth touched her arm. Beth was extremely popular among the moms even though she freely gossiped about one and all: the principal, the teachers, other parents, and other kids. Emmy guessed that everybody forgave her because Beth was so funny and it never seemed as if she meant to hurt.

Beth's kid Mark and Dan had become friends four years ago, in kindergarten. Mark brought out Dan's goofy side: he was all about spitting, farts, explosions, bad guys, and unusual weaponry. But, like his mother, his ways never seemed to actually offend anyone. Emmy thought that, with some people, you noticed the exuberance of the package more than the content.

"Hey, Beth, can Mark play today?"

"Uh, sure, but let me think. At 4:00 I have to take Jack to the dentist. How about if I swing by to get him at 3:30?"

It gave them only a little over an hour, but Emmy took it.

Emmy led the two little boys out to the parking lot, feeling as if she were picking up jacks because they just kept spilling beyond her reach. "Boys, the car's over here," she told them. They buckled in without interrupting their conversation. But because Dan was so bubbly, she was happy to be the silent chauffeur. When other little kids talked to her, especially in the car, she found it really hard to answer. Their thought processes were foreign, not at all like her own children's, and their comments always came out of left field, such as, "Hey, do you know my uncle Tim? He's strong." Or, "Our car is kinda like this, but a truck." Their chatter was all the more disconcerting when you had to drive and look at them through the rearview mirror.

"Guess what? I can do that fart thing with my arm," said Mark. He began the age-old boy trick of armpit farting as Dan watched with great appreciation. The noise and giggles were escalating, so Emmy really wanted to get home soon. It was distracting her, but she didn't want to have to tell them to quiet down.

It was a bit like the way she had dealt with Eric, she supposed. Not really asserting herself, letting him joke and make his messes all the time, even when it bugged her, then letting him drift away when she got preoccupied with the boys. She always let him do what he wanted, path of least resistance. Because often she ended up liking his path!

She remembered what happened with the breast-feeding, how he had convinced her that it didn't matter. But it did. It bothered her for years after the fact. She had felt as if she'd failed abysmally with breast-feeding Nick. She had done it for, like, three days, dutifully hoisting him to her blue-veined, football-shaped breasts and enduring the agonizing pain and the cries of an infant not getting enough to eat. "How can this possibly be such a good thing? How do people do this?" she'd asked Eric in teary frustration. She had made up a bottle of formula just to have it on hand but had been determined to breast-feed because all the literature said it was the healthier option. After three days, though, that bottle of formula was looking pretty good to her. She felt like an alcoholic eying a bottle of beer as she stared longingly at the tiny bottle with the yellow rubber nipple, feeling as if her own were being rubbed off with sandpaper.

"Come on. What's the big deal? You and I had formula. We're fine," said Eric over the phone from work a year later, when it still bothered her.

"You don't get it! It makes a world of difference in terms of their immune systems. I keep thinking it might have helped Nick develop differently—"

"Nick is fine! Stop saying that. He's just not like every other baby you see."

Emmy and Eric had that conversation constantly back then, when Henry had been born and Nick was two. Before they knew for sure.

"All I'm saying, Em, is maybe you have Daddy breasts and not Baby breasts."

Emmy started crying even harder. But she also started laughing. "Oh, Eric, I just suck at this."

"Too bad Nick doesn't." Then they both laughed hard. Emmy knew that the only thing Eric wanted was for her not to be crying all day long, and frankly, he probably wanted her body to return to normal. Emmy both liked his preoccupation with her body and resented it, back then. But because of this, and how hard it was for her to nurse, she had quit breast-feeding. Because it was so hard, and also to please him. *Diseased to please*, her friend Merle had once called it. Merle had bottle-fed from the start, deciding for herself what she'd wanted to do and feeling not an ounce of remorse.

Emmy knew she wasn't being fair, but this was the way it felt to her. As if Eric should have helped her breast-feed somehow. But how? It wasn't until she had Dan that she found the right kind of help. She learned about stacking up pillows under her nursing side so that she would not have to bend her back. And with no assistance from Eric, who just made tasteless jokes about his "dumb little ornamental titties." It had made her laugh, of course; joking was his way of dealing with everything.

Mark and Dan burst into the house, scrambled up the basement stairs, and kept going to Dan's room. That was Emmy's favorite kind of playdate for Dan: the kind where the guest went to Dan's room and stayed there, maybe surfacing once for a snack. She could get stuff done, like paying bills, which was what she was going to do right now. She'd had kids over who'd make a beeline for the little playroom on the first floor and wreak havoc in what she considered to be her space.

She remembered one kid who had pulled toy after toy off the shelves without regard to what Dan wanted to do. It was as if the exposure to all those new toys made him high. The mess would have taken her a half hour to get it all back into the boxes; it actually took forty-five minutes because Dan had helped.

She went back to her pile of bills, working as she always did, from the most important ones like the car insurance and the cable bill to the more minor ones like magazine subscriptions and charity donations. The phone rang thirty minutes later, at around 3:15. It was Beth. "I'm just calling to say I'm running a little late. How are they doing?"

Emmy poured herself some half caf and put it in the microwave. Late afternoon always called for a boost. It would taste like hot metal, but with enough Splenda and cream, it would be okay. Either that or a nap. With a playdate here, Emmy went for the boost. Nick would be home soon, so they would do something together, like the Grammar Trainer software that a friend was piloting, or maybe a thought-provoking problem-solving game like Pajama Sam. Either way, she really needed an extra push. Removing the mug, she said, "They're great, as always. Easy."

"Good," said Beth. "I hate it when it's work. Like, some kids, they hang around me the whole time. I'm, like, get lost! I'm not the playdate! Do I look eight to you?"

Emmy laughed. "And I hate the kids who have to touch every toy!"

"Oh my God, that drives me nuts!"

"But our boys don't do any of that, of course."

"Oh no." Beth laughed. "They're perfect, of course."

Just as she turned away from the phone, it rang again. It was Mom.

"Hello," Emmy answered.

"Hi, dear," said Mom. Her voice sounded full of concern, and nothing had even happened yet, Emmy noted. "Everything okay? How's Nick? And the boys? I feel so out of touch with you guys."

This was Mom's way of saying that Emmy had not called in a while. "Yeah. Just busy."

"You sound down."

"No. Just tired. What's up?" Emmy could not keep a slight edge out of her voice. She really did not need this conversation now, with Beth on her way and a whole playroom to straighten up in the next hour, not to mention Nick's imminent arrival from school.

"Just wanted to connect." Mom sounded friendly now, so Emmy warmed up. "Anything new? Hear from Eric?"

"I talked to him the other night. He's taking the boys this weekend."

"Oh, that's nice. And what will you do?"

"I'm supposed to see Merle for dinner."

"Great!" There was just a tiny note of pity in Mom's voice. For all that she had not loved Eric, she thought it was worse for Emmy to be alone. Mom had stayed with her husband all that time until he died five years ago—and Dad certainly was no bargain, with his cheapness and philandering.

Cradling the phone against her shoulder, Emmy walked to the foot of the stairs and yelled, "Boys, get ready. Mark's mom is on her way." While the two boys groaned and then went right back to their playing, Emmy started to pat together sloppy piles of mail and magazines that were strewn around the first floor, so it would look nice when Beth showed up.

"Who's that, Em?" Mom asked.

"Oh, Dan has a playdate."

"Playdate," Mom scoffed. "When I was a kid, it was just called 'playing.' Now everyone's got to have a personal secretary and one of those hand pilots or raspberries!"

"Mom, they're called 'Palm Pilots,' only no one even uses them anymore. And 'BlackBerries,'" Emmy said, marveling for a moment at how much she sounded like Dan when he got peevish with her. Raspberries! Could Mom really be that clueless?

"Well, excuse me for not being up on today's technology. I'm only a first-generation American, after all."

"Mom, you do just fine," Emmy said, exhaling, trying to relax and not sound cross, and started walking back up the stairs. She stopped at Dan's room. "But I should go and get this kid out of here." They said good-bye.

"Hey!" Mark called out. "I heard that!"

"Oh, you did? I thought I was speaking a foreign language with you guys."

Mark laughed. Emmy loved that kid.

She went in and tousled both boys' hair. "You guys going to help me put some of this crap away, or what?"

They both squealed with laughter. "Your mom said a bad word!"

When Beth showed up, they greeted each other with genuine pleasure. It had been a while since they talked. So they made arrangements for a future playdate at her house, maybe breakfast soon. It was all very relaxed and matter-of-fact by now because they'd been at it for four years. Mark and Dan got along so well, it was a real joy in Emmy's life, having something so easy for one of her kids.

Chapter 7

The honk of a horn woke Emmy up in such a way that she felt as if she'd never been asleep. It sounded like her horn, so she got out of bed and looked out the window, pushing the stiff window shade aside. Why was the dome light in her car on? Did someone leave the door ajar or something last night and she didn't notice? And what was that horn? There was no other car in sight, so she kept staring out the window trying to understand, but she couldn't.

She went across the hall to the bathroom, wondering if she could get to sleep now. It didn't feel as if she'd be able to, considering the way she'd shot out of bed and leaped straight for the window. On nights like these—and they were more frequent than she would expect given the alleged quiet of her neighborhood—her mind was a jumble of her worst possible thoughts.

It was all the random scary stuff that people think of when they can't sleep, like fear of fire, murder, or imminent poverty. Emmy would think about madmen breaking in to rape her and shoot the children after they'd been forced to watch. Sometimes she'd also see small flashes of things that happened during the day, or the last week, or even a month ago, and ruminate about what they meant, like the most recent time she saw Eric, and how he didn't seem at all interested in the fact that she'd found a new speech therapist for Nick. Actually, he'd seemed almost angry at her about it.

"You know, Em," he'd said, "it's just that they never work out. He gets aggressive, and then, you know, end of story."

Emmy had chewed her lip, not knowing what to reply. It was true, after all. Her stomach was in knots as she had interviewed this new guy over the phone to see if he would take on someone like Nick. Someone like Nick. Now *she* was thinking that way! "*Someone like Nick.*" What did that mean, anyway? He was just

Nick. But everyone treated him like some kind of creature to be kept at arm's length. Some kind of experiment gone awry. "You should know that sometimes, every now and then, he gets aggressive," she had told the therapist, by way of disclosure.

She used to feel as if she hated the world at times, especially the people whose kids were all "normal." She wanted to slap every one of them because they didn't know how good they had it. And then she'd catch herself, and her anger would evaporate. She knew it was not like that; no family was perfect. *No one* knew how good they had it. She didn't, either! Three healthy children! A home of their own in a decent town. And Nick was more than fine: he was the love of her life; all three of her children were.

Still, she felt frustrated by the way people stared at him. Why couldn't a person be different? Couldn't they see how sweet and beautiful he was, too? Why were Nick's odd ways viewed as something to be changed, stomped out? Or belittled and laughed at? She had said all this to Eric.

"Em, it's not that," Eric had said. "It's for his own good. The more he can fit in, the better things will go for him. You know that. He's got to learn to live in *this* world. You're not going to get the world to change for him."

"*In this world.*" What was so great about this world, anyway? Emmy thought, knowing Eric was right, hurting so much for her boy. She had said, "I don't know. Maybe some of it can change for him. Anyway, speech pathologists should be required to treat any case, no matter how challenging."

"Sort of a Hippocratic oath kind of thing?" Eric had been smirking, joking as always, but Emmy had not wanted him to. When it came to Nick, she felt dead serious. But Eric seldom was, and this made her feel lonely.

"Yeah, whatever," she had said, her voice curving downward, dropping away from him. *Fine, I'll deal with it myself,* she'd thought. Just like everything else.

She looked out the window again. The car was now dark. She

was shaking, terrified. Was someone in the car, trying to hot-wire it? Had they hit the horn by accident? That's what woke her up. And then—did they see her at the window? Were they now lurking in the dark, waiting for her to get back to sleep so they could steal the car?

It was so hard to live alone sometimes.

Against her better judgment, she dialed Eric's number, but hung up before it rang.

Emmy lay there a bit longer. Smaller problem thoughts would form, but then they burst like Nick's bubbles after he'd stirred the can too much, sudsy and weak. She could tell by the way her foot was rubbing rhythmically against her ankle that she was relaxing into sleep, at last. She closed her eyes, and just as she was giving herself up to blissful oblivion, the phone rang.

Her eyes flew open. "Hello?" Her heart was racing.

"Em, did you call me?" It was Eric.

"Oh yeah. Sorry, I thought I hung up in time."

"Nope."

An awkward silence hung between them.

"I called because I heard someone outside."

"Like what?" Eric sounded concerned.

"The horn, and a light on in the car. Then it was out. It was so creepy, and I got scared!"

Eric laughed. "Who'd want to steal that pile of shit?"

"The Volvo is not a pile of shit!"

"Em, it's, like, twenty years old. I doubt you really saw anything. Maybe you were dreaming?"

"I was not! God, why can't you just comfort me or something?"

"Or what? Have you forgotten I live in Cambridge now? I seem to remember that you requested that."

Even though he said this calmly, there was a harsh, raspy edge to his voice that made Emmy's cheeks turn red. "Yeah, I did. And now I remember why. Good-bye. Thanks for nothing." She slammed the phone down and flopped back on the pillow. Sleep would not come easily now.

It had taken months for her to get used to falling asleep without Eric there. For all the years of their marriage, they had always gone to bed together, at the same time. They had become completely dependent on feeling the weight of the other next to them, solid and warm. She hated to admit it but she'd even take his snoring now if he could be here. Just to get to sleep, though. Nothing else. She still did not want to have him around during the day, sullen and unhelpful as he'd been. Resentful of her with the boys.

Then again, she did want him around. She hated living alone. But the fact that she missed him, his stupid, really funny jokes, and his maleness made her angry. She was so angry. Still. Why? She wasn't even sure anymore. Just picturing his face, withdrawn from them, sucked into the computer, not dealing with the boys (Nick), had the power of a punch to the belly.

She shook her head, shut her eyes, and tried to meditate as she'd learned recently, from a magazine article Merle had sent: "Meditation Made Simple." She had laughed when she saw it. Funny thing was, sometimes it did make her feel a little better. But that was probably mostly because Eric had been kind of sweet. Even though he had been annoyed at her, he'd made sense about the car and she no longer felt afraid. This was one thing about Eric—he was always so rational, and sometimes it was (still) a great comfort. That was probably what she missed the most. Asshole. She didn't want to always be reminded of her need for him.

The next afternoon, Emmy collected Dan from pickup at his classroom, and they started to walk down toward the eighth-grade wing to get Henry. Usually he had lumbered over to them by now, so she wondered what was up. They bumped into him by the first landing. He was already taller than her, with bushy blond hair that touched his T-shirt collar. His cheeks were flushed, bringing out the swimming-pool blue of his eyes. To her, he was so beautiful that her heart skipped a beat when she saw him, but she smiled just a normal mom smile.

"Hey," he said in a very low voice.

"Hey, ready?" Emmy said.

"Uh, no, I actually have to take my English test," he said. "Remember when I was sick last week?"

She did indeed. He had not been sick at all—just in need of a mental-health day, but it happened so rarely that she let him have it. Henry was a good student. She trusted him completely, and probably to a fault. It was just that he had done some things in his life that were so breathtakingly kind, utterly unlike what one might expect from a young American boy, that she saw him with a kind of golden glow. Like the way he was gentle with Nick, or how he would just go and play with Dan, taking real pleasure in his little brother's long-winded banter and at the same time teaching him things like how to make movies and how to assemble LEGO kits. When he was little, Emmy used to say he was gifted in kindness, that that was where his genius lay. Eric used to snort, "People are gifted in math, or art, or music. You can't be *gifted* in kindness!" Well, she disagreed.

"So you'll walk home after?" she now said to him.

"Yeah, I guess," he said, hoisting his backpack and walking down the hall to his class.

Dan and Emmy had been home for an hour, sitting in the dining room going over his homework folder. How she hated it when he had spelling and sentences to write! It seemed to take hours for Dan to grind out ten sentences using words he'd known for years.

There was a jangling of keys at the door. Seeing it was Henry, she flung open the door eagerly but could tell right away that something was wrong. His eyes were strangely shiny and his cheeks looked hot.

"What is it? Why are you home so early?"

"I got caught cheating on my test. Smithers—Smith tore it up and sent me home."

Emmy felt as if she'd been kicked in the stomach. "What? Cheating? What happened?"

He couldn't maintain eye contact. "I don't know."

"You don't know? But what happened?" she asked again.

"I don't know. I guess I got nervous. I don't know."

Quit saying "I don't know!" Emmy wanted to yell, but she knew she couldn't come on too strong or he would take even longer to get it all out. "Henry, tell me how it happened."

"I was, like, doing the test, you know, and then I, like, didn't know the answer. I asked to go to the bathroom. When I came back, I kind of looked at my notes, and she caught me. She tore up the test and said I got a zero."

Emmy tried to take it all in, but questions were pouring out with the frenzied purpose of ants from a stomped anthill: What would this mean? Was there a policy about cheating, a consequence that would affect Henry? Could he be suspended? Would it damage his grade for the whole semester, even if he did better after this? Should she call the teacher?

And even more urgent: why did he do it? This was so unlike him.

She resolved to go in and see the teacher, with Henry, the next day. For now, she called Eric and told him. His response, thankfully, was much like hers, last night's argument entirely forgotten, or at least pushed aside for the moment.

"Huh? He cheated? Why?"

"I think he got nervous. What should we do about it?"

"How does he seem?"

Emmy looked over at Henry, who still had that funny look. She guessed it was guilt she was witnessing. "He seems to feel really bad."

"Well, I guess I'll talk to him about it tonight. Can I call?"

"Yes, sure," she said, warmed by that; she liked that he'd thought to ask. But then she remembered one more thing: "Eric, I think there should be consequences. For one thing, maybe he shouldn't be allowed to use the computer for a few days."

"Okay."

"And also, when I go in to talk to Ms. Smithers—"

"Smith," Eric corrected.

"Smith. Oh, man, I hope I don't slip and call her that. When I see her, Henry should come with me, right? I thought maybe I'd have him write an essay about this and how it makes him feel and what he thinks the consequences of his actions will be." She was breathless with anxiety, hoping Eric would agree—this felt so important to her. It was about Henry's character, after all! Henry, her knight in shining armor.

Eric was quiet. Then: "Yeah, that's a good idea."

Emmy was so pleased with this supportive response, so relieved that they were on the same page about this.

"Oh, by the way, Em? What's this I hear about you having a gun?"

Emmy frowned at the phone. What the hell was he talking about now? Then she remembered: Lucy. "Oh. Nothing. I don't have a gun. I was just jerking Lucy's chain," Emmy said, adding: "Her platinum chain." She heard Eric sigh in exasperation, and she smiled.

"Jeez, Em." Emmy said nothing. "She was practically choking when she told me."

"Okay, whatever. I gotta go."

Eric got off the phone sweaty handed, feeling as if he'd passed a test. Emmy could be extremely unforgiving, he realized, as Henry was probably about to find out. Eric, protective sympathy rising, felt sorry for his son. But then he realized that Emmy was still very much on Henry's side, and that she was mostly just concerned for Henry rather than angry with him. She would forgive Henry; in fact, she probably already had, and was racing toward how to help him by the time she'd called.

It was only for Eric that she felt not one drop of forgiveness.

And just like that, Eric sensed his smooth, benevolent concern for his son tip over, suddenly weighted with too many heavy feelings toward Emmy. It was all too messy for him to look at or think about for very long. Eric decided to check in with Henry privately on this to make sure he was all right, and put the rest of it out of his head.

Emmy told Henry that she'd spoken to Eric. She tried to get him to talk some more about what his consequences should be. She found herself mesmerized by his sad, faltering tones as he expressed his regret. His thin adolescent voice broke several times as he spoke, and this moved her perhaps more than his words, which were halting and slow, kind of how Eric could be when he was trying to fish out his emotions.

Her feelings about Henry's behavior were beginning to sink in and sadden her. Why had he done it? Had she expected too much of him? Poor darling. She wanted to take him in her arms and cradle him, make it all better. But not with this teenage Henry. This was new territory. She had to handle him differently, with boundaries. And she was not so good with boundaries. She figured she'd approach this talking to him from the standpoint of his own pride. Not punish him, but get him to see for himself how by his actions he had undermined himself. "You know, Henry," Emmy said slowly, "no matter what, there is no test that is so important that it's worth your honor. It could never be worth making people feel you're untrustworthy, a cheater."

Henry looked down at the ground. "Yeah, I know," he mumbled. She felt the tide of her emotions swelling up like a wave, needing to crash on something. *Why did they have to put so much pressure on the kids these days?* she thought angrily. They were just kids, but they were expected to perform at such an early age! Maybe he felt that and it had led to this. Maybe it was because of all the adults in his life, and their pressure—and their screwups. She thought of Eric, and her broken marriage, and all her moral outrage at the school petered out.

The next morning Emmy sent Dan off to class without walking him in. Heart racing, she hurried to meet Ms. Smith. She didn't know if the teacher would be reasonable, or if there was some other disciplinary action or consequence in store for Henry. She looked at him and saw that he had that hot red expression again.

"Ms. Smith," Emmy said in a voice that was more confident than she felt, "I think Henry wants to talk to you about what happened. He also wrote about it." Emmy looked her in the face and saw that she, too, was hot and red. *She feels like me*, Emmy thought. *She wishes it hadn't happened.* She turned to Henry and then took a few steps back, away from them, while he found the words to explain why he'd cheated. He was doing it well. She heard the roughness in his throat, the unmistakable prelude to tears; she also could hear the efforts he was making at holding them back and getting through this terrible moment in his life. He was doing it, and it was going to be all right. And then it was like a breeze on her face, lifting and blowing away the tremendous stagnant sorrow she had been feeling for him. Her tension broke apart, and her shoulders seemed to settle lightly downward. It was going to be okay. He was still Henry, after all.

Part II

March

Softening Ground

Chapter 8

"So this house of course needs work, but you can't get a better neighborhood than this," Emmy said. Emmy was standing in the center entrance at the foot of a massive staircase, in the exclusive Belleville Farm neighborhood. The man she was talking to was Will Cabot, a new client, up from New York; he nodded with his eyes closed and looked up at the ceiling, where a network of cracks fanned outward from the heavy plaster medallion in the center. He looked back at her, one eyebrow up, a slight smile on his lips. "A bit, yes," he said softly, more to himself than to her. He spun around and walked out of the room, leaving her there while he checked out the living room through the large archway. Emmy smelled a whisper of magazine aftershave, sharp and expensive. She gave him a few minutes, then followed him into the room.

This may well have been the most stunning living room she had ever seen, and she'd seen her fair share. You couldn't help but be moved by its beauty. She looked over at Mr. Cabot, watching his reaction. He was hard to read. He had his hands thrust inside his charcoal topcoat, his broad shoulders thrown back as he studied the marble fireplace. He reached out and touched it. Emmy knew you just couldn't help that, it was so smooth and rounded. The ornamentation reached upward, embracing a large old mirror whose silvered glass was fading. "Big enough to lie down in," he mused. He ducked under the mantel and looked up, surprising Emmy.

"Oh, it's probably really dirty. Be careful," she clucked. *What a strange thing to do*, she thought. His navy suit pants stuck out incongruously from the ash-filled fireplace.

He leaned back out, dusting off his hands and jacket. "You gotta get right in there with these old places. You can't be afraid of a little dirt," he said, grinning. "It's like falling in love. You see it, you just go for it, you know?"

"Yeah, I guess," Emmy said, thinking, *Whatever.* He kept making her feel as if he were trying to catch her off guard. "There's—um—a lot of room for a family," she said, hoping to get his mind back to buying this place, and to move him upstairs and closer to making an offer.

"Yeah, I noticed," he said. "Gotta get my wife back here to see it, I suppose," he said—again, not really to her, because he was walking away and heading for the staircase. "Or not." He laughed, but she couldn't see what was funny.

She knew she should not let herself start to dislike this client. Making this sale was important because she was still trying to dig out from holiday credit card debt. She had a feeling she could get him to buy. Refocusing on her surroundings, she wondered how she could draw his attention to the right things, the features that sell a house. Her eyes lit on the house's most magnificent feature: the bridal staircase. It swept sinuously upward from the center, dividing and circling around a center upper landing with two staircases, wrapped in deep brown wood.

"This is in pretty good shape, by the way," Emmy said, tapping on the smooth, shiny wood. But Cabot was already taking the steps, two at a time. At the top of the stairs, he paused. *Out of breath?* she wondered, then realized, no, he appeared to be in fantastic shape, for a fifty-something. She could see that he was merely studying the crystal chandelier. "Like water," he said, touching the droplets. "Beautiful." He stood back and pushed his hair out of his eyes dramatically, then put on a pair of tiny frameless glasses. He looked a little like a Kennedy, those same crinkly eyes, perfect white teeth, and tan skin, but with longer hair. *He must know how attractive he is,* she thought.

"Know the origins?" He seemed mesmerized by the chandelier.

"I'll have to get back to you on that," Emmy said.

He smiled and then poked his head into the remaining rooms, only a minute or two each. He did not linger in the old bathrooms. "Here's where you'll have to do a little work," Emmy said, almost apologetically, "but you'll see that it's all worth it. Such beautiful original fixtures . . ." Again, she realized he did not appear to be listening to her, which she was beginning to find annoying. But, okay, if he bought the damned place, all was forgiven. Actually, it was not the place that she was angry at: it was this job. And having to put up with prima donnas and jackasses like this guy.

He turned around and looked right at her now, taking off his glasses, that slightly twisted smile on his face. "How old are you?" he asked.

Utterly taken aback, Emmy couldn't respond.

He smiled slowly, warmly now, which made his eyes pull downward pleasantly at the corners. "I ask because I figure you've been doing this awhile, right?"

What the hell? She knew her face was flaming with anger, because it was suddenly hot. He laughed outright. "Don't look like that! You're fine! I'm just saying that you're not new at this, so you must realize that, yes, I want to buy this place."

I'm "fine"? He wants to buy . . . ? Emmy thought, not understanding his attitude at all. "Well, uh . . ."

"Yeah, so you can skip the selling bullshit with me, no offense. I know what I like, and I know what most things cost." He grinned—those white teeth, such taut cheekbone lines—and raked his hands through his receding, silvery-blond hair. He reminded her of someone else just then. Not so much JFK— that older tennis player? Björn Borg? But of course she couldn't put her finger on it. She never could these days, not since her fortieth birthday. Sometimes she felt as if her mind were disintegrating, neuron by neuron, like tiny bits of frayed cotton, disconnecting and falling apart in a long row, one after another. She sighed, not knowing what to say to this.

"Just let me do some figuring," he finished. There was a tiny chirping noise. He whipped out what looked like an iPhone and spun away from her, up to the third floor. She heard him speaking in clipped tones, probably to some underling at work. He was back downstairs in a few minutes, his aftershave preceding him.

She forced a smile, as a way of getting herself to let go of her irritation. She wished just then that she'd paid a little more attention to that meditation stuff from Merle.

"Aha, she smiles. Miss Graham, you may have got yourself a sale," he said.

She let the "Miss" go, though she sorely wanted to correct him in a frosty voice that would show just how above all this silly banter she was. He laughed again, as if he'd read her mind. Then she remembered something important. He was making an offer without even bringing his wife. How to raise this without blowing the sale? But, of course, if she didn't, and the wife hated it, she'd lose the sale, anyway. "Oh," she said, fumbling for the right words. "What about your—?"

"My wife? She'll love it," he said abruptly, and it was as if a dark curtain dropped over his eyes. "Gotta go." He rushed downstairs and held open the massive oak door. "Tiger oak," he said as she came closer. And then she thought she heard him make a little growling noise as she walked past him. Or did he?

"Uh, yeah," Emmy said. Why did this guy make her feel as if she'd lost even though she'd won? She tried again to let go of the tension that was squeezing her temples. She'd made the sale, and pretty quickly, but felt as if she'd screwed something up. *Okay, stop it*, she thought. It didn't matter. Bottom line, she had just made a two-million-dollar sale with very little effort. So what if she was just bit of a wimp when it came to handling arrogant men?

Chapter 9

Henry held the door for Sylvie, who passed through without looking up. She was flanked by two other girls, as always, and staring straight ahead. Sylvie hung out with girls who were okay, not too stupid—meaning they didn't whisper, giggle, and spread rumors too much. But they were on the young side: all leg, tiny bodies. Whereas Sylvie herself—well, she was definitely growing up fast. Big difference from last year, that was for sure. Henry lowered his eyes so that she would not see him looking at her.

"Let's go," barked Dan, who was standing next to Henry. "You always have to hold the door for girls, like yer some kinda grown-up!"

"Yeah, so what?" Henry said, reddening. Why did Dan have to call attention to the fact that he did nice things for girls? "It's called being polite. You should try it sometime." They passed through the doors behind Sylvie and branched off across the playground.

"Can we stop and play here?" Dan asked, as he always did.

Henry considered his homework load. He had an extra essay assignment now because of Smithers and the fucking cheating. He'd been such an idiot to do that; he hadn't even needed to, really. He'd just been kind of bored and pissed off at everyone.

In spite of his annoyance, Henry wanted to make Dan happy. "I guess," he mumbled.

"Yay!" shouted Dan, tossing his SpongeBob backpack on the ground and running for the glider.

Some things are so easy, Henry thought. Reading Dan was one of them. Dan was a good kid, but he was like a porcupine, especially this past year. Henry didn't remember feeling that crabby when he was that age. Only now. Henry pulled a book out of his leaden backpack and settled down on the wall by the play structure. The book was *The Red Pony*, by John Steinbeck. *Another coming-of-*

age story, he thought. Kids who struggle with tough situations and end up mostly worse off. Sad shit. Why did the teachers think that they had to learn that crap? They all knew what was what.

But Henry must have gotten pretty engrossed in it because the next thing he knew, he saw Dan standing a few feet away from him, his hands rolled into fists like a cartoon angry kid.

"What the hell's wrong with you?" Henry asked, knowing better than to laugh.

Dan glowered at him without answering, which Henry knew he would do. Dan got so mad so easily, he reached the point where he could barely talk.

"I asked you a question."

"Nothing," Dan said through clenched teeth.

Henry put his book away. "Dan, what is it?" he asked quietly.

Dan looked at him, his eyes bright with tears. "Why is he a retard?"

Henry blinked. "Huh? Who?" But then he knew. He two other boys standing close together, fourth graders, smirking and looking over at them. "Dan," he said, barely audibly. "You know he's not a retard." He wished he didn't feel tears coming. This would not be a good time to go emo.

"He is so."

"Dan. He isn't. You don't have to listen to those guys. They're idiots."

"He's a crazy nuthead, and I hate him. He can't even talk!"

Henry's stifled emotion burst into anger. He put his hands on Dan's shoulders. "Dan. Shut up," he said harshly. "Let's get out of here," he added, more quietly but still radiating heat. Without waiting for an answer, he gathered up his backpack and threw it over his right shoulder. He shook the hair back from his eyes and saw Sylvie standing ten feet away, by the playground parking lot, alone. Watching him. How long had she been there? "C'mon, Dan," he said, his throat dry.

"Henry," Sylvie called as they walked by her.

Henry stopped and swept his eyes down toward her. "Huh?"

"I was watching it. I saw. They were teasing your brother."

"Yeah, I know."

"I almost said something, but—"

Sylvie's brown eyes were round and wide-set. *Like a deer*, he thought. But the expression in them was bugging him. "It's okay. He's fine."

Sylvie raised her eyebrows. "No, it's not."

Dan was watching them both with interest. "They're bullies," he interjected, in an "isn't it obvious?" tone of voice. Then he shrugged with melodramatic indifference, tossing his unruly black curls like an impatient pony.

Suddenly Henry wanted to laugh and pick him up. Dan was such a funny kid—angry one minute, talking to Sylvie like an adult the next.

But Sylvie went on, "I know about your brother."

Henry closed his eyes. Everyone knew about Nick. Everyone wanted to be so nice about it, all the time. "Are you okay, Henry?" the guidance counselor always asked him. His mother, watching him, hovering. But no one did anything! Nothing changed.

Sylvie continued, "I mean, I know. Because mine is, too."

Henry had no idea what to say. He just stared at Sylvie as if she'd sprouted horns. He must have stared too long, or looked stupid, because eventually she said, "Anyway, I just wanted you to know. He's my little brother. He doesn't go to school yet. Just some people come to our house."

"Uh-huh." This news made Henry's throat burn. He did not trust his voice. He didn't know what to say, anyway. He looked at her warm brown eyes and her long, curling hair, and wished that she weren't so pretty. Or that she would go away. No, he didn't want that.

But she did. As she walked away from him, he noticed that the backs of her heels were all worn down. This made him want to run after her, he didn't know why. But he just stood where he was.

Emmy was still out in the garden when Henry and Dan came home. She felt, more than heard, the heavy front door slam shut. It was warm enough today to work out here without gloves and a hat. She never wore gardening gloves if she could help it. Even with all the dire warnings about Lyme disease, she could not bring herself to suit up to garden. Gardening had to be done like breathing—unpremeditated, spontaneous, and utterly necessary. So far she'd dodged the deer tick bullet.

She unfolded her legs, pulling herself up by the low-hanging trunk of the crab apple tree, which twisted sideways and then curved painfully upward, like an old crone with untreated scoliosis. From here she could see there were quite a few green bits unrolling curly leaves today, because of the recent unseasonable heat. The catmint was greening up, and so was the snow-in-summer. The phlox actually had visible buds; she'd forgotten how bright they were. She was always surprised anew by all the color of spring. She looked up, toward the apple tree in the corner of the backyard. There were green leaves all over, and soon pink buds would float up and down the branches like bibelots on a southern belle's sleeve. The wind rustled the buds and swirled around her neck, making her shiver in her sweaty clothes, but it felt like a shiver of pleasure.

All around her was the feeling of something good about to happen; it seemed today that the still, the stuck, the imprisoned, and the sleeping things of the world were beginning to stir and quiver with new energy. Maybe she was, too. She breathed deeply; a phantom scent of blossom floated on the edge of the cold air, and she inhaled again, trying to catch it.

"Mom! Phone call," Henry yelled from the porch.

"Okay." She walked to the back door and went inside. Taking the phone from Henry, she cradled it with her chin while she washed her hands. "Hello?"

"Emmy, 's Will Cabot."

Emmy's stomach did a tiny flip as she remembered his teasing. Then she thought: *The sale.* Was this going to fall through?

Be extra-friendly, she told herself. "Hi! How's it going?"

"Fine, just fine. Listen, I'm coming up that way again. Friday. Can you meet me to go over a few things?"

Friday. She visualized her calendar: there was only Dan's practice in the afternoon, and one showing at eleven. Eric was getting the boys for the weekend, and she was going to see Merle for dinner again. She had some paperwork, too, but nothing that would keep her from closing this sale. "Of course. What time?"

"How about around five? I'll buy you a drink and we'll tawk." She realized he was trying to be funny with a fake Brooklyn accent, and wondered again why he acted so strange.

"Will your wife be joining us?"

"Nope. She's on board, though. Showed her the pictures and the tour on the Internet. She'll love it. No, I just have to see you to tie up a few details about my offer."

"Okay. I'll see you at five. There's a place in The Point called Anam Cara. It's a nice Irish pub."

"Great! See you there." He clicked off, no good-bye. But then again, Will Cabot did not seem to be a "good-bye" kind of guy. Real pushy; slick, in fact, but what did it matter? She was going to make a lot of money from him. But that didn't quite explain why her pulse was hammering the sides of her head.

Chapter 10

Nick looked at his bowl of chili. He heard the clatter of Mommy setting down the other bowls. *Slam!* Dan took his seat, on the opposite side of the table from him. The air shook around him and went deep into Nick's ears. He lifted his arms in the air and opened and closed his hands, to push the noisy air away. "Hew, ssh," he said, which also helped quiet the air.

Nick looked at Daddy's empty chair, but he knew Daddy was not going to be there. A question-feeling formed in his mouth. He took a quick sideways glance at Mommy, putting her own bowl down and pulling out her chair.

"Whatisitnick?"

Nick turned away from her. He did not want words right now. He wanted to remember his question. But he could not.

"Nick. What. Is. The. Matter?" said Mommy, bringing her face close to him. "Why. Aren't. You. Eating?"

Eating. Nick smelled his food deeply. "Yes," he whispered. He wanted to eat. His tummy was empty and making noise. It had felt like that for a long time. He did not eat his lunch today. Margaret wasn't there, so he did not get chefboyardee. Margaret always made him that if he didn't like the lunch. But today it was Laura, and Laura did not know about chefboyardee, and Nick could not remember how to tell her.

The chili smelled hot and brown. Nick liked hot and brown smells. Chili, chocolate, leaf piles, Mommy's hair, and Mommy's garden were all hot and brown smells. But Nick could not eat because the chili had no powder on it. He looked for his spices, but they weren't there. Neither was his salsa.

There was also a smell that was very small but crowded his head, anyway, because he did not know what it was. The word for the smell was tiny, far away; it was a word he did not hear very often. It was a green word, he knew that. All of the words he knew had colors, and this sometimes stopped a word from coming out—because he was drawn to its color. But Nick knew that if he could find more words to say, the way Henry did, good things would happen, and his stomach would stop hurting. He closed his eyes to push the smell away, but that did not work because he could not close his nose. Most of the time he did not need to close his nose because smell was smaller than sounds. He decided to try one more time to catch the word, and he took a deep breath through his nose.

Henry looked out into the dining room from the kitchen, holding the door open. He blinked from the unexpected sunlight and surveyed the dinner table, where Nick sat. Milky light came through the red silk dining room curtains, turning their hems pink. It was close to six o'clock, but the sun had not set yet.

Now Nick realized the smell was coming from Henry, and so he said, "Henryshshshmellllllfeem," because he had to let some of the feeling in his stomach out.

"You talking to me, Nick?" Henry asked slowly with a quiet voice. He thought he perceived a dangerous heaviness to the air around Nick, so he stood three feet away from Nick, beyond his reach.

"No talking to me," snapped Nick. "Henry will go away." Nick was afraid that Henry's eyes would be looking at him now and there would be more words to hear. He felt so afraid that he brought his arm up to his teeth. He knew this would hurt, but it did sometimes stop words and other sounds.

Henry nodded, backing up another foot. Something was bothering Nick, but hell if he knew. When the arm-biting started, better to just back off.

It was pretty much Henry's responsibility these days to set everything out on the table, because Mom often forgot stuff. He looked over at Nick, who now seemed to be putting his nose right into his beans. Walking behind Nick's chair, he went into the pantry and came back with two small bottles, the chili powder and the onion flakes, and a small bowl of salsa. He set them down in front of Nick without a word.

"Oh, sorry, sweetheart!" Emmy said as she strode through the doorway, beaming her thanks at Henry. "What a kind brother you are."

Henry shrugged. "No problem."

Nick dumped the salsa into his bowl. Then he turned the chili powder bottle upside down and coated his beans with the ruby-red, shimmery, dusty spice. He did the same with the onion flakes.

"Ew, how can he eat that?" asked Dan disgustedly, stopping inside the doorway.

Emmy smiled. "I really don't know, Danny. I think he likes the way it feels in his mouth, don't you, Nick?"

Nick kept chewing, realizing that his mother was talking to him. He gave a quick glance around the table and looked back down at his food. He said nothing. He closed his eyes. Too many eyes, he thought, and he did not understand what Mommy had just said; he had only heard Dan shout. The air was crackling, and his ears thrummed with the noise. But even though his ears hurt, the powder on the beans brushed his tongue like butterfly wings, and he smiled down at his food. Also the small smell was gone because now he could smell chili powder. His stomach was smooth again.

Emmy sighed, as she often did at mealtime, because things rarely went as she hoped. Either they didn't like what she had cooked, or Dan was angry about something, or Nick seemed confused or in want of something, vaguely frustrated. Henry, well . . . Henry was usually the saving grace, like tonight—the one she could count on to bring good energy into the mix.

The phone rang, and she jumped up to get it, because they all hated the sound of its ringer. Eric had installed the new phone just before he'd moved out, and they'd had to live with its rusty robotic bleat ever since. "Hello?"

It was Eric. "Emmy, hi."

"Hey, Eric."

"Yeah, I was calling about the weekend."

Oh no! Was he going to cancel on her? That would just figure. He'd done that before. Working late, whatever. Their arrangement, where he took the boys on weekends, was nothing formal, just the natural result of their schedules. She worked more on the weekends, showing houses, and he worked more during the week. She had primary charge over the boys, because she was staying in the house and had more time for them, too. Plus—and this was something they did not speak about, though it was plain to her—the kids were closer to her, more attached to her. And that, she thought, was the problem in a nutshell. Eric had not been able to give to them the way she did. It was as if all he wanted was their old life, before kids, and he couldn't get over the way things had turned out, especially with Nick being the way he was. And it was this, Eric's inability to break through his own shit to reach Nick, that reduced her to blind fury every time. His emotional stupidity was how she thought of it. It trumped any feelings of longing she'd been having for him.

"What about it?" she snapped. She'd made plans to go out to dinner Friday night with Merle, which would now have to be after the drink with Will Cabot.

"I just thought maybe I'd get the boys early, like, Friday afternoon."

"Really?" Her voice was a little tight and wary from the unexpected good news.

But then Eric laughed, and it wasn't friendly. "Yeah, really. I'm their father, remember?"

Emmy didn't say anything to that. The fact that he wanted to take them early was so great, on so many levels—not only that she'd have more time to herself but that maybe it meant he was beginning to get it. Her heart felt soft around the edges as she let herself think for a moment about how wonderful, light, and easy things would be if Eric were back, *if* things were different. If he could do that extra bit for her, for the boys—if, if, if. But, of course, she could not live her life around "if."

"I have a light load, it turns out." Eric abruptly interrupted her thoughts, and she blinked, as if he'd poured cold water on her head. "I want to take them to the Science Museum. The *Star Wars* thing."

Emmy smiled into the phone. *Star Wars* was Eric's domain with the boys, one area from which she was excluded and didn't mind, either. Special effects trumped character development, action trumped dialogue, phallic light sabers sprang to life just when you needed them—these were male fixations that she could not relate to. They were all going to have a blast; even Nick would enjoy the softly lit rooms and the smooth carpet underfoot.

"Yeah, that's fine. That's great," she said warmly. "I have plans, you know," she continued, telling him about her upcoming dinner with Merle. Eric loved Merle, so she felt he would be supportive of her going. That is, unless he was jealous, which was quite possible, too.

While she talked, she stared at her face in the dining room mirror and was happy not to feel like flinching. She pulled her hair back, covering some of the strands of gray that she could suddenly really see. They seemed to burst from her part like tinsel. Overnight! *That's it*, she thought. *I'm calling the salon tomorrow and getting this colored.* Maybe some new clothes, too. The salon was in the mall, along with her favorite clothing store. She had not gotten anything new so far this year, and her weight was good, despite this being the all-you-can-do-is-eat end of winter.

"Hello?" Eric said, annoyed, realizing that Emmy did not seem to be listening to him. He felt deflated thinking of Merle. He realized just then how much he missed Merle and Alex, their get-togethers as a foursome. When he had left Emmy, he'd lost a lot more than just his home and family, he thought, his mouth twisting.

"Oh, sorry," she muttered.

"So, I'll get Dan from practice and swing by for Nick, too. Henry will be home, right?"

"Sure, I'll tell him. Thanks for this, Eric."

"Oh, don't thank me," he said. "I'm not doing it for you."

Then he must have realized how snide that sounded, and added, "I mean it's a total pleasure, is all. See ya."

She clicked off, fuming. It was that sardonic sense of humor of his that so often got in the way now. Not like before all their trouble. Back when he was her Extreme Opposite, and she could not get enough of that. His hard, lean WASPy ways and whiplike jokes used to drive her wild. But then she flashed back to the last time she and Eric had tried to make love, and almost cringed, remembering how badly it had failed. He had lost his characteristic self-confidence and was left with just anger and then, finally, indifference. He had been commanding, confident, always sure of himself. So sure of her. Definitely the sex had been the best part of their relationship. But even that had faded away when he'd started withdrawing from all of them, and then sex had become another unapproachable problem for them.

Was that all over for her, too? She could hardly bear it. No more sex? How could *this* be her life?

Then, out of nowhere, Will's face popped into her head, and against her better judgment, she smiled softly to herself. Hmm. Had he been flirting with her? Like, in a serious way? She laughed, thinking of him growling about the tiger oak, and now asking her out for a drink.

She was still married—technically—but she could flirt, couldn't she? Hell, she was practically divorced. Separated for more than a year, what did that mean? But Eric would be so pissed off, so jealous. But the truth was, flirting had been second nature to her before Eric.

But she was forty now. Wow, if she and Eric really did divorce, would she become a Susan Faludi statistic? Even though that depressing article had been debunked, how could it not be true—that someone her age had more chance of being kicked to death by a mule than meeting a good man? Or was that the chance of dying in a plane crash?

At any rate, she could try to have a little fun, see if she could still feel attractive, not invisible, to other men. Even if the "other man" she was flirting with was ten years older, overconfident, and a bit too suave.

Anyway, she was going to look her best for this little drink.

Chapter 11

Emmy shook out her hair, rotating in the chair with the mirror in her hand. Her hair was a sheet of shimmering brown, rolled under at her shoulders in a perfect curl. Lise had given her a semi-permanent warm brown—"chocolate," she had called it—as opposed to the "caramel" shade or the "honey-wafer." Was everything better when you could imagine tasting it? she wondered. But this *was* good. It was her color, but better. That line she realized, was from an old hair color commercial: "You, only better." But it was true! There was somehow more brown to the brown. The chemically engineered shine helped, too. "Wow!" she said, making Lise smile.

"You're welcome," said Lise.

"Now, on to Archaeologie for a little long-overdue clothes shopping," Emmy said, bending down for her bag.

"Ooh, lucky," said Lise, handing her the client slip.

Upstairs, Emmy moved slowly through the rows of sweaters, jackets, and blouses, touching each group, pulling out the lacy skirts. Immediately, a thin blonde woman buzzed out from nowhere, like a mosquito, and said, "Can I start a fitting room for you?"

Emmy smiled. "Uh, yeah. No. Not yet. I need to get stuff to go with these."

The woman smiled, baring her teeth and gums. *Nick would hate this face*, Emmy thought, realizing that she did, too. "Oh, I can help with that." She spun away as if to begin immediately.

Emmy said, "No, that's okay. I haven't been here in a while, and I'm eager to see the new stuff."

"Okay. Well, let me know if you need anything. My name's Susu."

Emmy's mom would probably have said under her breath, "What kind of mother names her daughter 'Susu'?" Emmy moved away from the woman, over to the section by the far wall, where there were blouses hung next to tiny cardigans. She sighed with delight; they looked like fairy clothing, as if spun from dewy grass and fresh new leaves. She looked at the label and laughed out loud: "Garden of Eden," the name of her fantasy business. What a good omen! As she hung up her clothing choices, she realized that her heart was beating quickly and that she was flushed and happy, something she had not felt in ages. It seemed good to have a reason for new clothes, and something to look forward to.

Emmy pushed open the heavy wooden door of Anam Cara and let her eyes adjust to the muted gray light. She saw groups of mostly students, with half-empty pitchers of beer between them, strewn noisily around the octagonal tables. There were dark wooden rafters and moldings with stark fleur-de-lis shapes cut into the woodwork, where light shone through in dusty beams. Red velvet curtains tumbled down to the floor, giving the whole place a medieval inn kind of air that was somehow in keeping with the raucous crowd.

She began to walk into the room, squinting more closely at each table. Where was Will? She noticed she was now thinking of him as "Will." When had that happened?

"Emmy!" She heard his voice, already familiar to her, but still could not see him. The voice was coming from the back of the room. She wove her way through the tables.

And there was Will, his back to the wall, a black leather jacket flung on the seat next to him, reading what looked like *Wall Street Journal* on a Kindle. He had on a light gray sweater over a lighter gray T-shirt. "Sit," he said, moving his jacket.

"Oh, I'll just sit here," she said, taking the hard chair across from him.

"You sure? This is more comfy," he said, peering at her over his glasses. Emmy had thought his eyes were brown before; she realized now that she was wrong. They were actually a kind of muddy gray, very changeable, depending on the light and what he wore. *Ooh, very interesting,* she thought. And then, *C'mon, who cares? On with the sale.*

"So," she said, sliding out of her coat.

"Whoa, looking good," Will said, doing that squinty JFK thing again.

"What?" Why did he always have to do stuff like that, and derail her train of thought? But why, also, was she blushing? Emmy was thankful for the semidarkness of the place. *Way to stay on top of things, Emmy!*

"That is a very lovely outfit," Will said, his voice softening like velvet. "Brown becomes you."

"I—uh, thank you," Emmy said, flipping her hair off her shoulder. What the heck—? He really was coming on to her! Excited and guilty at the same time, she flashed back to the comment about his wife and the house. "*Oh, I suppose she'll have to come up and see it—or not,*" he had said. Truly unconcerned, now that she thought about it.

"So, what'll you have?" He handed her a menu. "The beer's good. Drink beer?"

"Not really." She looked up at the waiter, who had appeared suddenly. "I'll just have a Diet Coke."

Will laughed. "Diet Coke? At least have some wine. Come on, it's Friday night. Happy hour! Bring her a glass of—white okay?" He looked at her closely, taking off his glasses. She nodded. "Sure. Thanks."

"Pinot Grigio? That would be my guess."

Has this guy ever experienced a moment of hesitation in his life? But still, Pinot *was* her favorite. "What does that mean? That I like Pinot."

"Oh, no biggie, just a little game I play with myself. A person's drink choice can tell you a lot about them. I figure you like an easy, gentle wine. Actually, why don't you just bring a whole bottle," he said, turning back to the waiter.

"Great," said the waiter, and left.

"Will, that's really not necessary. I won't be having that

much—"

"Don't worry!" He reached out and patted her hand. His touch was light and smooth. She drew her hand back. "Will—" she started to say.

"Shh," he said. "No worries." The waiter set down the glasses and opened the bottle. He poured equal amounts into the glasses, not waiting for them to try it. It was not that kind of place. Emmy looked around at the young crowd. Sighing, she lifted her glass to her lips.

"Here's to the Belleville real estate market," Will said, reaching over to clink her glass. She smelled his faint aftershave, blending lightly with the aromas of wine and beer. She swallowed the wine quickly, immediately feeling its heat radiate through her.

They sipped their wine, and he eventually went through every point that was holding up the sale. He was a shrewd businessman, getting the price down into the low one millions because of things that had already been taken into account in the asking price. Old termite damage. At one point, she forgot herself and slapped the table. "Come on, Will!"

He burst out laughing. "Okay, okay!" But then he simply continued with his list of what was wrong with the place. Needed new gutters. Old bathrooms. He was definitely very good at this. He tapped her hand—but just for a second, nothing inappropriate. "You're funny, Emmy," he said. "I'm not sure you belong in business, that's for sure! You're as transparent as this glass."

She frowned and told him point-blank to stop making fun of her.

"Nah, you don't get what I mean. I just see you in a warmer, more helpful kind of business than selling buildings. Ever do anything else?"

Although Emmy thought immediately of her dream garden business, she shook her head, afraid he'd laugh at her. Anyway, she was not at all bad in real estate, had made a decent living at it for years. Eric used to say that, too. Sure, she hadn't made a killing the way others had in the booming Massachusetts market, but she'd done all right for herself, paying off their house, making renovations, and starting college funds for Henry and Dan.

"That's too bad," he said, leaning back and messing up his hair. "I bet you're really good with people, or making things for them, that kind of thing." His phone chirped. Looking at the number on the screen, he said, "Gotta go." Now his voice was clipped and businesslike. He stood up and waited for her to do the same. She scrambled to gather her papers and stuff them in her pink Kate Spade briefcase. He tossed two twenties on the table—too much, but he wasn't the kind of guy to wait around for a twelve-dollar check—and held up her coat for her. "My little realtor," he whispered, "I think I'll keep her," bending close—too close—and making the skin around her ear tingle.

Pretending not to hear, she backed away from him and finished putting her coat on herself. He winked at her and raised his hand, then hurried out the door.

Will was flirting with her, that much was certain. What she didn't understand was why she was enjoying it so much. But then she thought about going home, to all her problems—to her darling, but complicated boys, ambivalent thoughts of her mercurial husband—and all that familiar terrible exhaustion swept over her. So maybe she did know why she suddenly found Will interesting. He certainly did not make her feel tired and pathetic. No, quite the opposite.

Chapter 12

"So how *are* you?" Merle asked. How long had it been since someone really wanted to know? Emmy smiled and basked in her friend's warmth. Even though she was a southerner, you could almost never hear Merle's drawl, except when she got excited and talked faster, and then her *a*'s would become very broad. She was always quite smiley, and something about how her fashionable black pointy glasses cut in on the shape of her eyes made her expression very intense.

They had the whole evening, in the South End. They were just planning to walk and walk, from Back Bay, and end up eating in the South End. A New Orleans–style place had recently opened down there that they wanted to try. Merle was from Louisiana but showed none of the snobbery people often have about others attempting their cuisine.

Right now they had stopped at a sidewalk café for lattes and a cookie. The tables were painted in different primary colors, with bright bouquets stuck in old salt shakers. This place was notorious for its butter-and-sugar offerings. Emmy did not usually eat cookies, but tonight she would.

"I'm okay, I guess."

"You look great. I love what you've done with your hair," Merle said. Merle herself had a cap of short, curly light blond hair.

"Oh, that was an impulse," she said, wondering again why she'd decided so suddenly to get a makeover. Was it because she was going out with Merle? Or was there some other reason? Will?

"Hey, what is it?" Merle said, nodding at Emmy's furrowed brow. "Eric?"

Emmy smiled. "Thankfully, no. Actually, he's been all right."

"That's good. Considering how it was, anyway."

Merle was referring to the bloody mess of their relationship just before the separation, which was fairly peaceful, comparatively. Just before Eric left, their fights had been so awful, and Emmy had called Merle once or twice afterward. Now there was only indifference or sullenness. A sigh escaped from Emmy before she even realized it.

"Yeah, well, now he doesn't give a shit. Not that he really did then, either."

Merle frowned. She always hated sad generalizations like that. She could never let them be, always had to smooth them over. "Well, he was just so broken up about losing you. He loved you, in his own way. Still does, I'm sure."

Emmy laughed harshly. "He had such a good way of showing it."

The waitress set down their lattes. Merle and Emmy both looked for Splenda and only found Sweet'N Low. "Oh, this will never do," Merle said in her best southern belle voice. "Y'all have any Splenda?"

The waitress rolled her eyes up to her brows, which were covered with little gold piercings. "Sure. I'll be right back."

Merle turned back to Emmy, peering into her eyes in that way of hers that refused to take no for an answer—another brilliant southern belle maneuver. "Emmy, what's going on? You seem a little weird. Down? Edgy."

Emmy sighed. She really didn't know. Was it the odd, slightly inappropriate drink with Will Cabot? Or Henry, cheating in English? Or Nick, just plain Nick, and poor, angry Dan? "You name it, I guess."

"Poor Emmy," Merle said, with such a delicate warmth that Emmy could have kissed her.

The waitress sullenly slid them a pink sugar bowl stuffed with the yellow packets of Splenda. "Thanks," Emmy called to her retreating back. She and Merle giggled. "Don't cry for me, Argentina," Emmy said.

"Well, I do worry about you, living on your own in that big old house. That big, wonderful house that you bought and fixed up with Eric."

"Yeah. You should see the house I'm selling now. It is amazing! Double staircase, huge marble fireplace—"

"Emmy, you have changed the subject!"

Emmy sipped her latte carefully. "There's this client who's really attractive. Like a Kennedy or something. Or Björn Borg."

Merle's sandy eyebrows went up, forming a capital A over her
flat glasses. "Björn Borg. Emmy!"

"He's—he's coming on to me. I think."

"Well, did you tell him that was inappropriate?"

Just like Merle, the southerner, to think only of propriety.
"No, I didn't. Come on, he's a client! You don't use words like
inappropriate with a client! Besides, it was kind of nice."

"Well, *I* would. But then again, I'm still living with my husband." Merle was a gracious drinks-on-the-veranda southerner,
but she also had a little bite in her sweet tea.

"What the hell's that supposed to mean? You know I was
miserable with Eric and he had to go!" She decided that she
could not tell Merle the whole thing about Will. Not that anything was wrong, exactly. There was nothing actually to tell, anyway. Not yet.

It was still light out, and the air was warm for March. Traffic
was slow on the street next to them, with most of the noise coming from couples passing by chatting. Emmy felt a sense of well-
being settle over her like a blanket. She looked at Merle and
smiled. Merle was absorbed in telling Emmy about a cousin of
her husband's who was getting married—in Provence, no less—
and they were going. Emmy felt the surge of excitement she always felt when people talked about weddings. Emmy loved everything about weddings: white satin; tight, round bouquets of
pale pink roses; men all dressed up; women looking their best;
matching dresses of polished cotton, tulle, or silk. She also felt a
pang of envy for Merle, that she still had weddings to go to; that
part of Emmy's life seemed long over. Merle told her about the
bridesmaid dress, and the pang sharpened: delphinium blue.
How perfect. Emmy told her about her longing, and how she

loved looking at wedding gowns and bridesmaid dresses and how she often replanned her own wedding and other people's in her head, always with better clothes, and they laughed. Merle said, "You're the only one I know who actually *wants* to be a bridesmaid."

"Yeah, well, I guess I should have spent more time planning my marriage than thinking about weddings," Emmy joked.

Merle looked at her with sympathy, and tried to get her to say more. "So, what's going on now?"

"Eric is such a jerk."

Merle sighed. "It's hard, I know. You're still angry with him."

It was definitely true. And Emmy had no idea how to get past this spot she'd been stuck in for more than a year. She thought again of Will, and the way he'd looked at her, relishing the tug of excitement in her stomach. As if something good was happening. Nothing good had happened to her for so long. She felt a rush of high excitement, like the one time in college when she'd snorted coke. She had bent her head over her roommate's Hello Kitty hand mirror, painted with the white powdery lines. She remembered how her heart had done a little flip. But she was going to try it, she just knew that she was, though it was furtive, secret, and against the rules.

And with Will, it was just the same. Naughty, and potentially dangerous. Just knowing she was desirable—wanted by a guy who was kind of aging-movie-star handsome at this unlikely point in her life—felt like a better high than she'd known in years.

But as close as she and Merle were, Emmy felt that she was taking a risk thinking, let alone talking, about Will. Merle would feel torn by her loyalty to Eric. Emmy felt her neck grow warm. She could almost picture the red flag flapping at her in warning, but then she just blurted out, "I find that this guy's so obviously attracted to me. You know, flirting? I don't know what to do with it. It's kind of wild."

Merle knit her brow. Her consternation was so pronounced, she reminded Emmy of how a child would draw "Worried."

Then her face cleared as if she'd figured something out. "Why do you have to do *anything* with it?" Merle asked. "You're attractive to men. You always have been. You're hot. You know that. Anyway, flirting! It's what men do. It happens to all of us."

Emmy considered this. She did not reveal to Merle the truth of how much she'd been fantasizing about Will, and so now either she had to forge ahead and take more of a risk, telling her everything, or leave it like this. Emmy had just wanted her to listen and laugh, relating somehow, or maybe to say something warm and helpful—not judge her, which was kind of how it felt. She struggled to regain her footing in their conversation. At last, she decided to change the subject, back to her marriage. "I feel like—well, with Eric, I don't know where to start. I don't know how to move us forward," she said.

Merle's worried and slightly patronizing face returned. This was starting to bug Emmy. She stumbled on.

"I worry that we won't be able to get back to where we were before. I mean, how can you go back to marriage when—?" She stopped. This was a mistake. Merle was a great person, but she could be a bit judgmental and old-fashioned. Plus, she had that loyalty toward Eric, which was really getting annoying.

Merle waved her hand as if she were batting away a gnat and said, "But *of course* you can go back," as if Emmy were a child afraid to go back to sleep after a bad dream. "He's your true love!"

Emmy slumped in her seat. That made her sad, and it also stung—probably because it was the truth. Or had been. She'd had always thought of Eric that way, from the moment they'd met—or the day after, the day of their "Coffee Confrontation," as she thought of it. Eric had asked her to go for coffee after only the second time they'd seen one another in passing on campus. They hadn't met or anything, but she had noticed how friendly he'd seemed. She'd laughed and shaken her head, saying she had to go. She remembered thinking, *Who invites a girl to coffee when he's never spoken to her?* They didn't even know each other's names. Then, later on that afternoon, she had seen him again.

"Hey." She'd nodded, friendly but not trying to encourage him. It wasn't that she thought he was a stalker or anything; it was more that he seemed different from other guys—nerdy, or too available, too openly interested in her.

Then Eric had said, "Hey, you missed out on one great cup of coffee." He stood, head thrown back, hands on hips as if challenging her. The sun was glinting off his golden hair, lighting him up from behind, making him look superheroish, like Hercules or something.

"Yeah, well," she said, not sure why she suddenly felt foolish. She knew he was kidding her, but now she felt as if she really *had* missed out on the opportunity of a lifetime! What was it about this guy? she'd wondered. She felt tongue-tied. Over a coffee! "That's how it goes," she'd managed to say.

He shook his head as if he pitied her. "I don't know. This kind of coffee comes along only once a decade or so . . . and I'm talking more than just decaf and French roast. Well, you really missed out." He folded his arms and leaned back a little, a crooked Rhett Butler–like grin slowly snaking its way up the right side of his face.

And just like that, she had fallen.

"You just go back, that's all!" Merle was saying. "You both get over it! You're a wonderful couple! And, anyway, it's not like you did anything, except kick him out in the first place. And it's not like either of you *slept* with another person or something!" She turned her head to look at Emmy, and the light slid off her glasses, making her eyes look sharp and too bright.

Emmy looked away, feeling the connection break between them. Her disappointment flooded her. Suddenly she wanted to cry.

"Right?" Merle repeated. "Em, I hope you won't do anything impulsive with this flirtatious stuff . . ."

Em couldn't look at Merle. She felt muddled, tongue-tied. She tried to get a grip on her scrambled thoughts. Eric, Will, fidelity, lust. *Anything impulsive.* Was she? All her life, she'd been responsible, careful—so careful as a daughter, as a mother. And where'd it get her? Alienated husband, autistic son!

A knife of shame sliced into her heart for thinking this way.

But it was true that you couldn't exactly call her methodical and thoughtful when it came to men. She had thrown Eric out without realizing what was happening, without ever discussing it with anyone. It had sprung up like a hidden volcano, from deep within her, all this anger at him, and his inability to share their tasks, or the real issue: his inability to connect with Nick the way she had. She had not questioned her out-of-control anger; she'd just run with it. For the last year, all Emmy had really done was live day to day, problem to problem, in reactive mode. The only thing she could plan, it seemed, was her garden. Which was actually a trial-and-error kind of thing. She had simply stopped dealing with her feelings about her husband, slipping into a robotic routine so that she could function for her kids and her job.

And now? With the new little bit of excitement coming into her life, she was noticing feelings that had been buried, pushed down inside her like crocus shoots under a heavy weave of leaves and mud. There were desires left unnourished; she now saw this. She was suddenly aware that something inside her was starving, and the thought of Will was kind of making her mouth water. She felt crazy-hungry, imagining herself to be like one of those cartoon wolves who looks at the little chicken sidekick and suddenly sees him as a tasty roasted dinner. But even as she acknowledged this, she realized that she was being buffeted by forces all around and within her, and not actually controlling them or thinking them through. And this, she admitted to herself, seemed to be her modus operandi with men. Look at how she had just kind of become absorbed with Eric, then with his children, and then she'd just kind of let him go.

She turned to Merle with a sad little smile on her face. "I haven't done anything impulsive, no." She sighed, thinking, *Not yet.*

Usually it was this practical, knowing-what-was-what aspect of Merle's character that made Emmy feel so safe with her. Merle's certainty and levelheadedness were something she took refuge in. But not now. She could see the colossal implications of what

Merle was saying, but she also saw how she felt—her nascent crush on Will—and she suddenly sensed that familiar tremendous pressure again, like books collapsing on top of her. Because even though she hadn't done anything with Will, she felt herself being pulled, inexorably, in an unfamiliar direction. And with it, a small but sharp rift opened up between her and her best friend. She stared at the flowers on the table, gerbera daisies in red, yellow, and orange, so vivid they almost seemed fake.

Chapter 13

"Here's our stop, boys," Eric said as the train pulled into the Museum of Science elevated subway station. They clattered down the rusty iron steps and crossed over to the museum. When Eric saw the long line of people in the corrals, he sighed, feeling the familiar streaks of apprehensive panic start to spread through him. Would Nick be able to deal with this? he wondered. But mercifully the line did not take as long as it looked.

He looked around as they waited and noticed two teenage girls staring in their direction, nudging each other and giggling. He followed the line of their eyes directly to Nick, who was squeezing air and talking softly to himself.

"Nick, Nick," he pleaded in a whisper, trying not to get irritated. He hated when people stared at Nick. It was as if they were staring at Eric himself, and finding him lacking somehow. Maybe because Nick had never grown into enough of his own person, who could be responsible for himself, Eric always felt as if Nick were a reflection of him, a part of him. A part of him that was all messed up. Bright red shame flared up in his face. He did not want to feel these feelings, or think these thoughts. But he'd never learned to just shrug, the way Emmy did. "Quiet hands," he whispered. "Quiet silly talk." Goddamn it!

"Okay, yes," Nick said. Then he exploded into a very loud cough, mouth open, spit flying. The family in front of them turned around. Their little boy looked up at Nick, wide-eyed, and remained turned around for the entire rest of the wait. *Even a five-year-old can tell he's not normal.* Eric's face got hot and he took another glance over at the girls, but they were no longer staring overtly at Nick; they were all texting on their phones. He checked his watch. Here five minutes and he was already in a sweat. But Goddamn it, he was going to do this. It had worked last time. All three of them had made it through the electricity thing a while back, and all three had seemed to like it. Today, the *Star Wars*. Just an hour. Then they'd have McDonald's and call it a day. After that, videos, homework, snacks, whatever. He was not a fuck-up father.

The phrase bounced around in his head like a spiky mace, hurting everything it struck. Well, maybe he kind of was. He was here *alone* with them, after all. Actually, that made him a fuck-up husband, but maybe a good father! He looked back at the girls, happily txting on their phones, heads down, fingers flying, and suddenly felt the way he used to in high school, hoping the popular girls wouldn't notice him and laugh at him for one thing or another: weird hair, wrong pants, bogus-brand sneakers. Only now it was Nick he was afraid for, but his problems went far beyond fashion.

Henry wanted an iPhone, like the teenage girls were using, Eric knew. Emmy was totally opposed to it, but Eric didn't think it was that big a deal. Yet, the way they had always done things, especially when they'd been a working family, was to defer to the one who felt more strongly about something. Usually it was Emmy. The only things Eric felt really strongly about had to do with how you designed buildings, and how they were then built. The right way to create shape, and the wrong way. Maybe the Red Sox. But that was it. Everything else was too amorphous; he could never quite get his head around stuff like what children should and should not do, unless it involved danger or health. Things like whether to let them have a smartphone—Eric could not muster passion about something that did not move him personally. He had a phone to make occasional calls. That's all. Maybe txting Henry. He knew intellectually that kids did far more with them than that, but it didn't bother him. He had been an excessive kid, too, in the geeky sense. Buildings, buildings, and more buildings. And geometry. These were his passions, his indulgences, the things that had made *his* mother worry about *him*.

At last, they were inside. They strode purposefully through the museum, not stopping to check out the Rube Goldberg sculptures, the strategically placed gift shop, or the musical stairs. They were going to see the dinosaurs, and that was it. They were men with a mission, thought Eric.

As they passed the elevator, Nick said, "Go in elevator."

Eric knew they really didn't have to because it was just one flight down and the stairs were right here. But he also knew better than to say no to an articulated request by Nick, especially if it made some iota of sense.

"Oh, why do we always have to do what he says?" asked Dan.

"Go in elevator! Go in elevator!" replied Nick, his eyes dilating, his voice rising.

Shit. "Nick. We are. Right now. Push the button." Eric glared at Dan. "We don't always do what he says." But his stomach hurt as he said it, because he knew it was sort of true, what Dan was saying, or at least he should respond differently, but—

Nick pushed the Up button.

"Yeah, in fact, we pretty much never do, because he doesn't say much," agreed Henry.

Dan turned toward him and said through his teeth, "That's because he's a crazy nuthead."

"Dan, will you give us a break!" Eric said, jabbing the Down button hard, over and over, in a futile effort to counter Nick's push. The elevator binged with the red arrow pointing up. In a flash, Nick slipped through the sliding steel doors.

Eric leaped forward. "Nick! Get out!" He thrust his hand into the slot, but the doors were very heavy. Something was wrong with the mechanism, because his hand made no difference: it did not make them stop moving together. It felt like a giant set of jaws clamping down on his wrist, trying to swallow his son. He yelled, "Stop!" knowing there was nobody to stop it.

Nick looked at him blankly through the closing doors.

"Jesus fucking Christ," Eric muttered, punching the closed elevator. A guard started walking toward him.

"Can I help . . . ?" His eyes had a stretched, wary look that told Eric he had only one chance to explain himself.

"You just said a bad word," Dan muttered. Sweat seemed to be pouring out of every crevice in Eric's body. He whirled on

Dan. "I swear to God—" But then he saw Henry scrambling up the stairs two at a time to intercept Nick when the elevator stopped. "Come on, Dan," he said, following Henry, leaving the guard standing there.

They reached the elevator just as it stopped. Panting, Eric reached through the slowly opening doors and grabbed Nick, who was alone in the car.

"Go in elevator," Nick said.

"Yes, you did, didn't you?" said Eric, jumping inside next to him. "Now let's take it down to the dinosaurs." They rode down in the humming quiet of the closed elevator, which, to Eric, felt like the sacred silence in a church.

Chapter 14

"Mom, how 'bout we make clay figures?" Dan was across the room from Emmy at the dining room table, his head just making it over the table's edge. A squooshy dark brownie sat directly on the table in front of him, uneaten. He was more interested in his water bottle, which Emmy had thankfully saved for him from last week's excursion to the pharmacy. He had asked for "his" water bottle today while in the car driving home, and for a moment Emmy had thought, *Oh no*, but then remembered being smart enough to have saved it. Never knowing when Dan was going to insist on something from the distant past, she'd learned to keep things, just in case.

She was standing at the granite counter with her laptop open. If she could, one eye would always be on that screen while the other took care of all other business. But she also loved having an excuse to sit with Dan and study him. Would she ever stop marveling at his perfection?

Bing, she got an e-mail. She was dying to see what it said. It might be from one of the other realtors who had fielded a call from the couple who were interested in that town house. She was also hoping maybe she'd hear from Will.

And what would that mean to her?

She tried to think, but all she got was a wildly thumping pulse and sweaty hands.

"Come on, let's make clay figures," Dan said again. Emmy sighed, wiping her palms on her thighs. This was Mommy time, after all. But she couldn't help it; she was reluctant to play because of the tantalizing unread e-mail.

But also, sometimes her sons' invitations to play made her tired before they even started. Maybe because of how it had been with Nick, who had not played with toys, always preferring wiggling string or sunbeams. She had felt so unhappy sitting on the floor with Nick, who was more like a kitten than a toddler.

But it was also the sheer energy it took, to get into play the way Henry and Dan did. Child play with Henry and Dan was fun, but it was amorphous, unpredictable, running on beyond bounds of mealtime, daylight, convention, responsibility, so it took a lot out of her. The boys also did things like mixing totally different toy types. McDonald's Happy Meal dolls played with teddy bears. Miniature fake food shared a plate with Play-Doh birthday cakes. Dan would put LEGO men into a Playmobil castle; stuff would be taken completely apart, or the bits got scattered under dressers, rugs, beds, never to be found again. Things could remain permanently disassembled, or parts got put away in the wrong boxes—but it all worked, somehow. The toys seemed the better for it. The boys had a kind of exuberant imaginativeness that she herself experienced only when she was gardening: a letting go of formal thought, which then paradoxically led to an enhanced level of thought and creativity.

Another *bing*. She jumped up and looked, then scrolled down and clicked. Oh, well. Just Gifted and Talented Parent Advisory Committee (G/T PAC) announcements. "Dr. Cindy Fang, renowned specialist in differentiated instruction, to give workshop at Bowker School, 7:00 p.m., Wednesday." Emmy used to be an active member of that group, back when she began to suspect that Dan, like Henry, was tremendously gifted academically and the school was doing nothing for it. *Delete*. "Okay, Dan, let's do it." She closed the cover with a determined snap.

They searched for the clay, and for a moment she was afraid it was on the third floor, in the attic playroom, which she had not been heating. It was so cold up there, and frankly, a bit creepy. They used to have bats coming in through the attic bathroom ceiling, where there was a wide-open vent from the roof. That was the scariest thing they'd ever encountered. She didn't care what the environmentalists said. Bats might be beneficial outdoors, but you got one indoors and it was a horror movie. They flew erratically and were huge with their wings open. They might be more afraid of you, but they sure didn't act it. They were known to carry rabies, an incurable, horrible disease; and they swooped right at your head. She never wanted to hear Henry cry the way he did that night, and she couldn't protect him, Goddamn it. But eventually Eric did. He got their neighbor, who had also had bats, to come over and help. Together, they trapped the thing when it came to rest in the bathroom, suddenly as tiny as a brown leaf. A leaf nestled on the bathtub rim. A leaf that was soon crushed under a tennis racket, swept into a Baggie, and brought to the state lab in Boston, where its brains tested negative for rabies.

But Dan uncovered the clay somewhere in his room, sparing them a trip to the attic. She looked down into the shoebox he held out to her and saw primary-color chunks of plasticine, with varying amounts of hair and dust clinging to them. Some pieces were mottled green-red, blue-green, hopelessly and eternally joined. She tried to pull apart an old volcano, to separate the red lava from the little green mountain. It was futile, and her fingers become sticky and green.

"Mom, we're making tikis," he said in an exasperated tone, as if he had already told her a number of times—which he had not. "Oh, you took apart my volcano."

"Yeah, I hope that's okay. I want to use these colors," Emmy said sheepishly, wondering what he meant by *tikis*. She didn't know why she had pulled the thing apart; she was actually getting a little bored and felt like mindlessly squeezing something. But she knew it would go over better with Dan if her destruction seemed purposeful, as if she were with the program. So she had pulled the volcano inside out like a minigramophone. Now it was a blob. Maybe she'd make an animal out of it.

"It's okay," he said, satisfied that she was making an effort, and he pressed a clown-like character into shape. It was quite good; the arms were tucked against the sides, and there were little yellow hands. As always, seeing Dan's talent for art buoyed Emmy and made her smile. It also made her remember, a long time

ago, when she had told Merle that Dan seemed to have an apti-
tude for art. Merle was an artist, and a very good mother. Emmy
figured she would have some great advice, like enrolling Dan in a
baby art class or setting aside time to draw with him every day.

"What should I do?" Emmy had asked her.

"Get him some paper," she'd said.

Good old Merle.

"Wow, Dan, I like that one," Emmy said of his clown.

"That's William," he explained, as if that were all she needed
to know, and suddenly she wanted to clutch him to her and kiss
him all over his smooth, tiny face.

Emmy restrained herself, of course, and instead settled in and
started pressing her own tikis, which, it turned out, were little
clay heads with some sort of weird aspect to them—like, one had
a removable skull top and an egg inside instead of a brain; another was all blue with a red tongue sticking out. Emmy took the
blue one and formed a little catlike body. The first Sphinx tiki.

Dan liked it. "Hey, Mom, you made a cat!"

She made a few more and so did he. They worked in companionable silence, and it felt so good. The floor was warm, and her
clothes didn't constrain her too much as she sat cross-legged
with Dan. Adult limbs could be so ungainly, and well-tailored
clothes did not bend easily when playing; today she was wearing
old jeans, a pair of Eric's sweatsocks, and a stretchy cardigan. She
made a two-headed guy with pizza in his flaccid hands, and then
put a small body on the removable-skull guy. She also took a
little red head and put it on a green tree trunk. They were working in the small playroom downstairs, in between the living room
and the dining room, surrounded by LEGO boxes stacked up
against the wall along with old Hot Wheels boxes; piles of the
soft pastel foam letters with the bumpy surfaces, which no one
had played with in years; and a tray overflowing with Playmobil
parts. There was a large bay window, and the sun moved around
back of the house, so it was often sunny there.

This felt so right. It was what she was supposed to be doing:
just playing on the floor with her little son. She wished that this

simple way of being would happen more often for her. She gazed dreamily at Dan's head, bent on his delicate neck as he dexterously gave life to tiny monsters. He demanded nothing of Emmy, except to keep him company as they formed their creatures. Being so close to him, she could smell his hair very faintly—a clean-skin smell.

Hearing a horn somewhere outside, she looked around—and immediately noticed her computer sitting there in the dining room. She felt the flow of the moment stop and drain away. "I'm going to go clean up, sweetie. My hands feel uncomfortable with all this clay on them, okay?"

"Okay." Dan did not look up. He was still working. She felt that maybe it was okay that she was done. A job well done.

She checked. There it was. Just two lines. But her insides contracted when she saw the familiar name: wcabot@gmail.com.

"Hi, E—

"Can we meet again? —W"

She straightened her back and sat perfectly still, trying to think clearly and assess the situation. The left side of her head tingled, and her cheeks felt hot.

This time, it was not about the house. Otherwise, he would have said so.

She thought of the way he had patted the bench next to him, commanding her to "sit." The smell of his black leather jacket. The decisiveness of his movements, his unconscious ease with himself. She did not let herself think about his idiotic remarks, his blatant sexism, his wife. Nothing penetrated this hot haze in her head. He was attracted to her. And he was very attractive, in a bad-boy way. And he wasn't Eric. Her fingers were poised over the keys.

"OK"

She pressed Send. Her heart was pounding and she felt slightly nauseated, but she pushed the realization away. Now she watched the mailbox, hardly able to sit and wait for whatever might come next.

Part III

April

Preparing the Ground

Chapter 15

Nick pulled the seat belt over his body and felt it click into place. He loved the fastened seat belt. He loved the car. In the car, everyone looked ahead or out the window. People talked but you didn't have to. He could just look straight ahead and at the lines in the car leather, watch them blur and then sharpen, blur and sharpen, creating gray thicker lines that shimmered and waved. He loved things that shimmered and waved.

He had first discovered the shimmers when Mommy had picked up Floppy Bunny and tossed him into the air, shouting, "Hi, Nick! Hi, Nick!" in a squeaky voice. Nick knew that Floppy Bunny did not really sound that way—Floppy Bunny was always quiet and soft when he was alone with him—but he didn't mind the squeakiness because he loved the way Floppy Bunny wiggled in the air and gently tumbled downward, blurring into an airy waterfall before his eyes. The downward shimmering of his bunny washed over him like cool water, such a beautiful motion that Nick felt like laughing with joy. Bubbly giggles had escaped from his throat, surprising him. But they felt good, so he kept doing it.

After that, Nick always tried to reproduce the downward shimmering of objects, but nothing worked that well until he discovered ribbon. He wiggled and twirled some white curly ribbon, left over from a birthday present. He was standing in the front hall, where the sun streamed in from the long window at the top of the stairs. As he wiggled the ribbon, the sunlight caught each edge of the ribbon's curl and shone silvery white. Nick's eyes were bathed in the snowy light that quivered in his hand, and he could not move. His insides swelled up and he felt the bubble laughter again, coming out of his mouth, floating around him and wrapping him in weightless sound while the ribbon filled his eyes with light.

But then a hand had wrested the ribbon from his little fingers.

The sudden sharp contact made his hand throb. "Nick! Nick!" Mommy yelled. "Say, 'What, Mommy?'"

Nick looked at his empty hand.

"Say, 'What, Mommy?'" She had pushed her face right in front of his, filling his eyes with her eyes. He looked to the side.

"Say, 'What, Mommy?'" Again.

Now Nick remembered. The way to get the string back was to say what he heard. "What, Mommy?"

"Good boy!" Mommy showed her teeth and pulled her face away. She slipped the ribbon back into his hand. She pulled out another ribbon from her pocket. "Look, Nick," she said. She lifted the ribbon up toward the sunlight and proceeded to twirl it as he had done.

Nick had watched, mesmerized. He looked at the ribbon, then at Mommy. Her teeth were showing a lot. He drew his lips back and showed his teeth. "Nice smile, Nick!" Mommy said, her voice getting bubbly. Nick liked it when her voice got bubbles in it. Bubbles and shiny, shimmery things were best.

Now Nick crossed his eyes together, staring fixedly at the lines in the leather. Dan, who was next to him, could feel the taut concentration in his brother's body. He looked at Nick, who appeared hypnotized by the seat in front of him.

Dan felt a jab of irritation and sharp embarrassment whenever he caught Nick doing things like that, things that no one else did. Even though Nick had been like this all Dan's life, the older Dan got, the harder it seemed for Dan to accept. His experience with Nick was like being lost in that maze at Story Land, or the house of mirrors—only not fun. There were few paths that led him to anything clear with Nick; in fact, it was like more and more of the turns he took were wrong.

"What are you doin', ya freak?" whispered Dan, unable to stand it anymore. He could see Nick squinting at the back of Mom's seat, as if he were reading it. Nick only did weird things, never normal things. Henry did mostly normal things but sometimes was mean to him. Still, Dan preferred Henry because Nick was like a baby, even though he was big.

"Yes," Nick replied, without looking up.

"I said, 'What the heck are ya doing!'" shouted Dan. "That's not a question you answer yes to!"

Henry heard Dan's sharp tones and lurched around from the front seat to glare at him.

"Danny, what is Nick doing?" Emmy asked at the same time, in a sighing voice.

"He's staring cross-eyed again!" Dan said with great exasperation, and waited for his mother to yell at Nick. A balloon of hope and frustration inflated in his throat, pushing all the way up into his eyes. He wanted her to yell at Nick. Say something. Do something about him. Though after Mom yelled at Nick, sometimes he felt angry at *her* instead of his brother.

The tension in the car pressed in on all of them. Then the car hit a pothole, which had burst open in the road from the constant freezing and thawing during the past month, and they all bounced in their seats.

Emmy listened for any new rattles or clanks in the Volvo; Eric was always warning her to avoid potholes. She sighed again. "Nick, do you want to listen to some music?"

"No listen to music," Nick said, then shouted, "NO LISTEN TO MUSIC!!"

"Quiet!" Dan yelled back. He made a fist and shook it wordlessly at Nick, who said, "Yes," again.

Henry turned his head away from them, gritting his teeth. *Thing 1 and Thing 2*, he thought, watching them from the corner of his eye. Why couldn't Dan ever get it? And, naturally, Mom was clueless. She was kind of like the mother in *Cat in the Hat*, come to think of it, the one who left a fish in charge of her two little kids. He dug his earbuds out of his pocket and inserted them, then stared out the window for the rest of the drive.

Eric sat at his desk, idly pressing the magnetic chip sculpture flat with his fingertips. He was thinking about Nick and how he never seemed to need people. This was one of the first things he'd ever realized about Nick, and it had been when he was still an infant. He hadn't told anyone, because he knew it was ridiculous, he was just reading into everything. But from the start, he hadn't felt something from Nick that he thought he should. Something had been missing, and it had scared the hell out of Eric.

But now—he had to admit that sometimes he felt a little like an autistic himself. He loved being by himself, and most other people were mysteries to him. He hated small talk and social niceties. Growing up, he'd had few friends and even fewer girlfriends, preferring to dwell in the world of perfect shapes and lines. Landing a girl like Em had been a totally freak occurrence. He was on the nerd track from day one.

And it didn't help that he now worked in an isolated building in North Cambridge. That meant he was often tucked away from the noise and social distractions of people. But what could be done about it? This was the best rent he could find, and more important, it was quiet here. Eric took off his glasses and rubbed the bridge of his nose, thinking about the meeting he'd just led, and how noisy they were, the young turk architects, like eleven-year-old boys. Or like Dan. He laughed out loud thinking about his youngest son, who delighted him despite his occasional rudeness. Deep down, Eric was even delighted with the rudeness because to him it meant that Dan would never be consigned to the world of the wallflowers; the quiet, shy geeks with no girlfriends; the fashion challenged. No, Dan was a man of the world already, at age eight. Eric laughed again, noting as always how bizarre a thing laughter is, especially when done alone. How much stranger was laughter in a silent, lonely room than laughter with others. One was okay, the other was not.

He stretched his neck and back; he'd been sitting at this table far too long. He would go get a soda. Replacing his glasses, he buttoned his collar, then retied his tie, a dark green silk paisley that had been a gift from Emmy. Emmy had told him that it "went great with his eyes," or some such thing, which he didn't understand at all, since his eyes were blue, not green. But she would know, since she studied such things; he only knew about architecture and math, so he took Emmy's word for it that it became him.

He locked the door to the conference room, his keys jingling in his hand as he slipped them into his pants pocket. He began whistling "Bohemian Rhapsody." Eric still loved Queen, and had ever since discovering them in seventh grade. He walked down the corridor to his office, where his projects awaited him. Where he was on top of his game and rarely disappointed anyone.

He just kept thinking about Emmy and the boys. Hey, wasn't today the day Nick started with the new therapist? He frowned. That was a fool's errand. He'd wanted to tell Emmy not to bother, but she was hell-bent, of course. But he knew how disappointed he'd be— Well, he meant, how disappointed *she'd* be— or did he? He chewed on the inside of his cheek.

The waiting room had been full of kids half, a third, of Nick's size. Nick's knees had sprawled forward from the little-kid chairs. Eric could sure see how out of place Nick looked. Maybe even Nick could tell. Who could be sure what Nick knew, really? Eric was saddened by the thought; he was not used to considering what Nick's feelings might be in a given situation. And that was exactly what Em was always on him about.

Nick's therapist had been a short young woman named Jackie. Jackie reminded Eric of a tiny brown mouse with scared eyes. Her face was filled with naked dread when she came out and called Nick's name. She obviously already knew about Nick's "aggressive" profile.

Nick had shot out of the chair like a cannonball and followed her into the room. Not five minutes went by before Jackie could be heard yelling, and there was a muffled bump, then the door flew open and she had shouted, "Mr. Graham!"

Eric had jumped to his feet and moved quickly. All the parents in the waiting room were watching. All the kids, even the very self-involved ones, paused in their play to witness this drama. Eric had stumbled over a toy fire truck, one of those fat red-

and-white Little Tikes ones that his boys had played with, and half dragged himself, half leaped into the therapy room. He was in time to see Jackie trying to pin Nick's arms behind his back, with his face wedged up against the wall. Nick was yelling, "No push! No push!" over and over. It made Eric feel a sharp, sudden pain, like a finger jabbing his belly. "What's going on?" he had yelled, placing his arms on Nick's. "Let go!" he had said to Jackie angrily. Nick was flailing in his arms, but Eric could tell that he would not punch him. Nick knew that Eric was here to help him. Somehow he knew that. This had made Eric want to sag onto the floor in a heap, but he didn't, of course. "I am going to try to forget what I just saw," he'd said to Jackie through clenched teeth.

Jackie's eyes had widened, and two pink spots blazed from her cheeks. "I did what was necessary," she'd said, gulping. "He attacked me out of the blue. He's an awfully anxious kid. I don't think this is really for him. It might be that—"

Eric cut her off, spitting her words back at her: "You're damned right this isn't for him. But then again, maybe that's because of you. Come on, Nick, let's go home."

"Okay, yes," Nick had said quietly.

That was the last time Eric had ever taken Nick to anything alone—until he and Emmy were separated, that is. And they had tacitly decided to forgo any more speech therapy while Nick was like this. *Like this*, he thought. That was three years ago. Nick still needed to learn to talk, but there was no one they felt could work with him. Plus, there was that question that skittered across Eric's mind every now and then like a furtive rat: at some point, were they going to have to decide that this was the most they could expect of Nick? He considered himself a practical person, but even he had never been able to voice that idea to anyone. And he certainly wouldn't expect Em to.

Eric rubbed his hair and squeezed the bridge of his nose. Sighing, he turned back to his work.

"We're almost there," Emmy announced, looking into the rear-view mirror. It was 5:30, and still pretty bright out. The smaller, ornamental trees were all in full leaf now, and the early-evening light gave their new green an almost neon look.

She was still feeling her early-spring free-floating optimism from the other day in the garden; the thaw was very real, and it was obvious that winter's back was truly broken. Even as a little girl, this phrase had evoked powerful images for her. She liked to picture Winter, a crawling, stumbling gray monster, its hands like twisted, leafless trees; its back snapped by a big, strapping, green-booted giant: Spring.

"Big whoop-de-do, speech therapy," mumbled Dan.

"Hey!" said Emmy.

"SOR-RY," said Dan, obviously not. "Besides, why do they call it 'speech therapy'? He's not giving speeches or something."

Emmy snorted but did not answer. She eyed Nick in the rear-view mirror. He looked calm. He was staring out the window, not even squeezing air with his hand. "So, Nick. Do. You. Want. To. Hear. What. We. Are. Doing. Again?"

Nick looked up for a split second. "Yes."

Very slowly, Emmy repeated the words she had told him three other times on the way over: "We are going to a speech therapist. He is a nice man named Tom. He is going to help Nick—you—learn how to talk."

"Yes." Nick was watching her eyes in the rearview mirror, intent on hearing the same thing yet again so that he would know what to expect. Such times were the only moments when he looked at people willingly.

"We'll sit in the room for a little bit, and then Tom will come out and say, 'Hi, Nick!' Then you and Tom will go into the other room to play some games and practice words."

Nick could hear and understand this. He remembered what happened in speechferapy, anyway. He had done it lots of times. He also remembered that there was too much yelling and talking. His stomach cramped up. "Noise, feem," he said.

"What noise, sweetie?"

Nick shut his eyes. He understood what she was asking him, but he knew he would not be able to say any of the words for her.

Mommy blew air out of her nose. "Okay, darling, and you're going to stay calm, right?"

"Right, okay, yes."

Emmy sighed again, only then noticing her tight grip on the steering wheel. Her stomach slightly knotted, she pulled into a parking space at West Newton Speech Associates and found herself shaking. She whispered a tiny, brief prayer to God-knew-who, that this time it would work out. "He needs this so badly," she prayed.

Henry watched his mother surreptitiously, keeping the earbuds in but the sound turned off. Jesus, with her eyes closed like that and her lips moving, it looked like she was praying! *What the hell for?* he wondered. But knowing his mother, she'd tell them all about it on the way home. Mom never kept a secret for too long, especially if it was about her favorite subjects: autism. Nick.

Emmy filed the boys into the waiting room. She settled Dan quickly with a *Highlights* magazine—even though he protested that it was for babies—and Henry took out his earbuds again. Although it had looked from the outside as if the office were in a worn, nondescript brick building from the 1960s, the waiting room was softly lit and yet also bright with sunlight, due to a strategically placed skylight. A large bulletin board adorned the facing walls, sporting kid art, and another wall was filled with announcements of conferences on autism, social skills, behavioral issues, bullying and teasing; books for sale; ads for respite workers and babysitters. The chairs were navy cloth plush, and in good condition. There were waxed wood floors in the entryway, and the windows were clean. The burnt-sugar smell of fresh paint tickled her nose.

Emmy looked over at the door that was opening. A very large man walked out. *A bear*, she thought. Everything about him

seemed ursine and grandly proportioned: his little round ears,
spaced widely apart above either cheek; his round shoulders; his
height; the fleshy paw that he was holding out to her; his benign
smile. Emmy met his eyes, smiling, suddenly happy that she was
here. Tom Palmer appraised her in a friendly, approving manner,
eyes crinkling at the corners. His skin was a little bronzed, as if
he had just been out on a walk in the woods, and in fact he
seemed to smell a bit outdoorsy, sharp pine deodorant or something. She looked down at his L. L. Bean boots, noticing he had
one jeans leg tucked into one of them and the other pulled out.
She felt herself warm toward him, but just as quickly, her defenses came up. She sighed, remembering other times therapists had
seemed nice, raising her hopes. The slight improvements, the
regression. The aggression. And then, as always, "Sorry, we're
going to have to end our work together."

She scooped up her bag and rooted around in it for her health
insurance card. "So, assuming this works out, I'll bring him the
same time, every Wednesday?"

"Why wouldn't it work out? What are you looking for in
there?" Tom asked, nodding toward her handbag. His voice was
deep, but had a husky, soft roundness at the edges. *Kind of like
him*, she thought and almost laughed.

"Oh, my health insurance card. Don't you need that info?"

He grinned. A nice smile, but Emmy noticed his slightly une-
ven teeth, the top left one angled just a bit toward the right. He
also seemed to have the habit of peering at people over his eye-
glasses. Except for his massive rugby-player build, his face
looked like a college professor's, with that heavy gray curly hair
and those small, rimless glasses perched down his nose. One
hardly ever came across guys like this—older men—in this pro-
fession. In fact, thinking back, she had *never* seen a male giving
speech therapy. It was always young, perky women.

"Nah," he was saying. "I'm going to figure that your school
system will come through, even though they're already sending
him to private. Belleville's pretty good that way. A boy who
doesn't talk needs speech therapy, don't you think?" He winked

at her.

"Um, yes, but—"

"So we'll just cross that bridge when we get to it." He turned to Nick, who was standing and opening and closing his hand, whispering softly to himself. "So, Nick," he said, almost imitating Nick, and very quietly.

Nick looked at him, then, as Emmy predicted, he looked away. "Yes."

"Can we go and play for a little bit?" Tom asked, not touching Nick but standing very close to him, not looking in his face but at the wall ahead of them.

"Okay, yes." Nick started marching out the office door.

"Hey, not out there!" Dan yelled, shaking his head. "What a freak," he muttered.

Emmy opened her mouth, but before she could say anything, Tom said, "Hey there, buddy, would you do me a favor and go get Nick? I think he forgot where he was going." He winked at Dan conspiratorially.

Dan frowned at Tom and muttered, "My name's Dan," but then did as he was asked.

"Twerp," Henry muttered. Tom looked at him and then at Emmy, raising one eyebrow the tiniest bit.

It was just a second, but something flashed between them, and she knew he really got it. All of it. And Emmy suddenly felt the way she did when she was about to lower herself into a hot bath: an utterly breathtaking sense of perfect comfort and relief suffused her as she realized how long it had been since any other adult had helped her with her boys. She said, "Well, I really hope this works out." Her voice caught on the last word.

Tom tilted his head and looked at her closely. She knew he could see the tears starting in her eyes, damn it! She tried to force a smile, blinking them away.

"We all *hope* it will work out, but I *know* it will," Tom said warmly.

Now Emmy smiled for real. "I guess things get kind of emotional around Nick."

"I can see why. Ah, Nick! There you are. Thanks, Dan." And he led Nick into the therapy room.

Chapter 16

Emmy smoothed the powdery dirt in her vegetable bed and poked holes with her fingers. She knew it was a little early to be seeding, but she could wait no longer. And this had been such a mild spring, weren't the chances good that there wouldn't be any more frost? The packet read, "Sow in May, or after last frost." It was almost May, anyway! Imagining the crop she would have—the first peppers, the sweet surprise of little jewels of red and green peeking out from under their leaves; the tight, shiny yellowy-green globes that ripened into soft, squat tomatoes—she had to take the chance.

Today she was meeting Will for lunch, at the Oak Room in the Copley where he was staying. They had decided on this plan after a few back-and-forths via e-mail, because he was just not satisfied with carrying on their business over the phone. Nor would he come to the office. The guy was simply used to everyone else bowing and scraping, Emmy figured. Fine. If this is what it took to reassure him that he was getting what he wanted (as usual!), then she would force herself to have a nice, fancy lunch with a handsome client in the middle of the week!

But she had a liquidy feeling in her stomach whenever she thought about this appointment. She had to admit she was a little worried—and excited—about whether he had other intentions, and what she might have to deal with. She still couldn't quite believe how much of a thrill the flirting was, but that's all it was. *Right?* He was married, after all, and of course, so was she. But she was also sick of feeling hopeless, and as if her life as a desirable woman were over. Because if Eric was really gone, didn't that mean all of that was gone, too? What was she going to do? Date, with her complicated family situation? She couldn't even imagine it.

Her cheeks were warm as she tore open the seed packet and

sprinkled the small sweet peas into the holes. These little life-bearing dots. Tiny beads of hope. They'd come to life, even though they seemed dead. Well, maybe she would, too. She covered them over and stood, pushing up off the soft, wet ground; her knees ached and could not straighten on their own. Her fingernails were rimmed with black dirt, and her feet were caked with wet mud. Turning her face to the sun, she closed her eyes, hoping that they would all do okay in the crazy conditions of early spring—her seeds and herself.

The Oak Room was filled with the low-voiced rumble of mostly businessmen eating lunch. As Emmy stepped into the room, she felt as if she'd entered a different world. It was almost like a movie set, of a business lunch or a men's club, with nearly everyone in suits and the confident clink of ice in glasses. Emmy smoothed the wrinkles in her black wool skirt, which was at least five years old and was clinging to her thick tights. It had seemed like a sophisticated choice at the time but now felt a little dowdy.

The sepia-toned lighting made it seem later in the day than it actually was. Very flattering to the older faces that sprinkled the room. Emmy thought she saw a familiar face. A local anchorman? She scanned the room and saw Will in a discreet corner table.

She took her seat kitty-corner to him—as far away as she could. No threat of knee brushing. Will looked genuinely handsome, dressed in a crisp navy jacket with a red silk tie; his glasses were perched on his head, like another set of eyes. He made no attempt to disguise how he was looking at her, as if it were his birthday and she were the present. Pleasure and excitement practically hummed in the air around him.

She reached for the menu and their eyes met. She looked away immediately, still trying to keep him at some sort of distance while she collected herself. It had been months, maybe a year, since Eric had wanted her this blatantly. And even though she did not like Will's personality all that much, his man-of-the-world demeanor, good looks, and overt desire made her feel very sexy; even his superficial air was kind of appealing because it felt dangerous and one-night-standish.

Her hands were shaking. Grasping for composure, she glanced at the choices on the menu and identified a goat cheese salad that looked good. The waiter appeared out of nowhere like a magic trick, and she murmured her choice to him. If only her face were not so hot; that was always a dead giveaway (although Eric always said that everything she felt showed up on her face as plain as day).

Will was still looking intently at her, and she saw that he had not even opened his menu. He flicked his hand toward the waiter, who nodded and backed away. His left hand was spread across the white napkin, the wedding band flashing gold against his tanned skin.

"Not eating?" she asked. Her throat was dry, so she took a long gulp of her subtly lemoned water.

"Not . . . yet," he said with a smirk. He leaned forward with his hand folded under his chin.

"What?" Emmy said, not drawing away, though she wanted to. She was starting to feel engulfed—by Will's physical presence and by all her own confusion. She had completely lost control of this as a business relationship. Now she could see no clear path she was supposed to follow. "Maybe we should just go over everything, since your closing is a month away."

"A whole month without seeing you again," he whispered. He reached for her hand. His fingers were heavy and warm splayed across her knuckles. Suddenly, the lighthearted flirting was slowing down, morphing into something heavy and opaque. She looked away again, not knowing what to do. Her breath was shallow. She started to think, "What if . . . ?" An image spread out before her, of a big white hotel bed and lean-muscled arms reaching for her. Body heat, wet mouths . . . It had been a long time. She felt herself pulled tantalizingly forward, upward, like the breathless ascent of a roller coaster.

Oh God, she thought. This is how it happens. People did this all the time, right? Although none of her friends ever did . . . she supposed. Who talked about this stuff?

Didn't everyone face these kinds of situations, with really powerful attractions?

But was this the point she'd reached now, as an almost-divorced woman? The thought gave her a moment's pause, a small, cool breath in the middle of the turmoil in her mind. Her eyes darted around the room like a pair of startled birds and finally alighted on a table in the farthest corner, where there was a small family. People actually brought their kids here, she thought, amazed. Her family had never been that simple. Had they?

Then the mother brought her face in close to the toddler, strapped into the wooden booster. One of those spontaneous, mindless gestures mothers automatically did, all the time. She pulled her face back, and brought it in to him—or her—again. This time, the child squealed with laughter, understanding the game now. Suddenly, this small, utterly simple interaction seemed miraculous to Emmy. She felt a deep, warm longing all the way from the center of her chest to her belly, as if this were her own baby, her moment.

That's who I am, she thought. The heat in her neck and face quickly receded like the tide, and she sat back in her chair. There were no more thoughts in her head now, just the certainty of her pounding pulse. She slid the navy-blue folder with its gold-embossed letters over to Will's elbow.

"Looks like this is one goat cheese salad I'm not going to eat," she said, standing up. She marveled at how the air felt almost crisp around her, with bronze light shining in from every window, and the ocean-like roar of Boylston Street outside. Emmy cleared her throat, ignoring Will's soft chuckle, his protests. "I think the rest is self-explanatory." She stepped out from her chair, careful not to come too close to him, then strode out of the room, her legs and hands still shaking but her head held high.

Back at the school, the boys piled into the car, absorbed in their own thoughts. "I don't know why we couldn't walk home," mumbled Dan. "And play in the playground."

"Do you see the rain pouring down, doofus?" Henry asked, eyes drooping, sliding his earbuds in place.

It was raining so hard the windshield wipers were going like propellers. Fat raindrops were landing with tinny thuds on the car roof. With the doors shut, the windows fogged up. The inside of the car smelled steamy and organic, like a pot of corned beef. "Henry," Emmy said, looking sideways at him. Henry looked even messier than usual, his long blond hair hanging in Rasta-like strings all around his head. Had he looked like that this morning and she failed to notice? "Honey, maybe we should get you a trim," she said softly, reaching out a hand to smooth his hair, which felt coarse under her palm.

Henry jerked his head away from her. "No way," he said.

"Excuse me? 'No way'?"

"Mom, let it go," Henry said, pulling as far from her as he could. This stung, but Emmy let it be.

Henry was staring out the window, watching Sylvie with her little band of friends, standing on the island by the flagpole, umbrellas open overhead. Every single one of them had some word stretched across her ass: *Juicy*, or *Abercrombie*, or *U Mass*. Even Sylvie.

Did they know how they looked to him? Could they possibly understand that doing that meant he could not look at anything else while they were standing there? He watched, mesmerized, as Sylvie laughed and tossed her hair, in that way of hers. He almost hated her then—almost. Then he felt a pang, as he remembered how she'd been close to crying when she told him about her autistic little brother.

He forced his mind away from all that. He had to do a paper on *The Red Pony*, and he had to do a really good job or else Smithers would have his head on a plate. She was gunning for him already, because of the cheating. Why the fuck had he done that? He couldn't figure it out, even now. It's not like he didn't know the answers. It was more like—he'd just suddenly been so bored, or pissed off, or something.

"Mom, can we please just play for a little bit?" Dan asked plaintively.

"Jesus Christ!" Henry exploded.

"Henry, that's enough! Danny, sweetheart, how 'bout we go to the video store on the way home?"

"Okay, but do I have to watch my movie with Nick?"

Emmy could not help sighing. "Well, that would make him happy . . ." But then she caught herself. Dan needed something that made *him* happy. Just him.

Did she do that regularly, lump Dan's wants right in with Nick's? Sure, it was easier for her to have them watch a movie together, and not have to worry about what Nick was doing or whether Dan needed anything, but—wow. Her eyes were stinging; her arms practically ached with wanting to pull Dan to her and tell him she was sorry for being so cavalier about his needs. What Nick didn't know wouldn't hurt him. "Oh, okay, you can watch it by yourself now."

"Yay!" Dan shouted, with a naked joy that made Emmy smile. *Well. At least I can learn from this*, she thought.

Chapter 17

Inside the therapy room, it was quiet. Nick sat with his chair pulled up tight against the table, a pile of LEGOs before him. Tom sat across from him with his own pile of LEGOs, building a small, rectangular structure.

Nick liked the soft lights in speechferapy. His eyes did not hurt from them, and he also liked their smooth whiteness. But on the table in front of him, there was a scattered bunch of LEGOs. He did not like LEGOs, because they were very sharply shaped, and he especially did not want to look at them right now because these were piled in a mess, all different colors—and no orange. LEGOs were never orange. This made his stomach hurt and his teeth feel bitey. He raised his hand and grabbed at the soft white air until he found just the right rhythm. "Ehhh, 'GOs, 'GOs. Hoo, hee, orange," he said, even though the orange was not there, and started to feel happier just seeing orange behind his eyes.

Tom said, "Hmm, orange?"

Nick stopped, and his hand dropped down on the table.

Tom looked around him for something orange. There really wasn't anything that was orange. The pile of LEGOs he'd just thrown down were only red, green, blue, and yellow. Tom said very quietly, "You're right, Nick. We are missing orange."

Nick found that he could hear all the words that time, because the manforspeechferapy spoke slowly and quietly, and about the LEGOs, which were really bothering him. "Yes," Nick said, and braced for the shouting and the touching. People always made so much noise and touched his body when the words were there, in his mouth. They shouted when they were happy with him. He never really understood when it was going to happen, but he knew that when he did understand their words, they usually had to touch him or yell, or move their mouths apart and show their teeth.

Tom got up from the table, slowly, the way he did everything, then crossed the room and began rummaging in the LEGO bucket. He pulled out a handful of pieces and sifted through them, finding a few off-brand orange ones and throwing back the rest. He placed them down in front of Nick. "That was good talking, Nick," he said in a whisper, not looking up.

Then Tom started to build a square structure, next to the rectangular one.

Nick exhaled sharply at the sweet glow of the orange LEGOs and raised his hand and started squeezing the air again. He was happy about the orange, but he also felt on edge, in case the loud talking happened soon, anyway, and he whispered his words this time, because he did not want manforspeechferapy to hear him and say what he was saying.

But Tom did hear, and said, "Feem?"

"No feem!" Nick shouted, and bit his arm, which hurt, but his teeth loved it.

Tom watched Nick, his expression purposefully blank. He reached across and pulled Nick's arm from his mouth. "No feem," he said quietly, dropping Nick's arm gently. He went back to building his structure. "Nick. Will you build this, too?"

Nick complied by picking up a few LEGOs and haphazardly clicking them into one another, obviously not interested.

Tom watched and then put his hand on Nick's building. "Okay," he said. "We'll build yours." He took apart his shape and started to copy what Nick was doing. Nick paid no attention and soon put the pieces down and resumed squeezing the air.

"Nick."

Nick looked at him, then looked away. Then he remembered something: Tom, the man's name! "Tom, feem," he mouthed.

"Hey, that's right. I am Tom. Nick, build mine." Tom dismantled Nick's structure and his own, and put together a simple square.

Nick picked up the orange LEGOs and started to copy Tom's. Although he hated their sharp edges, he loved the hard, snapping way the pieces fit. They always fit! And that made him happy. Nick was nearly done and then abruptly stopped. He lacked certain pieces that kept him from finishing his structure.

Tom watched without helping. He waited. He knew that this was going to be frustrating to Nick. But he also knew that this was the only way to get Nick to become aware of the need to communicate, *and* that he could get his needs met by other people. Tom knew that even this was not intuitively known to Nick, or at least, he never showed it. Either way, Nick's profound lack of communication was his biggest challenge.

Nick put down the square and started squeezing the air again.

"Nick."

Nick did not look at him. "NO."

"Nick. What do you need?"

Nick looked toward Tom, then away. "No need." His stomach was squeezing with anxiety, that he was not doing what he was supposed to do. Even though his words were there, he could not feel happy or relieved by them because he knew there was something going on that he did not understand, something Tom wanted him to do. He knew the words, he felt them, but they were swimming under a layer of pictures in his mind, snapshots of everything that he had looked at in the last few minutes. The sounds around him slashed across these images, and all the while, the feel of the air around him caressed him gently. The confusion was almost too much to bear. He started rapidly patting the air, swinging his hands and making a small breeze, which felt good.

"What do you need?" Tom asked again, his low voice dispelling the breeze.

"What do you need?" Nick said. He thrust his arm into his mouth and bit down, suppressing a scream.

Tom plucked it out without a word. Nick put it back and hit at Tom, who ducked. Nick's eyes were black now. He thrashed again at Tom, pulling off his glasses.

"Yes, Nick, what do you need?" he said quietly, and picked up first his glasses, then Nick's cube. "I need . . . ," he prompted.

"I neeeeeeed . . . ," Nick said, stretching out the words until they made no sense.

"I need . . . ," said Tom again.

Then Tom said in a quieter voice, "I need a L—"

"LEGO," Nick said, and raised his squeezing hand. "I need a LEGO," he said, perfectly.

Tom smiled. Nick was flapping as if he could fly out of there. But Tom stayed quiet and still. He soon noted that Nick's eyes were ebbing back to blue again. His whole body seemed relaxed, softer. Whatever it had been, it passed. Same as the last few weeks. There was always an outburst, always around a demand— nothing unusual there—but then there was a sudden snap of a change back to a calm, soft Nick. Even his eyes would look different, seconds later. Tom thought he was beginning to be able to predict it, when the snap would occur, and today, he'd been right, and had ducked just in time. It came, of course, when Nick was at his most frustrated about not being able to find the words. But Tom did notice, too, that even when Nick used his own language, often a relevant word would be tucked inside, a little bit of light peeping out from behind clouds.

He reached into the bucket and quickly pulled out the piece Nick needed. "Here," he said quietly, as if nothing had happened, when something most certainly had.

The door opened and Emmy leaped to her feet. Tom couldn't help but smile at how nervous she looked. "Don't be so worried," he said. "We're doing great."

"You are?" She looked at his rolled-up shirtsleeves, below which showed a scratch, a thin red slash of blood glowing through the black hair on his forearm. His glasses were a little bent. "Great, huh?"

"You can't expect this to be easy for him," Tom said, dabbing at the scratch with an alcohol pad, from the mug on the reception table where they were kept. Next to the mug stood a glass jar of Band-Aids, and Tom reached for one and peeled it open. "There," he said, smoothing it into place.

Just then Nick ran out of the room and grabbed his coat off the hook.

"Nick, wait!" Emmy yelled. Nick stopped at the door and started squeezing the air. Emmy turned back to Tom. "So, what did he do?"

"He put together a LEGO structure, the way I asked him."

Emmy blinked. "No, I mean, what did he do to you—?" Then she realized what he'd just told her. "He did? He built a LEGO structure?" Her mouth hung slightly open in disbelief.

Tom smiled. "He got a little frantic with my demands. Nothing I haven't seen a thousand times before. Nick!"

Nick stopped squeezing the air and turned toward Tom, eyes closed.

"You did a great job, buddy." Again, Tom said this in a slow, barely audible voice.

Nick turned away and went back to flapping, a trace of a smile on his lips. Emmy wondered, as always, was it because of what had been said to him, or was it some internal happy thought?

"I think he liked LEGOs," Tom added, as if guessing her thoughts.

Emmy looked from Nick to Tom. "He played with LEGOs," she whispered. "Hah. Wait till I tell Dan."

"Oh, I don't know if I'd do that yet," said Tom.

"Look, I'm desperate," Emmy said. "You see how it is. How they are."

Tom raised his eyebrow. "Where are they today?"

"Today I tried leaving them home, with Henry in charge of Dan."

"Does that work?"

Emmy searched his face for signs of judgment. She was so sick of people who didn't know her life but still judged her for the decisions she made. The decision to send Nick to private school. The decision to separate from Eric, and go it alone. The decision to make things easy on herself and get Henry to babysit. But staring at the leathery planes of Tom's face and the soft, round eyes, all she got was a sense that he was going to laugh any minute. In a nice way.

"I think so. Henry is so good. You know."

"I *don't* know."

Emmy's eyes widened in surprise. "What do you mean?"

"I think Henry's got a lot going on. Hey, I don't mean that you're wrong to trust him with Dan. Hey!"

Emmy was mortified to find herself choking back tears. Tom put a hand on her arm, warm and heavy. She stepped back, to get him to remove it.

"Emmy, Henry's a great kid."

"Then why'd you say, 'I don't know'?"

"Here, sit down." He guided her to the soft chair behind the receptionist's desk. Why was there never a receptionist? she found herself idly wondering. Nick was flapping and talking to himself, so she let herself settle in for a moment.

"I just think that Henry is not 'so good,' as you put it. He's only a kid. A good kid, but maybe not as good as you think."

"Excuse me? What the hell do you know about my child? Or what I think?" Emmy reddened because she was losing control of herself like this. She was terrified of what she might hear, of what Tom—a stranger, but a smart one—had noticed.

"You're right. I don't know what you think," Tom said. "I'm just commenting on the 'so good' characterization. I think that the sooner you see Henry more for who he is, what he's going through, the better for both of you."

"And how do you propose I do that? What am I not seeing?"

Tom thought for a moment. "I think he might be smoking pot."

"What?!"

"As a former pothead, I'm very familiar with the sweet reek of marijuana, and I smelled it on his coat last time."

"You really think so?" Emmy's heart was pounding.

"I do." Tom said.

Emmy was quiet, lost in thought for a minute. *Oh no, oh no. Henry!* Then she sighed. "God, I've been so focused on Nick and Dan!"

"What about them?"

"Well, I mean, things are so bad between them—" Emmy faltered. She hated the bad blood between Nick and Dan. She knew, or she felt, that Dan's meanness toward Nick actually hurt Nick, even though he did not seem to understand the actual words. But she could not bring herself to say, "Dan, he did that because of what you just said," because she didn't know how Dan would take that. He could be so literal, he might think she was saying it was *all* his fault. And she never wanted Dan to feel as if he were the cause of the autism. He was too young to separate it all out.

"I noticed." Tom paused, then asked, "Has either Henry or Dan been in . . . therapy?"

"Huh? Why?" Emmy was suddenly annoyed again by Tom's prying—and by

the fact that he may have been right in both cases. At the same time, she wondered if the boys should be in therapy. Dan with his ready anger. But he was so young! Could such a little boy go to therapy? Was it anger or just personality? Would therapy help either way? She made a mental note to call around—discreetly—for a therapist for Dan.

But Henry? Wasn't he okay? Was Henry hiding some kind of psychological burden?

"Sorry, didn't mean to intrude," Tom said, watching the emotions skitter across her face.

"No, no, it's okay. I just—I hadn't really considered it. I don't know why, actually. I've done it for myself, after all! But the boys—they're different. They're just kids. They are who they are. Nick's the one who really needs help. He's so lost—"

"You know, he is really aware of the stuff that's going on," Tom interrupted.

Nick stopped squeezing the air. "Yes."

Emmy looked at Tom and then at Nick, utterly surprised by this. A messy knot of feelings tightened in her throat that she could not even begin to put words to.

Who the hell *was* Tom Palmer, anyway? How had he known

this about Nick? How had she missed it? Was he right about Henry, and the pot?

She had to get out of there and just think. "Well, um, thanks. I've gotta be going," she muttered, and slipped out the door, holding Nick's hand.

As Emmy rinsed the casserole from the mac and cheese, Tom's words came back to her. "I know the sweet reek of marijuana." *God, what a pompous way of talking*, she thought. Suddenly she felt angry, knowing on one level that it was easier to be pissed off than to deal with the more complicated guilt she was also feeling. Tom had no business commenting on her other two sons. *Who the hell does he think he is?* "The sweet reek." Jesus, could the man get over himself? She reached for her empty wine glass and swung too wide. It tipped and clunked against the hard white enamel of her sink. The glass broke in two pieces, and a ribbon of blood cascaded down from her left hand.

"Ow!" she yelled.

Henry appeared at her side. "You okay? Oooh," he murmured, staring at the blood.

"I'm fine. Just get me a paper towel, okay?" She did not reach up for it even though the roll was right over the sink, because she wanted to hold her hand under running water and get some of the blood rinsed off. As she moved her hand under the faucet, she tried to see how big and where the cut was. There it was, a weeping half-inch slit in the padded part below her thumb. "Shit," she muttered. Henry reappeared with a wad of paper towel and some alcohol.

"Thanks, darling," she said, and pressed the paper towel to the cut.

"Bleeding, yelling," said Nick from behind her. "Hoom, bleeding, feem."

"What happened, Mom?" said Dan.

"Boys, all of you, I'm fine, I just cut myself." She touched the cut with an alcohol-soaked square of paper towel, and then winced.

"You said a bad word," said Dan.

"Yes, I did," said Emmy tersely. "Grown-ups do that some-times when they're very upset, but you should not."

"Can I have dessert?" asked Dan.

Emmy looked at Henry. "Can you get him something?"

"Yeah. C'mere, Dan, let's go to the pantry." When Henry mo-tioned to Dan with his head, Dan followed, and so did Nick, whispering softly.

"Get something for Nick, too, okay?" she called out. The pa-per towel was not soaked with blood as she'd feared. She pulled it away and peered at the cut again. It was a superficial slice, not deep. *Thank God*, she thought.

What was I thinking about, before? She knew it was something important, but the glass breaking had totally wiped it from her mind. She pulled down some new paper towel and stood with it on her hand, turning quietly to look over at the boys. Henry was holding an unwrapped Yodel, saying in a high-pitched voice, "I'm not a Yodel, I'm poop!" while Dan squealed with laughter. Nick sat at the table licking the crumbs from his Yodel remains. There was a glass of juice sitting next to him, too.

Look at how good he is with Dan, Emmy thought, smiling. How Henry knew what to do and just did it so graciously. Henry—yes, that's what it was. Tom and his observations. He saw something about Henry. Emmy continued to look at Henry and pick through her memory for clues, signs that he was smoking pot. What did Tom see?

All she could see was this grinning fourteen-year-old, wild blond hair, a face that was both young and mannish at the same time. Could he be smoking pot? It just did not feel true to Em-my. But was she seeing all of Henry, or only the Henry she want-ed to see? What would Eric think? She could ask Eric.

Just then Henry met her eyes. He raised his eyebrows as if to ask if she was okay. She gave him a half smile of reassurance, made a kiss in the air, and closed her eyes. She wanted to keep these thoughts to herself. She believed in Henry. He was in her blood. He was *of* her blood. She would know if there were trouble. Next time she saw Tom, she would have to ask him. Ask him what he saw, what he meant. And maybe also just thank him, very pointedly, for his hard work with Nick (Nick, and not her other sons, thank you very much) and not let him talk about the rest of her family when he obviously knew nothing about them.

The phone rang. It was Mom.

"Hey, Mom," she said, a little tense because she didn't want to give away anything about her concerns over Henry. Mom would go right to panic, leaving no room for anything else. "What's up?"

"What's wrong?"

How did Mom know? But Emmy knew these things, too, about her own kids. Mother-radar. "Nothing, Mom, I just cut myself."

"Are you all right? Want me to let you go?"

"No, no, I'm fine. How are you?"

Mom sighed. "Well, you know, dear, it's been ages since I saw the boys."

"Yeah, I guess it has." Em thought back to the last visit. They had all driven down there, to Armonk, the little Westchester town where Emmy had grown up. "Wow, Chanukah, I think."

"Right! Too long," Mom said. "How are they? How's Nick?"

Most of their conversations began this way. Somehow, Mom always had to ask about Nick in a separate category. "Good. They're *all* good," she snapped.

But if Mom noticed, she gave no sign. "So, I was thinking of coming for a visit. Would next weekend be good for you all?"

"I'll make sure I have the boys." Why not? All she had been planning was some kind of outing with Beth, easily rescheduled. It would be nice to see Mom and have her take over for a few days.

"Okay, good!"

"See you soon. Love you."

"Take care of that cut."

When Emmy hung up the phone, she marked the visit in her

calendar, and noted that she would have to let Eric know about the boys. Then she went upstairs to get ready for bed.

Chapter 18

Ping went Emmy's computer. She clicked Get Mail and saw that there was one unread message. Wcabot. Her heart sped up, but at the same time, her stomach turned over. Why was he e-mailing her? But of course she knew that he hadn't gotten the message. Apparently, he liked the chase and now figured they were going to have an affair. *Wrong*, she thought. Yet instead of deleting immediately—she couldn't, because he was a client—she double-clicked, feeling as if even the nanoseconds of waiting for the message to load were too long to sit through.

"Where have you been? —W"

She typed back, "I'm right here. Everything going okay? Getting ready for your closing?" and sent. She had already taken care of that potential can of worms: she'd gotten a friend to handle the closing for her.

After two minutes passed, she clicked Get mail. And then, one unread message from wcabot:

"I'm ready, all right . . . I'll be back there real soon. Will you visit me at the Ritz-Carlton? I still owe you a lunch. —W"

The druggy aura of flirtation was seeping slowly through her, despite her previous resolve. *No*, she thought. No. She recalled the stupid southern-style twang in his voice. It was a mistake. But the pleasure of feeling wanted like that rose up to her throat nevertheless. Swallowing hard, she typed, "I'm sorry, but I don't think that's a good idea." And sent.

Almost immediately a new message read: "Okay. For now."

There was no e-mail for the rest of the evening, even though Emmy checked every few minutes. She wanted to keep e-mailing with Will. It was such a rush, she admitted that. But it would have been a horrible mistake to go out with him. Probably the worst mistake she could ever make. It didn't work to try to justify it by saying that she and Eric were separated, that it wouldn't really be cheating. She knew, and Eric would agree, that it *would* be cheating. Eric wouldn't even like the way they'd been flirting.

Feeling tired and a little sick, Emmy stretched and stood up, then climbed the stairs to her bedroom. She took out a fresh towel, hung it on the silver hook in her bathroom, set the nozzle to pulsate, and undressed while the bathroom steamed up. After her long, hot shower, she lay in bed with the Sunday *Times* crossword. This always made her sleepy. Yet tonight, her nerves felt like old rubber bands, stretched tautly, near the breaking point. Even though she knew she was exhausted, even drowsy, it took Emmy a long time to fall asleep.

Emmy had two back-to-back showings the next morning. The spring season had really picked up, and she was busier this year than she could remember being in a long time. The first was a condo in the upscale Belleville Farm neighborhood, an over-priced two-bedroom that had a rooftop patio with a Japanese gravel garden and a kitchen that was completely custom. She led the couple, a Cambridge doctor-lawyer professional duo, up the stairs. The man seemed to size Emmy up and dismiss her the moment he heard what neighborhood *she* lived in. His wife had expressed his thoughts for him, just in case Emmy hadn't under-stood their contempt the first time: "Oh, we thought that The Point was *working-class*."

Emmy couldn't help but answer, "Oh, no more than The Farm is nouveau riche." She smiled guiltily, knowing she should resist making jabs at clients, no matter how deserving they were. She waited in the dining room while they finished opening clos-ets and whispering. The whole appointment took about forty minutes, door-to-door, and by the end of it, she had a decent offer. Being from the area, the couple knew the market, and to their credit—and Emmy's surprise—they did not bid outra-geously low.

The second showing was in Belleville Corner, an area of multi-family Victorians, where most middle-class families lived. There were two schools within a mile of each other in The Corner, a real draw to the families who wanted their kids to be able to walk to school. The client was a fortyish woman who said she had three daughters. Emmy thought this Philadelphia-style side-by-side two-family would be just the thing for this family (the woman said they were from Philadelphia, too), with three floors of living space and four bedrooms.

"The baths are old," Emmy said, pushing open the heavily painted door. "Like all bathrooms in Belleville," she added quickly, remembering Will's joke about how she wasn't that great at selling. The floor was tiny white hexagonal tiles, the tub was a freestanding claw-foot, its enamel pitted and graying, but there was a white marble sink on legs off in the corner. "But you can imagine this with gleaming white paint and a white muslin shower curtain draped over here." She made a sweeping gesture to call to mind a bishop's sleeve–shaped curtain.

Emmy loved it when a client allowed her to do her thing, the virtual redecorating. This was the only part of her job she truly liked. And this woman was even more amenable to her ideas than most. "Oooh, yeah," the woman agreed. "Look at that," she said, pointing to the tiny leaded-glass window near the ceiling. "I've always wanted a bathroom like this. Reminds me of my grandmother's in Brooklyn."

Emmy smiled. "Hey, I've got relatives in Brooklyn, too!" she said. "So, anyway, notice how that windowsill is so wide? Big enough for little silver vases or makeup jars. And there are two more just like it on the other floors!" Emmy smiled, feeling the sharp pleasure of work when it went well.

Emmy's cell phone rang. "Excuse me," she said, and walked into the hallway. It was the boys' school.

"Hello," she said.

"Emmy, hi, it's Ben Taylor."

The principal! "Oh, hi," she said, her voice small and her heart pounding. For the principal to call midmorning, it had to be something bad.

"Hey, would you be able to come down to the school sometime in the next couple of minutes?"

"What is it?"

"It's Henry."

Henry! "Oh my God, is he all right?"

"Well, that's why I'm calling. He was caught rolling a joint in the bathroom today."

Emmy's stomach churned. "What?" she asked. She listened to the whole story again. "Okay, I'll be right there," she said, throwing the phone into her bag.

"Are you okay?" the woman asked.

"Yeah. Well, no. That was my sons' school. I have to go."

"Oh, I hope nothing's wrong." The woman was smiling kindly at her.

"Well, something kind of is, and so I'd better—"

"Sure. Hey—" She paused and seemed to think better of what she'd been about to say.

Emmy looked up, her heart racing as she thought about getting to the school.

"It's just that—I'd like to come back and see the rest. When you can show me, okay?" She reached out and patted Emmy on the arm.

Emmy smiled, in spite of how upset she was. "Thanks, okay."

As Emmy pulled up into the circle in front of the school, she found herself wondering how she'd gotten there. She literally could not remember the lefts and rights, the stoplights, the flow of the cars around her. The whole way, she'd been picturing Henry, knowing very well how he must be feeling: humiliated. He had a huge sense of shame, always had. As a little boy, he had avoided speaking up in preschool or with friends, even when they'd done something wrong, for fear of being wrong himself. He was never one to raise his hand, to volunteer. Always had to be completely sure before he put himself forward.

She punched the dashboard. Why had he done this? *Pot?*

Then she remembered Tom's strange admonition about watching out for Henry, that he smelled smoke on his coat. Oh God! How could she have been so stupid?

She pushed open the office door, and the receptionist looked up, an old dragon of a woman who had been at the school forever. Mrs. Riordan. Betty. But no one really called her Betty, probably not even Ben Taylor. Mrs. Riordan looked at Emmy, narrowed her eyes, then smiled coldly. "Your son is in there." She gestured toward the closed office door behind her.

"Can I—go in?" Why did she feel as if *she* were in trouble? Of course she could go in! He was her son, damn it! Without waiting for an answer, she got up and strode past Mrs. Riordan, hiding her trepidation but annoyed at herself for feeling it. She raised her hand to knock, then decided to just be assertive and walked in. As the door clicked closed behind her, Ben Taylor and a police officer looked up. Henry, huddled at the end of the couch, did not. His cheeks were a deep, blotchy red. She got a sudden flash of memory, of baby Henry, whose cheeks often looked like this, because he was constantly hot as an infant. People were always thinking he had a fever, but Emmy had known that he just ran hotter than most. Her heart turned over, and she longed to pull him into her arms, gangly defensive adolescent or not.

"Emmy," Ben said warmly, interrupting her thoughts. "Come in. This is Detective O'Connor."

Detective?! Emmy looked at the officer, a handsome, square-jawed gray-haired man in his sixties, who smiled kindly at her. "Hello," she said, holding out her hand, which he grasped lightly, the way old-fashioned men shook hands with women. She sidled up to Henry, who stared off out the window.

"Emmy," Ben began softly. "This is a pretty serious matter. I'm sure you know that."

Emmy looked up and, to her chagrin, felt the sting of tears. *I'm not going to cry now!* But a big tear spilled out traitorously into her lap. "I know," she said, and dug in her bag for a tissue. Ben held out a fresh one for her, like a prom date offering a corsage.

The cop spoke up. "Look, it's the first time. He's a good kid, an A student, from what I understand. Also a minor, of course."

Henry looked over at them, his eyes a dull gray-blue.

Emmy squeezed his hand. He did not respond, but she heard him exhale just a tiny bit. "What happens now?" she asked. "Suspension?"

Ben shook his head and said, "Community service. Good, hard work, around the building."

O'Connor nodded. "Henry here will do some community service," he said, repeating what Ben Taylor had just said. Emmy thought it was ridiculous that the cop was even there in the first place. "Okay by me," she replied. Clearing his throat, the detective leaned forward, very close to Henry's face. "Young man."

Henry looked at him. "Uh-huh?"

"You understand how bad this is, that you were smoking a controlled substance like this? I'm not even talking about the law right now. Do you know what this stuff could have in it? You don't know where they get it from. What they might put in it. You think you're getting some decent dope, a nice buzz, right? Then—bam! You get a hit with PCP in it. Or worse, something like detergent. Make you sick as a dog."

Emmy wondered if Henry was thinking what she was—that the cop, who was trying to speak Henry's language, or what adults thought was Henry's language, sounded like a dork. She shivered slightly, embarrassed for the older man.

"Yeah, I'm serious." He hooked his thumbs into his belt. Emmy suddenly noticed his gun and handcuffs, and swallowed hard. "These dealers, they cut the junk with lots of stuff on hand, either to hook you more or to maximize their profit. Nasty people, dealers. They don't care if you live or die."

Henry nodded, keeping his eyes down and his hair half hiding them.

"Do you understand that you're getting a break here, that you'll never get another one if you do this again? Mr. Taylor thinks you're a good kid who's goin' through a rough spot now, with the family and everything." He looked over at Emmy sympathetically, and she realized, embarrassed, that Ben must have told him about the separation. Did everyone know? Or maybe about Nick? Something twisted in her belly, and her head hurt. She longed to lie down. But of course she couldn't just wilt now. She had to be strong, for Henry.

"Yeah," Henry muttered.

Ben spoke up. "Henry, what I'd like is for you to check in every few days with Mrs. Whitney, our guidance counselor. You know her, right? And you're also going to do some work here after school every day. Helping out the custodians, the teachers, whoever needs a hand. You're a strong kid. I think we could use your muscle." He winked at Emmy. His leniency and kindness were the last straw. She felt another tear threatening to spill out.

"Okay," said Henry. "Uh, thanks." He looked at all three of them, clearly wanting to leave.

Ben stood up, and the detective put his hands on his hips and nodded. He held his hand out to Emmy again. "Take it easy," he said, shaking her hand limply and smiling at her, fatherlike. Ben opened the door for Henry and her, and they left together. Henry would have to go back to class soon, but Ben understood that they needed a few minutes alone.

They sat together outside on the bench. "When did this start?" she asked, fingering the spaces between the old wooden slats.

"I don't know. Maybe a month ago."

"So—why?"

Henry sighed. "I don't know."

"Come on, Henry. You owe me."

Henry was silent. "I guess it's—I don't know—I was thinking of Dad and stuff. Kids have it. It's hard *not* to get it, you know what I mean?"

Emmy nodded, although she hadn't realized that drugs were that rampant at their beautiful school. Things had certainly changed since her junior high school days.

"But you're not going to do it anymore, right?"

Henry looked down at the bench. "Yeah."

"And, sweetie, what do you mean about Dad?"

Henry looked at her. "Huh?"

Emmy said, "You said you were thinking of Dad and stuff when you started smoking it. What did you mean?"

Henry frowned and turned his back. "I don't know." He put his cheek against the back of his hand.

"Just say it."

Henry groaned. "I guess I'm—I'm kind of—fed up with him, you know?"

Emmy nodded, hoping he would go on, because she really had no idea what he meant. She only knew what *she* thought. *She* was fed up with Eric, sure, but Henry?

Henry said, "He's so . . . perfect. Mr. Clean. All my life, do this, do that, be a role model, '*Help your brothers, Henry.*'" Henry did a dead-on impersonation of Eric, and it was so accurate that Emmy couldn't help but smile. She bit it back, not wanting to stop Henry from talking.

"It's like, he's so good and all, so I'm supposed to be, too. But *they* don't have to be! And then, he just goes. Walks out the door without looking back! How's that for good?" Henry's voice broke.

Emmy's heart pulsed hard in her chest. She hadn't realized how much Eric's leaving had hurt Henry. But of course it had! He'd been abandoned by his own father! Emmy felt a surge of self-righteous anger, followed by a tiny flicker of self-doubt and guilt. She did not want to think about her part in this; it was much easier to just be angry at Eric. He was the one who left, after all. And yet, there was that flicker of doubt—of shame, even—that she had failed at two such important things: her marriage and especially her son's well-being. She looked at Henry, wanting to hold him and soothe him the way she had when he was a little boy, not entirely sure he would let her. She settled for standing close to him and smiling into his face.

Henry's little outburst was so like Henry. So articulate, so right. So rare. But of course, he had not said anything to her about any of this until it had practically been ripped out of him.

"I know, sweetheart. I know." She stroked his hand, and he let her. The flicker inside suddenly glowed, warm and insistent, and she felt compelled just then to say, in the softest whisper, "And you know, in the end, I was the one who asked him to go."

Henry turned to look at her, and she saw tears starting. Quickly, he turned away, to think his own thoughts, which she knew she would never get to hear. He'd already given away so much more than he usually did.

Chapter 19

Emmy drove straight home from the school. There would be no more appointments today. She had somehow managed to call her office and get the assistant to rearrange things. Her head was pounding, and all she could think about was how bad everything in her life was.

When she pushed the car door closed, it just barely latched from her weak swing. She felt shaky as if she had the flu. Maybe she did have the flu, she thought, but more likely it was because of the stress about Henry. Then she walked into the backyard.

The daffodils were fully open. When had this happened? Yesterday they'd been like fat yellow-green eggs, bent over and still tightly closed. Today, rows and rows of yellow faces stood before her, stacked up on the little slope over the stone wall, like a chorus of happy children singing.

She climbed up the small stone wall and knelt before the fluffy mounds of flowers. Reaching in, she pinched the thick, artery-like stem of a hyacinth, her fingers getting gooey and wet from the nectar. She smelled her sticky fingers, breathing in the sharp, alive scent, and then wiped them on her pants. Some of the headache she'd had in the principal's office subsided for a little while out here in the refreshing spring air.

As she dropped flower after flower on the soft peat moss next to her, the found herself thinking of Eric, but for now without rancor. She hated the way things were now. She felt aimless, stuck. Going through the motions and not enjoying anything. She knew that what she had was good—healthy sons, a beautiful home, a job she didn't mind—but she wanted more. She wanted a partner, a lover, a husband again. Someone to share everything with: jokes, stories, the boys. Why had it gone so sour with Eric? He'd given her all that. And what did he think about it? What went on in his head, night after night, alone, without her and the boys? How was it okay with him to just live apart from them? Didn't he feel guilty? She would never be able to live with herself if she missed out on so much of the boys' lives. Why was that fine with him?

These thoughts made her pulse quicken in anger. So easy for him to just go on. Was it a male thing? Women usually ended up with custody, so maybe it was nature's way.

But how stupid was that? She knew it was ridiculous. Certainly men could be nurturing, and hadn't she read just recently about those dads who felt that sole maternal custody was child abuse? She laughed bitterly, thinking about where her primary caregiving had led Henry. To cheating on a test and smoking pot!

Now she was worried again. Would Henry be okay? What else could she do for him? She looked up at the flowers, bobbing blithely in the breeze. Was it enough that he would check in with the guidance counselor and do the community service? How was she to know? She'd have to remember to talk to Eric about it.

She felt a chill from the wind, and could no longer find the feeling of equanimity that had come over her when she'd entered the backyard. Another unwelcome thought floated into her mind. When would she and Eric make their separation permanent? What would that be like? All she knew of divorce was what she'd seen on TV shows: couples sitting with well-dressed lawyers, saying horrible things about who got the house in Malibu, who was a dirty cheat, and so on. She didn't feel that way about Eric. He was a jerk, but there had been no wrangling. He'd left her with everything, and had his little apartment with a few of the things that had been his before they'd been together.

It had been very quiet, after that last painful fight a year ago when she'd kicked him out and he'd actually gone. They had simply fallen into a routine of terse conversations about when he would have the boys. She supposed they'd never talked about the separation because Eric didn't talk that way, period. Eric worked, Eric joked, Eric made love, Eric complained, and Eric fought. That was the man she knew. They'd remained apart because it was more normal for them *not* to discuss such things than to examine, and fully understand, what they were doing.

She had never asked him for money, because her job brought in enough and the house was already paid for. Besides, it had been really cheap when they'd first bought it. Emmy had never realized just how relatively easy things were, financially, for them both. She saw now that actually they were very lucky in that they didn't have to squabble about money, only kids. She felt a warming gratitude for that, right then, knowing how much worse things could be. But this feeling seemed to unsettle other, more troubling emotions, which were less black and white than her anger. Sadness mixed with longing and floated upward, silvery blue. She had not realized these feelings were even there.

She decided, pinching the last perfect blossom in a row and setting it down, that she was not going to be the one who asked for the divorce. She had no desire to push things further apart. It was bad enough for them to live separately, but they were managing that pretty well. Why rock the boat? Let sleeping dogs lie, and let separated husbands remain in Cambridge, with uncertain status. Or something like that.

As she gathered the bouquet, she realized that things were far from settled. She wanted more out of her life, more than just coping. She wanted someone to share her thoughts with. To feel whole again, successful. No, that wasn't quite right. It was about feeling as if she was part of something. Everything right now was in pieces, not whole. Sure, the boys were her family, but she wanted a partner. They needed more than just her, and she wanted to be able to give them that kind of fuller family life. But how? She and Eric had been so acrimonious about everything. They'd experienced so much pain, mostly around Nick.

She let herself remember that day, the last day, the last straw. Eric had just come home from work, and Emmy wanted to run out to Brickman's, their convenience store, for some salsa. They were out of it, and Nick loved chips and salsa. In fact, Nick had gotten it into his head that he was going to have them right now, and he was starting to get really worked up.

Eric put his briefcase down slowly, not taking his eyes off

Nick. Emmy remembered how he looked: like a hunter, his eyes slanted and dark, moving carefully around his startled, dangerous prey.

"I'll be right back," Emmy said, keeping her voice upbeat, knowing that Nick would get even more upset if he thought she, too, was tense.

"Why does he have to get what he wants all the time, when he wants it? Don't any of the rest of us get a break?" Eric cried out.

Emmy snapped her head around at him, immediately on her guard. "Eric," she said quietly, "now is not the time. Look at him."

Nick was jumping up and down, smashing his feet into the floor. "NO LOOK AT HIM, NO LOOK AT HIM!" he shouted.

"Okay, okay, honey," Emmy soothed. "No one's looking. Mommy's going to go get your salsa."

"CHIPANSALSA, CHIPANSALSA!"

"Jesus Christ," Eric whispered.

Emmy felt tears of frustration welling up behind her eyes, and her throat tightened. "Shut. Up," she said through clenched teeth. "You are not helping.

"And giving in to his every whim *is* helping?"

Emmy took a step toward Eric, but just then Nick rushed over and started slapping Eric in the head, screaming and jumping. His face was contorted and red, his dilated pupils were glittering like blackened lava, and his arms were flailing, pummeling his father.

Without thinking, Eric brought up his arms to fend off the attack, pushing against Nick's chest. Nick went hurtling backward, onto the hard foyer floor.

All was quiet. Nick was wide-eyed, his face now drained of color. Emmy rushed over to him, lifting his head, carefully feeling the back of his skull. Nick was too shocked to resist her touch as he normally would have done. Emmy felt for anything bumpy or wet with blood; satisfied that he was okay, she ran into the kitchen to get ice.

Eric was still standing a foot or two from Nick, saying nothing. His eyes were now matte blue, like old, worn sea glass.

Emmy looked up at him from where she knelt next to Nick and said, "You bastard. I can't believe you did that. You hit him. You hit our child."

Emmy had been spanked many times as a child and had vowed never to do the same to her own children. She and Eric had agreed easily on this issue in the early days of their marriage. This betrayal, this horrible wrong thing that had just happened, thrust itself straight into her heart and would not let go.

Until Eric said, "He was out of control. I—"

Then she cut him off, and the shouting and mutual cursing followed, the memory of it etched sharply in her head forever. The terrible back-and-forth that had ended with her telling him to leave.

Emmy was crying, and the dirt around her was wet. The fist was there, in her chest, all over again as if it had just happened. "Oh, Nick," she said out loud. And then, remembering Eric's stricken, glassy eyes, the ache in her heart worsened. "Oh, Eric," she said. As she stood up, the wind blew, whispering and cold on the perspiration at her neck. Suddenly she didn't want a bouquet. What a stupid, useless thing for her to do, to pick flowers, with her life like this. What was the point of that? She dropped the blossoms on the ground and sat next to them, unable to stop crying.

They were seated at the dinner table, mashed potatoes piled high on their plates, along with some strips of leftover chicken. "Why was Henry in the principal's office?" asked Dan, shaking salt all over his food. Henry rolled his eyes.

Emmy jumped in before trouble could start. "He had to explain something he'd done that wasn't right," she said.

"What was it?" Dan was flattening his potatoes with his fork.

"Have salt, please," Nick muttered, getting up and taking the salt from Dan.

"GIVE ME THAT BACK!" Dan shouted.

Nick jumped up again and put the salt back without using it. He started to bite his arm.

"Jesus, Dan!" Henry reached for the salt and slammed it down next to Nick.

"Mom, Henry said a bad word," Dan said, shoveling the potatoes into his mouth, not looking at anyone, but not taking back the salt.

Emmy reached her hand across the table and touched Dan's fork. "Dan. Listen. You can't yell at Nick that way. He asked nicely for the—"

"He asked like a baby!"

"Talk about babies," Henry said.

"Henry, that's not helping," said Emmy, her head starting to ache.

"Salt, sssh," said Nick, who was burying his potatoes in a layer of salt and pepper.

"Ew, look how he eats!" said Dan.

"Look how *you* eat," said Henry, flinging his hand at the salt spread far and wide across the table, looking as if someone had shaken out a beach blanket on it.

As difficult as it was to listen to the boys bicker, Emmy was relieved it gave her a momentary breathing space. And Dan was not pestering her to talk about the pot. She had no energy to explain the ins and outs and the gray areas to him tonight. Dan seldom saw gray, anyway. And she'd need her energy, for soon, she knew, she'd have to call Eric and tell him.

As if on cue, the phone rang. She looked at Henry, who didn't move. She rose to get it, noting the unfamiliar name on the caller ID. "Braddock." Braddock?

A girl's voice. "Is Henry there?"

Emmy felt a rush of color in her cheeks. She was embarrassed, because she knew he would be even more so. "Um, who's calling?"

"This is Sylvie, from his class."

"Hold on." She pressed Mute. "Sylvie from your class," she said quietly, even though the Mute was on.

Henry scrambled to his feet. "Okay," he said, trying to suppress his excitement, taking the phone and moving quickly into the playroom.

Emmy looked at Dan, waiting for a sarcastic remark. But he was completely absorbed in finishing his dinner. Even though there was just a cirrus-thin layer of mashed potatoes smeared across the plate, he was running his fork over and over it, to scrape up every last bit.

Nick put his hands over his ears because of Dan and the scraping. While Dan had his head lowered, Nick looked at Dan's hair, which was fluttering down over his eyes. This was Nick's favorite way of seeing Dan. The shiny black curls dancing downward were like Mommy's, and also reminded him of the ribbon, springing up and down, the ribbon he used to play with. Daddy hated the ribbon. But Daddy was not here. Nick knew by his calendar that Daddy would be here in a few days—he now knew about days because the calendar showed him. Margaret had made him the calendar, and then Mommy started making them. They said, "School, school, school, school, school, no school, no school," across the page, over and over again. Nick loved the pattern, except when suddenly there was another "no school." No school also meant "stay home," but sometimes it meant "see Daddy." Nick liked to see Daddy, but he did not like going to a different house. And he did not like it when Daddy yelled.

Nick stared at Dan's hair, mesmerized by its movement. One thin lock was lying across the rest, a tiny loop out of place. This really bothered him. It made the lines all wrong. Nick's hand went up to push it aside, but then he thought better of it and squeezed some air instead, saying, "Hhhhairrr," as quietly as he could.

"Mom! Nick is staring at me," Dan said, glancing up. Nick looked away immediately.

Henry closed the door to the playroom and sat heavily in the computer chair. "Hey," he said into the phone.

"Hey," Sylvie said. "I heard about—what happened."

"Yeah, everyone must know by now. What're they saying?" He flipped the computer on, listening for the crackle and feeling its vibrating click under his fingers as it started up. He had recently assembled his own server, which he kept on the third floor, and was using it to help administrate the online game Uru Obsession, a game far superior, he felt, to World of Warcraft. As soon as the screen flickered and burst into color, the instant messaging squares started blinking on.

"That you—were caught with a joint. Henry, were you? What's going to happen? Will they arrest you?" Sylvie sounded as if she were crying. Henry felt something turn over in his stomach.

"No."

"No?"

"No." He knew she was too polite to press him further, and the thing in his stomach cramped harder. He glanced at the IMs. JR needed help getting online to WOW, as usual. A couple of his other friends were telling him about bugs they'd found in Uru.

He'd lost track of what Sylvie was saying. "I'm sorry. What?"

"I asked if you were okay. Are you in trouble or anything?"

"I'm fine. I just have to do some after-school junk for Taylor. I'm, like, his personal slave for the next month."

"That's it? But I heard the police were there."

"Yeah, well, don't believe everything you hear."

"Oh. Okay."

His heart was pounding. "I gotta go. Dinner, you know."

"Oh, sure. Sorry."

"No, it's okay."

"Bye."

"Uh, bye." He clicked off. *Thanks for calling. Want to go out with me?* He stared at the screen for a while, then rose to go back and finish his dinner. At least Dan would be done by now.

After sponging off the counter, Emmy slid the last remaining fork into the silverware rack and snapped the dishwasher closed, then started up the wash cycle. She could smell something sour and realized that yet another sponge had gone bad. Must be the unusually warm spring air. She smelled her hand and went to wash it, opening the lower cabinet with her knee. She withdrew the last pink sponge from its plastic wrapping, wetted it and soaped it up, and turned to clean the counters again.

She wondered what she ought to do about her shifting feelings toward Eric. Because she had no doubt that something had changed. That moment in the flower garden, when her sympathy for her wounded child had suddenly stretched out and wrapped itself around Eric, too. *Please don't let me start crying again*, she thought.

She heard the water running overhead as Nick started up his shower. Dan was in his room, getting undressed supposedly, but she could hear the telltale clatter of LEGOS. She imagined him hunched over the sharp, colorful pieces, his deft little fingers intent on creating whatever nightmarish creature or vehicle of death seized his imagination. It was in these moments that she loved her Dan the most. The stark contrast between the ferocious LEGO worlds and the pure innocence of the boy who built them never failed to make her heart tender and soft. "LEGO happens," Eric used to joke, about this obsession that he had shared not only with Dan but once with Henry, too.

Suddenly she wanted to call Eric. She had to tell him about Henry and the pot anyway. Sighing, she picked up the phone and pressed his number.

"Hey, Emmy," he said after three rings.

She dove right into it. "Eric, Henry was in trouble at school today."

"He was? How?"

"Caught rolling a joint in the bathroom."

"What?!"

"Yeah. A detective was even there."

"Jesus."

Emmy let him absorb it all for a moment before saying, "I know."

"That's a little bit of overkill, don't you think?"

"I guess. I figure they're trying to scare him away from ever doing it again. So I suppose it's okay."

"What did Henry say about it?"

Ugh. She knew he'd ask this. She didn't want to have to tell Eric what Henry had said about him. She knew how it would hurt, and she wanted to shield Eric from this—she didn't know why. "He said it was because drugs are easy to come by."

"So? That's always been true. Since when is he interested in anything but his computer?"

"Eric, first of all, I think he's got more going on than that." She thought of the tremulous Sylvie, wondering what she looked like, and hoping she was a kind girl and not one of those mean Queen Bees she'd read about.

Eric laughed harshly. "Well, sure, he's a fourteen-year-old boy!"

"Eric, he said he was angry at you," she blurted out, because he was such a know-it-all.

Silence. Bingo. *Good, you prick*, she thought, and immediately was ashamed of herself. She held her breath, poised for either an explosion or some cutting response.

"Fucking hell," Eric muttered.

Emmy exhaled and said, "I know," tired and defeated.

Eric noticed Emmy's resigned tone. He was not used to that; she was the one who always had so much energy for everything, even unpleasant things. Eric sighed. He imagined Henry, too, and how scared he must have been. He felt his own energy rise, realizing that he could help them. "Uh, should I talk to him?"

Emmy was warmed by the direction of Eric's reaction; instead of just being angry or upset at Henry, he was thinking about how to parent him. That was kind of new. Maybe this distance from them had actually done Eric some good, she thought. But she also felt that Henry had had enough talking for one day. Whatever Eric might add would not even sink in at this point, probably. "Well—yes—but maybe not now. Soon. There's already been a lot of talking today!"

"Okay, how about this weekend? I've got them."

"Yeah, that might be a good time." And then she remembered Mom. "Oh, this weekend, my mom is coming. Can I have them for some of it? So she can see them?"

"Uh, yeah, I guess . . ." He didn't want to fight with Emmy, but he was disappointed, because he saw little enough of the boys as it was. And he knew how her mother was, after all, and that Em generally did nothing about it. That was the one area in her life where Emmy was passive, a complete doormat. Where her mother was concerned, she was a total child. "How about I bring them back at three, or late Saturday afternoon?" So, okay, he'd get more work done. Maybe he'd even see Lucy on Sunday; she'd been asking him to come to dinner for weeks now. And unlike Em's mom, Lucy was perfectly content to see him without *les enfants terribles*, as she called them, always with a smile, so he couldn't exactly complain. It was meant to be their little joke, or something, but he actually never thought it was funny. She also called them *les dauphins* and *les petits princes*. Lucy seemed kind of hung up on French royalty, and Eric didn't get it; did she think the kids were spoiled or something? Or was this a dig at Em? So he'd always just ignored it.

"Yeah, that's perfect. Thanks." Emmy's voice was lighter now, so Eric felt that he'd done the right thing.

"So what's gonna happen?" Eric changed the subject back to Henry, whom he was feeling very worried about.

It took a second for Emmy to understand what he was talking about. "Not much, I think. Community service, they call it. He does odd jobs around the school for a while. Keeps his grades up. I think it's because of his grades and, frankly, our separation and maybe even things with Nick that made them all take it easy on him."

"Well, thank God for small favors," Eric said, but the anxiety for his son was still gnawing at him.

"You think this will scare him enough to stop?"

Eric was silent for a moment. "I guess. I don't know. Let's see how he seems, with the community service." He liked the fact that Ben Taylor had a solution of sorts—and one that involved more at-school oversight of Henry.

This seemed reasonable to Emmy, who did not know what else she could do for Henry. He seemed okay otherwise. She went through her mental list of things she thought were indicators of Henry's well-being: his grades were up (well, except for that cheating incident); some friends were calling the house; he was still willing to babysit his brothers. "Okay, I'm going to go now. Anyway, I wanted to tell you as soon as I could." She felt wrung out, and had no energy right then to try to figure out what else she needed to do about Henry. Although Tom's words still haunted her, she just felt that therapy for Henry at this point would be overkill. He would have to learn his lesson by working at the school. And she'd keep her eyes open for signs of drugs.

"Appreciate it. You okay?"

"Um-hum." She liked that he asked but was not about to get into anything with him now. She was too vulnerable from the whole afternoon and just wanted to lie down.

"I'll be there around nine on Saturday."

"Okay. Bye."

After hanging up the phone, Emmy realized she hadn't mentioned Dan and therapy. She almost called Eric back, but thought maybe she'd sleep on it and ask Beth for a name tomorrow.

Then out of the blue she thought of Will, and their flirtation, which had been completely sullied by the reality of his hand on hers. Guilt trickled through her, because Eric had been so nice. And because she'd suddenly felt sorry for him on that awful day.

Eric cradled the phone and stared blankly at his desk. He was worried about Henry, sure. But he'd smoked dope as a kid, and he couldn't bring himself to believe that this was such a big deal. Emmy and he had gotten high once in grad school. Surely she hadn't forgotten that night, when they couldn't stop laughing in the McDonald's?

Anyway, he knew that Henry was a good kid, with his head screwed on right. Henry would be okay. They could always depend on Henry.

Having this problem to talk about with Emmy had left him feeling a new sense of peace. He rested his head on his palm and found himself remembering something from a few years ago, when he was in bed with Emmy, trying to get her to have sex with him. It was always so difficult, after Dan had been born, and in the years that followed, for her to get in the mood. She would tell him that the idea had to come from her in order for her to want it (and she never wanted it) and that all she ever felt was pressure from him, which then killed it for her.

"So what am I supposed to do?" Eric had asked. "Pretend I *don't* want to have sex with you? That's kind of hard," he'd added, grinning pointedly.

"Stop it, Eric! Joking isn't going to help!" Emmy had rolled over in disgust.

Eric had known, after all these years, that the thing to do next was touch her shoulder gently, seriously, and bring her around. The old dance. But he hadn't done it. Lying on his back, so obviously wanting her and having her reject him, he'd felt like a stupid clown. And he was suddenly so angry at her, so humiliated, that he rolled over, too—away from her.

He could feel the sheets quivering as Emmy wept silently in the darkness, but he'd done nothing.

How had things come to that? he thought now. Was that the beginning of the end? Was it when they realized they couldn't even get sex right anymore? Why couldn't he and Emmy talk—just talk? *There were always so many things in the way, that's why.* One child or another would interrupt, and they—or she, really—would be carried off by the kid's need. And even if Nick was perfectly calm and settled, he took up so much of the emotional and psychological air in their life. So how could Eric break into her consciousness, her child-care-induced obsessiveness? How could he matter to her again?

Until this moment, he hadn't even realized how much he *wanted* to matter to her. He'd simply been angry for so long. A whole year of seething from the hurt of being kicked out. A year of keeping his distance from her and thoughts of her. And now—they had connected. It burst right through his angry stupor, like a bowling ball headed straight down the middle. He was so surprised to have these feelings. He didn't want to have these feelings, either, because with feelings like these, he didn't know what to do next. And Eric did not like to be indecisive.

But if Eric was anything, he was honest. He and Em had connected. Just for a second, but still . . . It was something. And, stranger than anything else, he realized that, along with all his confusion, he could feel the thrumming of happiness, fluttering at the edges of his consciousness like a tiny hummingbird discovering a cache of nectar.

Chapter 20

The therapy door opened and Nick came bounding out, right past Emmy to the coat hook.

"Nick—" Tom said, a little warning note in his voice.

But Nick pulled his coat on and started zipping it up, oblivious.

"It's okay, Tom, he doesn't have to—" Emmy murmured, gathering her bag and coat.

Tom held up his hand. "Nick," he said, softly. Nick looked at him this time. "G—"

"Goodbyefankyou," Nick blurted, looking at Tom, then looking away.

"Good job, Nick." Tom smiled, and Emmy realized with surprise that his large face seemed much younger when he smiled.

Emmy smiled, too. "I owe you an apology," she said.

"Huh?" Tom raised one scraggly eyebrow.

"Well, it's nothing you're aware of, but I was really angry at you last week."

"Oh?"

"The pot remark."

"Mmm."

"Yeah, it . . ." Oh, shit, she was tearing up again!

But Tom understood. He looked down at the floor and let her recover.

"Well, I just wanted you to know you were right," she said, sniffling slightly and gathering her bag.

"I usually am," he said. She jerked her head up at that. He was smiling warmly at her. "You let me know if I can help in any way." Emmy nodded. "See you, Nick," he said.

After dinner, Emmy took her laptop and sank down into the

living room chair and a half. Blue mail bubbles lined the entire left side of her screen. She zeroed in on the interesting ones: those from wcabot.

"E—

"In town briefly next week . . . ? —W"

Her heart thumped. Damn it, she thought he'd gotten the message.

"I can't," she typed at last.

Emmy closed her eyes and rested her head against the flowered cushions, feeling sad that she couldn't figure out what she wanted in life—all she knew was what she didn't want.

The next day was Saturday. Eric would be coming for the boys at nine. But it was already eight, and none of them were even awake. Emmy couldn't believe the capacity Nick, especially, had for sleep, but he was a teenager and they were famous for that.

"Boys!" she called. She opened Dan's door, and he immediately threw the covers over his head to hide.

"Where's Dan?" Emmy played along. "Jeez, I thought this was his room. Maybe I made a mistake. Maybe a magician came along and made him disappear. Maybe—"

Dan's giggling was her invitation to come over. She jumped on the bed and dove under the covers for Dan, inhaling the smell of his sheets, which were soapy sweet and also salty, yeasty and bread-like. She scooped him into her arms, and for a brief moment, he laid his head against her body and she could remember how sweet he was as a baby. She could still find that boy sometimes and felt momentarily blissful about that.

"Mommy?" he asked, from within her embrace.

"Mmm?" She grazed his head softly with her lips.

"Do I have to go with Daddy?"

"Oh, Dan! I thought you had fun over there."

"Naw, it sucks."

"Dan! *Stinks.*" Immediately regretting this, she said, "Sweetie, how does it stink?"

"It stinks. There's just one room for all three of us, and Nick makes noises the whole night. And Henry just listens to his stupid iPod, and Dad acts dumb."

"What does he do?"

"I don't know. Tries to make us laugh and stuff. Also, his house smells. Do I have to go? Can't I stay here with you?"

Emmy felt a surprising pang of empathy for Eric. She was really glad to hear he was trying so hard with the boys; too bad he wasn't very good at it. It was really kind of sweet, she thought. "Actually, you won't have to sleep there, because Grandma's coming here this weekend. But you should go; Dad has a fun day lined up for you. I think he's taking you to the Science Museum."

"Again? We were just there." So like Dan to protest something he loved, such as the Science Museum, just to be obtuse.

"Yeah, but that was for the *Star Wars*. This is different. Dinosaurs, I think."

"Dinosaurs are for babies," Dan said dismissively, conveniently forgetting how important they were to him two weeks ago when he'd begged for a T-rex set: a mother and babies. "Mom, can I bring LEGOs with me?"

"Sure you can! Bring whatever you want."

"Yeah, Dad doesn't have any toys over there. Just stupid books and a bad TV."

"What's bad about it?"

"He doesn't have cable. He only gets, like, six channels."

Which was more than enough in Emmy's day, but she didn't say that. She still remembered her first color television, which had been her grandmother's. And she could suggest that Eric get a few toys—nothing wrong with a friendly suggestion for how to make his home more comfortable for Dan. "I'll ask him about that," she said. "Get dressed, Danny Boy. He'll be here soon." Watching his small body go about the serious task of collecting LEGOs, she felt a swell of adoration and sang out, "Danny Boy, the pipes, the pipes are calling!"

"Oh, Mom, stop!" he yelled, but she could see he was trying not to smile.

They had just finished bringing their cereal bowls to the sink when Eric arrived. "Hey, all!" he shouted. Emmy watched from the kitchen doorway as Eric put his arms around all three boys at once, his angular face creased into a bright smile. He had a few days' beard stubble, which was quite unlike Eric, and she said so. "What's with the beard?"

Eric turned to her now, his smile dimming slightly as he looked her over. She suddenly wished she'd thought to brush her hair, or put on a little eyeliner. She dismissed the idea. How stupid. Eric's opinion of her shouldn't matter anymore.

He released the boys and said, "I don't know, just felt like it."

"Really? That's a change!"

"The old geek loosening up, eh?" Eric's mouth twisted to the side. He had been letting his hair and beard grow, but only out of laziness. He hated to shave. Still, he wasn't surprised that Emmy would read meaning into it.

"No, that's not what I said! Not at all. Hey, it looks nice."

"Well, thanks. So do you. Guys, you ready?"

"Mmm," mumbled Henry, looking down. He didn't want to have to talk to his father about the pot, but he knew that Eric knew and would try to make him talk. Henry scowled. He always had to talk, inform, be helpful. But, he thought, no one else did. Nick couldn't, and Dan wouldn't shut up.

Eric glanced over at Henry, noting how the boy seemed taller since even the last time he'd seen him. He took in the hunched shoulders; long, stringy hair; baggy clothes. He noticed, for perhaps the first time, that Henry's chin was long, like Em's, and where he'd looked like Eric as a boy, he was now looking more and more like his mother. This realization made Eric inexplicably sad, because he felt as if he'd missed something important—something that had moved too quickly, while he was away.

Then he remembered the pot, and a stab of guilt shot through him. Emmy had said it was about *him*. How? Was it true? Or was it about the fact that the two of them were not together, at a time when Henry really needed them to be a unit?

He looked over at her, smoothing her hair, glancing surreptitiously in the dining room mirror. Without makeup, without any tight-fitting clothes, and her hair a cloud around her face and shoulders like this, she was a total knockout. She never got that. As she buttoned up her cardigan, which she'd always used instead of a bathrobe, Eric watched, against his better judgment, for that button across her chest to strain and gap. Emmy could never get a sweater that would fit her right—or at least the way she wanted them to fit. Emmy deep down wanted to look like a J.Crew girl, like the ones he'd gone to prep school with. Curvy Emmy was never going to look like one of those, thank God. Even now, Eric felt like smiling, despite the fact that he was simultaneously feeling a little blue over Henry. Being here was overwhelming, a whole mess that he just didn't have the energy or time to sort out. *Ah, life with Emmy*, he thought. *The roller-coaster ride of a lifetime*. Well, he was done with that. She had forced it to be that way. Ugh, not exactly true; he had lost control of himself. "Come on, guys," he said, a little gruffly.

They hurried out the door.

Nick buckled up in the backseat behind Daddy. He sniffed the air. It smelled right. Mommy's car smelled like flowers and brown, very sharp but also soothing in his nose. But Daddy's car smelled like skin and coffee, more like a hungry smell. Daddy's car made Nick want to eat. He rubbed his stomach and fixed his eyes on the pattern in the cloth of Daddy's seat. He liked the way the tiny black squares ended exactly at the dark gray line running down the seat. The line held them in perfectly, and the squares swam together the more he stared. A sigh escaped him and he began to feel happy, even though he had been upset to leave the house. It had not been on his calendar. Yet he knew it was a Daddy day, because it was Saturday and because he had been home last week. No school, Saturday. No school, Sunday. School; school; school, school; school; no school, Saturday. Daddy comes. But it hadn't said that. He squeezed his hand open and shut.

"You okay, Nick?" Eric asked, glancing in his rearview mirror, then quickly looking away, knowing how Nick hated being looked at, especially in the mirror.

"Okay."

"He was going cross-eyed at the seat, Dad," Dan informed him.

"Yeah, okay, Dan," said Eric crisply. "How was soccer?"

"We lost, but I scored."

"Fantastic! Wish I could have been there."

"Mom was," Dan said sullenly.

With the iPod turned way down, Henry listened to all this without appearing to. He thought about the little bag of joints that he'd stuffed into his top drawer, where his underwear was. He'd decided that his dad's apartment was too small to risk a smoke. He hoped his mother wouldn't do a white laundry; he figured she wouldn't because she just did one yesterday—he remembered the pile of clean and folded briefs sitting on his bed—so his stash was safe.

Emmy had a bunch of appointments strung throughout the day, until three, starting after lunch. The weekends, of course, were her busiest times. And although she did not have to do a laundry today—she'd forced herself to do an extra load just a day ago—she still had to clean the house. She kept her PJs on and took out her vacuum cleaner and the Pledge. They could no longer afford a housecleaner now that Eric had his own place, so she was (for now) cleaning the house herself. And doing a lousy job of it, because she hated the chore. She made the boys vacuum their own rooms and bathroom, but, of course, being kids, they worked only in broad strokes and never went behind or under anything. Nick simply went for the clumps of dust and spaced out, sometimes just vacuuming the same spot over and over until she told him to move. Dan complained every step of the way. And she got so tired every time that she never finished the whole house at once. She hated living with the feeling of unseen dirt lurking somewhere at all times, but what could she do? She rolled the vacuum cleaner over the dining room sisal rug, which really hid dirt well, and listened with some small satisfaction to the crackle of crumbs disappearing into the tube. Afterward, she put away the vacuum cleaner and went upstairs to throw on dirty clothes. Time for a little gardening, a little fun. Communing with the plant-a-loons, as Eric used to say.

Eric. Who cared about Eric? she thought, annoyed at herself, realizing how she missed his humor. Grabbing her rake from the shed wall and a few large paper leaf bags, she started swinging at the yellow grass. She was not going to let herself get all sentimental about him again. What good did it do? Her stomach growled just then, as if in response. She'd skipped breakfast, which she often did on weekends.

She walked to the center of the backyard and started bouncing the rake there, more gently now, as her father had taught her to do. "You want to make the grass stand up, and get all the dead pieces to come out," he would say. She felt her arm muscles working hard and figured she could skip a workout if she did this for a half hour. It wasn't that she loved raking, but she did love the results: the overnight unfurling of lush green grass, like a siren letting down her hair.

It would do no good getting all forgiving toward Eric, she thought, when he hadn't done one thing to change. Given the same frightening conditions, of Nick's losing it, would Eric push him again?

And there they were, her eternal companions, Grief and Shame. Goddamn it, when would they go away? When would she be able to resolve this thing, or at least move past that terrible moment? Even Nick had let it go. She hoped. *Who really knew what Nick knew, anyway?* And the burning in her stomach grew stronger.

The hard work eventually helped dissipate a lot of the feelings. She fell into a rhythm of raking and bagging, hearing herself breathe and occasionally pushing her hair back away from her sweaty face. Once she finished getting the grass to wake up, she'd fertilize with an organic mix of cornmeal, manure, and lime, and in a week it would start to be brilliant green. Never, of course, as consistently green and smooth as the lawns of her surrounding neighbors, who used services and lots and lots of chemicals, but a basically green gestalt, which was good enough for her. And the birds. The birds flocked to her yard more than anyone else's because, frankly, it had gone to seed and birds couldn't get enough of it. But still, it was a green meadow to her, filled with life, and safe soil, no pesticides or poisons that would harm her children. That was what was important. Not so much how perfect something looked as how much happiness it gave in looking the way it did. If her children could play on her grass and be healthy, then the grass was beautiful. This was the way she would view her clients' gardens—if she were ever to have that gardening business. The arrangement of their outdoor space would be about stirring the soul, feeding the human need for beauty—natural beauty. Nothing artificial (no plastic anything, nor chemical fertilizers) and nothing forced (no tropicals in their hardy New England climate, nothing too dainty for their demanding weather and rocky, acidic soil) but only plantings to bring out the beauty of what was already there.

Thinking about Gardens of Eden renewed Emmy's energy. Even if she could not start it up, except in her dreams, she felt that the idea of it kept her going, and made her feel strong, like her younger self, the botany student full of hope and piss and vinegar. Gardens of Eden let her see that she had a life and interests beyond discontented soon-to-be divorcée, or struggling mother of three.

But it couldn't happen. She had to keep working as a realtor now that she was single, without Eric's income. And she'd be the struggling mother of three for years to come, as well. So what did *that* say about her and her future life? She shook her head and rubbed her right lower back. A red ball-shaped robin bounced along the stone wall. A sudden wind rushed up at her from the underbrush, roaring over and around her like current in a river. The bird startled and flew higher, into the craggy branches of the crab apple. *Rain's coming*, she thought.

She knew how to do the garden plans and the work, but she just did not know how to start or run a business, and when she'd told Eric about her idea, he'd made it quite clear that this kind of enterprise was not for someone like her. *Someone like me*, she thought, frowning as she gathered the piles of dead grass, careful to bend her knees to preserve her back. She flashed on Nick, how people said, "someone like Nick," as if he were in a category completely unto himself.

She flapped open the musty-smelling paper lawn bag and wondered if things would ever get easier. Her big little boy. Forever innocent and dependent. Shy, quiet, pretty much untamed like a forest creature. But also a young man. She sighed and stretched. A blister was already starting in her right palm. For this, she would wear gloves. She went to the shed to get her floral cotton ones.

Emmy did a half hour more of raking, attacking most of the lawn, and then sprinkled fertilizer, while she thought more about Nick. She had tried to get him interested in the outdoors—grass, flowers, animals—but his interests were only internal. Aside from salsa, chili powder, ribbon, and bubbles, she had no idea what Nick liked. There was nothing anyone could share with him, nothing he could get from anyone else. People did not make him happy; only certain sensory experiences could do that. She felt a small, old, familiar ache in her heart, that this was a child of hers—she, who got so much out of being with people! Not that she was judging Nick; no, it was that she grieved for him, what he did not have, what he did not know. And she could do nothing to fix it.

But, she thought then, and not at all for the first time, there must be something that he could love—something that she could do for him, with him. But nothing came to her.

She walked to the house and turned around, as she always did, to see how it would look if she were just now coming across her yard for the first time. A haze of white grass shimmered, alert, interspersed with some brown and some green patches. Not bad. Her arms and back ached. Her sweat smelled tangy. She felt done, worn-out, and threw her gloves into the shed, just as the first fat raindrops started to fall.

Chapter 21

This was Emmy's last client to get through before going home, where Mom would be arriving. She swung the Volvo into the tiny driveway on the side of the row house and waited for Sally Frye to show up. Sally had loved the Philadelphia-style house last week, when she'd first seen it, that morning that Henry had been caught with the pot. Now she wanted to see it again because, frankly, it had not been a long enough showing and had been overshadowed by Emmy's precipitous departure.

Sally pulled up at the spot in front of the house. Emmy was grateful there was one; this block was tough during the day. She didn't know if Sally realized that, but at least there was the little driveway, so Emmy didn't feel nervous about mentioning it. If anything, Emmy disclosed too much to her clients, a habit that Eric had made fun of and that she knew didn't help her make too many sales. *Yeah, I guess a better salesperson would conveniently forget about the bad parking conditions here*, she thought. A better salesperson but a lousy person. She would always opt for being a good person. No matter what it cost her. And with that thought, she could just imagine Eric laughing and saying, "Oh, Em, it doesn't have to be one or the other."

"Hi! Come on in," she called out, forcing Eric from her head.

"Thanks," said Sally.

She held the door for Sally and followed her inside. "So, why don't you just wander through and see what you'd like to see; I'll follow along, okay?"

"Yeah, that's fine," said Sally.

The showing took a bit longer than Emmy had anticipated, because Sally had fallen completely in love with the place. She had gone up and down all the stairs at least twice, and they'd spent a little time going over possible bidding prices. So she was late getting home, and her mother arrived just as Emmy was pulling up. Eric and the boys were already there, waiting on the front steps.

"Oh, sorry!" Emmy called out. She left her work in the car and slammed the door.

"Hello, princess." Mom held her arms out to Emmy and pulled her into a deep embrace. "Mmm, my sweet girl," she whispered into Emmy's hair.

"That's because I'm wearing your perfume, Mom!" Emmy kissed her mother, surprised as she always was lately by the feel of Mom's cheeks, now that she was seventy: her skin no longer seemed firm, but actually more gel-like, as if you could press on it and change its shape.

She looked over at Eric, who was watching them hug. "Well, now that you're here, I guess I'll take off." He walked over to Mom. She turned to look at him, her eyes wide, as if to say, *"You're not going to hug me, are you?"*

Eric stopped short, remembering whom he was dealing with. He patted her on the shoulder and winked at Emmy, who made a pouty smile at him and rolled her eyes the tiniest bit. He had the feeling that she would have wanted him to stay. It had always been this way between them when her mom was around. Something about Em's mom brought out the wench in Em, the mischievous sexy side. He was surprised, though, that this was still true, and he was a little tempted to stay because of it. But he'd promised Lucy he would come by this weekend. He knew better than to tell Emmy where he was going, though. "Take care, you two." He strode off before they could reply.

Mom watched him go and then shrugged. *"Nisht ge fayleh,"* she muttered.

"Mom, you forget I know Yiddish, too."

Mom raised her eyebrows. "Mmm?"

So she was starting already! Emmy went on: "Anyway, you're right. There's nothing to be done. It's over between us, and that's that."

"Who said anything? So, is anyone going to take this suitcase?

So many big, strong men around here!"

Dan ran forward to hoist the suitcase, which he managed to lug off using both hands. Emmy noticed that he looked over at Henry with an expression that said, "See?"

Henry rolled his eyes and walked into the house, letting the screen door slam behind him.

Emmy tried not to think what she was thinking: for this I gave up my weekend? But she'd never learned how to say no to Mom, and she wasn't about to start trying now, at forty. What was that thing Eric used to say? Oh yeah: "Mothers. Can't live with them, can't kill them." She looked wistfully at the spot where his car had just been and wondered why it was that she thought about Eric's words more now that they were over than when she'd been living with him.

"I don't know, Lucy," Eric said to his sister. He took his glasses off and rubbed the bridge of his nose. Eric and Lucy were sitting on her sumptuous white couches in her bright living room, where they usually spent his visits. A silver tea tray was set before them on a cherry coffee table. It was filled with scones, a silver pitcher of heavy cream, another pitcher of strawberry preserves, fine china teacups, and of course, a brimming teapot. Lucy was the only person Eric knew who actually "took tea," English style, and not green, chai, or herbal. The real East India thing. Usually, it amused him. After all, they'd grown up in Vermont, two middle-class kids, with no English relatives whatsoever—only the distant ones, who had come on the *Mayflower*, or maybe some lesser ship. But Lucy had always been one for ceremony and theater. Even as a child, she had done more than play house: she'd played manor house. Now, a grown woman with a successful interior design business, she could indulge her highly colorful fantasy life as much as she wanted. "And they pay me for it, can you beat that?" she would say, laughing. Most people who knew Lucy thought of her as a lucky person.

Eric especially. For Lucy had it all, plus a husband, Jordan, with whom she enjoyed "true love," or some close approximation, and their wonderful daughter, Katie.

"But, Eric, you must know what's bothering you. You just don't want to say, that's all." Lucy poured him coffee and, without asking, threw in three lumps of sugar and handed him the cream. She watched him pour it in until its swirls spread over the black surface, changing it to a thick, soft, tan color.

Eric was such a boy, still liked everything so sweet. She smiled. But when he didn't smile back, she became worried. Was it Nick? Was he somehow troubled by the autism again, like the year after his diagnosis? She shuddered inwardly at the thought of those days, when her gentle, life-loving brother had been unreachable, lost to her. He'd come out of it, thank goodness. But he hadn't really picked up with his life, now, had he? Living on his own. Not that she missed Emmy. But still. It was sad. One didn't want one's marriage to break up, for heaven's sake, even a mediocre one!

Although Eric usually seemed happy enough this past year, lost among his drawings and his math, it had always bothered her how much he seemed to have aged since the separation. She nudged him with her elbow. "Eric, just tell me. What is it?"

Eric studied his sister's pretty face. She had as strong a chin as he, but the resemblance ended there. Where Eric was thin, gaunt even, Lucy was soft and rounded. Even with her auburn hair starting to gray like his, she was quite a pretty woman. "Well, Lucy, I don't really know what it is. I think I'm just alone too much."

He sipped at his coffee—he hated tea, and she knew it—and reached for a scone. "Good scones," he said, biting into the spongy pastry.

"At least take some jelly, Eric. You're so thin. You could eat all you want!"

"No, too sticky. You sound like Mom! You talk to her lately?" He continued to eat and Lucy grew visibly impatient.

"Yes, of course," Lucy snapped. Even though he knew she loved their mother dearly, Lucy had no desire to be like her.

Eric thought for a moment about their mother, whom he rarely spoke to. He had parted ways with his parents since he'd gone and married Em. Vaguely disapproving—of Em, of Jews, of God knew what else—they'd stayed put in Vermont and that was that. Eric said, "How is she?"

"Mom? Same as ever. Nothing will ever change her." Lucy rolled her eyes.

Eric took another sip of coffee. "Emmy's got it pretty tough these days."

"Emmy? I guess." She looked down at her lap, not trusting her expression. She still felt miffed over the whole gun thing; Emmy was such a child! Even if she did have it tough, that was all the more reason for her not to spurn Lucy's attempts to help.

"She seems different."

Lucy raised her eyebrows. "Hmm," she murmured. "How so?" Just like Eric to fall for Emmy's histrionics.

"I don't know. Looking at me and then looking away. Weird."

Lucy paled slightly at that. Maybe Emmy wanted them to get back together? "Looking at you? Oh, *looking* at you! What do you think it means? That she wants you back?"

"That's what I'm wondering. No. I don't think so. I just don't know."

"Well, you said she seemed troubled and was looking at you. Maybe she just can't talk about it to you. Do you want more coffee?" She reached for the coffeepot. "Or maybe—hmm."

"Hmm?"

"Maybe she's interested in someone else."

Eric looked startled. "Low blow, Luce." He couldn't believe how hard his heart was beating at the thought of this. He'd never considered it before.

"Why? Just a possibility." Lucy helped herself to half a scone. She whispered, "Just a half," to herself out loud. But Eric knew she'd finish the whole thing before he left. Lucy had been struggling all her life with her weight.

"Hmm. I doubt it," he started, then wished he hadn't said it.

"I have to get back. I really want to finish up a project by

Monday." He stood and stretched. "Thanks for everything," he said as he walked to the door.

"You know, I'm sure everything is okay," Lucy said.

Eric smiled, because he knew how much she had to love him to say something kind about Emmy. He turned and caught her raising the last bit of the scone to her lips. She stopped, her mouth still open.

"They *are* good scones," he said, grinning. "I'm sure that little bit won't hurt. Practically a crumb, really."

"You get out of here, you idiot!" She threw a round velvet couch pillow at him.

Part IV

May

Planting

Chapter 22

It was the end of another weekend with their father. The boys filed into the house, and each went to the place where he was most comfortable. Nick sat in the dead center of the living room couch, Henry pulled out his homework on the dining room table, and Dan got out his pad and paper and sat down on the floral chair and a half in the living room. Each barely acknowledged Emmy's joyful greeting.

Emmy had missed them so much, as she always did on Eric's weekends, but they didn't seem to notice her now. She was as much a part of the background in their lives as the sofa and the coffee table. She knew in her head that this was how it was supposed to be, with boys, but still—it made her feel sad and alone, more than it had in the last year. She didn't understand it, why she could not adjust to things after all this time.

Eric stood in the doorway, knowing, of course, what she was thinking. "Yeah, it's a bit like pulling teeth," he said softly, catching her eye.

"Want anything?" Emmy asked him, which was usually his signal to leave, but tonight she seemed to mean for him to stay, because her tone was warm. He raised an eyebrow and said, "Uh, got any decaf?"

"No, but I'll make it. I like it at night, too, you know."

"I know."

Eric followed her into the kitchen. He couldn't believe how nervous he was. His heart was thumping away like a scared rabbit. He passed Nick, where he sat on the couch in the living room, his tall, thin shape silhouetted in the gray semidarkness of the unlit room. His hand was raised, opening and closing. "DaddyMommy, feem," he said. "DaddyMommy, foooom."

Em got out the chocolaty brown Peet's Coffee bags and started scooping coffee into her coffeemaker.

"So, how was it?"

"It was." He looked around the kitchen—their "dream" kitchen, as Em liked to call it—and the loss hit him anew, remembering how they'd pored over designs together. Even the arguments about prices of things made him feel nostalgic. Ahh, he shouldn't have come in. Remembering his flood of feelings for Em the other night, on the phone, Eric wanted to turn and run. He rubbed the back of his head. Why had he consented to stay? It just hurt to be there.

"'It was.' This is how you describe your twenty-four hours with your boys?"

He frowned at her. "Yeah, I guess so. It wasn't much fun. None of them was particularly charming. They didn't want to be there. Dan snipes at Nick. Nick—well, it's hard. Henry kept talking about the homework he had to get back to. By the end of today, I was so fed up I almost asked him if he had any pot."

"Eric!"

Jesus, she still couldn't even tell when he was joking! Eric's mouth twisted into a lopsided smile. "Sorry. Bad joke. Don't worry; *I* was a good parent."

Something about the way he said it made her look up suspiciously. "What's that supposed to mean?"

"Nothing."

"Eric, don't give me that. You're implying that he got into the pot under my watch, right?"

"Well, I didn't say that—"

"You didn't have to! Well, that isn't what he told me, for your information. He told me it was about you walking out of here—"

"You know, Emmy, I don't need this." Eric rose from the barstool. It scraped along the floor, irritating Eric even more because he remembered adding felt pads to those stools for just that reason. Where had they gone?

"Eric, wait."

"Emmy, what? It's late. I'm tired." But he sank back down onto the seat.

"Eric, we have to talk."

"I thought that's what we were doing. Kind of. Talking plus shouting. Equals fighting."

"Eric." She walked over to him and set down an empty mug. His favorite, a round, black misshapen thing that Henry had made and glazed in his one and only ceramics class. He turned it over and read the scrawled name with the backward R. He smiled. In spite of the tension, it felt good sitting here, just looking at her. Like normal, the way it used to be.

His smile gave Emmy courage to tell him. "I just thought you should know. It doesn't mean anything, but I've been kind of—I was—someone was interested in me," she said, "kind of a lot." Eric didn't say anything. The coffeepot burbled and sucked, and suddenly spat out some steam, signifying the end of the brewing cycle. Emmy stood up and got the carafe.

When Eric finally spoke, his voice was tight and dry. "Really." He wouldn't look at her. "Who?"

Emmy shook her head. "What does that matter? It's not going anywhere. That's not what I meant, in bringing it up. I just wanted you to know how conflicted it made me feel!" She wanted Eric to see that she missed the attention of a man, but now that seemed like too vulnerable a thing to admit.

"Some guy's fucking my wife, I think I'd like to know his name. And how he managed it."

"Eric! Shut up! That's horrible! That's not at all what happened!" She swallowed, and tried to regain control of the conversation. Eric was taking this completely wrong. "He's a client, but that doesn't matter, and his name is Will."

"I don't care if his name is Fuckface! Why the fuck would you do this?"

She reddened, not knowing what to say—and poured the coffee, gathering her thoughts. The earthy smell filled her nostrils. Coffee always relaxed her, inexplicably. It forced her to sit down—too much motion would cause the hot liquid to spill— and the careful sipping caused time to slow.

Now, feeling wrapped in this moment, of Eric back in her kitchen, sharing coffee just as they'd always done, she was filled with a strange sense of hope. "Eric," she said softly, feeling a new generosity and gentleness toward him. "I didn't do anything! It was a harmless flirtation! I only told you because I liked the feeling! I was trying to be—I don't know, completely honest with you! Something's missing in my life. I don't know, but the thing is, I wanted to tell you and see if we could try to talk a little more about . . . us." She pushed the sugar bowl over to him and reached for a spoon.

Eric laughed, but it sounded to him like a rusty hinge. "Us? Is there really such a thing?" He hid behind his coffee for a moment, taking a long sip. He knew he was being unreasonable; and he did believe her that nothing had happened. Yet still he wanted to slam the mug down and break it into little black shards. And he didn't know why. Why should her being honest and gentle make him this angry?

Because it was easier for him when she was being a loud, self-righteous shrew. If she was going to start being sweet and considerate, where did that leave them? He gulped his coffee, pushing down a lump gathering in his throat.

"Yeah, there is. You're my husband. You're also—you were—my oldest friend. You know me best."

"So now we're 'friends'? Oh, excuse me, we 'were' friends?" His voice cracked on the word *friends*, which really bugged him. Just when he was trying to be tough with her, the old testosterone just petered out. *Now that was a good pun*, he thought incongruously. In the old days, he would have told Emmy, made her laugh. But that seemed so long ago; she wasn't going to laugh with him now.

His frustration, his impotence over their relationship, made Eric's anger stronger and hotter, driving him to some terrible precipice. He had to leave. He wanted to be home, alone, and not here, which was also home—yes, it still was. His chest hurt, his nostrils flared, his eyes were blinking a lot; he was *not* going to cry now. "You know what," he said, his voice shaky. "I don't want to hear this. Any of it. I don't need this right now." He pressed his hands down on the counter, watching the fingers turn white and red. He stood up. "And I am not your friend," he added, a bitter tang to his words.

"Eric! Look," Emmy said. "I'm sorry. I feel really bad. It was nothing, I swear. I did not mean to hurt you, I meant to—" But now she didn't know what she meant to do, because he was angrier than she'd seen in a long time. She had not thought this through enough, because it never occurred to her that Eric would show so much emotion about it. She dropped her eyes, feeling like a child about to be punished.

"Yeah, what? What did you mean to do? Talk about our marriage? You've got a funny way of doing that—by flirting with some guy. And who knows where that will lead? After all, where there's a Will, there's a way!" The joke had just flown out—old habit—but neither of them acknowledged it. This made him feel even worse. And to his horror, his lips started to quiver. He pressed his mouth with the back of his hand and started toward the kitchen door.

"Eric, please, listen. I just needed the fun, the pleasure. I was so depressed when you left. I felt like a has-been. Will made me feel good. Beautiful. For that . . . moment, anyway."

"Well, you *are* beautiful," Eric said hoarsely, still walking away. She really was so beautiful to him. Never more so than right now, standing on a distant sandbar while he tried to get to her as the tide rushed in. He had to escape. There was no dealing with this right now. He was going to cry, or scream, or something that he just could not do here. He pushed open the door. She didn't follow him.

Nick was the only one in the living room, still sitting in the middle of the white couch. The room was dark. He was talking quietly to himself. Eric listened for a moment, trying to pick out real words. But he couldn't. It was all just singsong nonsense syllables strung together. *Like baby talk*, he thought bitterly. In this moment, he became conscious of wanting something so badly he felt himself flayed open, a kind of Prometheus who finds himself once again in the same familiar and horrible and inescapable situation. *Please*, he thought, hard, beaming his wish to Nick the way he'd done as a kid during ESP experiments with his friends. *Just look up. Say, "Good night, Dad." Please.*

He gave it a moment, then left as quickly as he could.

Emmy was determined to stay busy after Eric went, so as not to think about what had happened. Her e-mails had really piled up. One by one she pierced the tiny blue e-mail balloons with her cursor arrow and took care of business. A question from sallyfrye@aol.com. "How is your boy?" Emmy smiled at this, thinking how sweet Sally was to remember that. She sent a quick thank-you response.

There was also a request from the Pearls to see a completely different neighborhood, which they wouldn't be able to afford. An e-mail letting her know of a new Multiple Listing Service house in her area. Another staff meeting reminder from her firm and a PTO newsletter from the boys' school. Nothing from Will, which was a relief.

She sighed and shook her shoulders, trying to clear the creeping complicated feelings out of her head. How upset Eric had looked! She didn't want him that upset! After all, they'd been apart for over a year. And everything had become so bland, so rote between them. But he'd been surprisingly emotional over Will.

She was also surprised by how that fact went straight to her heart. It hurt, but it was a relief, too. It meant Eric still cared.

So it really wasn't over with Eric? There was just no simple answer to that.

Work. The only solution for feeling this way. She went into the MLS database and familiarized herself with all the new listings in her area. She started to gather comparables ("comps") for some neighbors down the street who had intimated that they were thinking of selling, provided they could be assured of a certain price. There were about five other comps, so she ran them off and collected them in a bright red folder. Then she turned to her other client e-mails and dashed off some quick replies. She fished out her calendar and gave Sally a few appointment options, for her to come in and make her offer. She wondered if the offer would be reasonable, and had a feeling it would be, though you never knew how people would be about their money. But Emmy really liked Sally, and felt determined to make this deal go through for her. She knew the sellers were a little flexible, because they'd left the state to move to North Carolina, where life was much cheaper than here in Boston.

She shut the lid and went to check on the boys getting ready for bed. "Dan, brush your teeth, especially behind, okay?"

"Mom, I know." He shuffled off, wearing beige camouflage boxer shorts and a matching T-shirt.

"Hey, I almost didn't see you because of the camo!"

Dan rolled his eyes. "Mom, it's for the desert, not *here*." But she could tell he was pleased.

"Oh yeah."

She saw Henry shoving books into his enormous gray backpack. "All done?"

"Huh?" He still had his earbuds in. She motioned for him to take them out.

"All finished?"

"Yeah."

She sat gingerly at the foot of his bed. "So, sweetie, how was it with Dad?"

"Okay."

"Did you guys talk?"

"About—?"

"Oh, anything other than what to eat?"

"You mean the pot?"

Emmy smiled. "Yeah, I mean the pot."

Henry frowned. "No way."

"No way?"

"Yeah."

"Henry, he's your father. Don't you think you guys should talk about important things?"

"I guess." He shrugged, then stretched. He looked pointedly

at the clock on his desk.

What had Eric said? Like pulling teeth. Well, she was no dentist. She knew she should probably do more about this pot thing—or Eric should have—but she just didn't have the energy. Ben Taylor would keep an eye on Henry while he was in school, and she would keep a better eye on him at home. As long as his schoolwork was going well—other than the cheating—wasn't that the key to it all? Her stomach fluttered nervously, but she ignored it. "Okay, good night, sweetheart." She leaned across the table and kissed his oily skin, remembering, with a little ache in her heart, when this was the sweetest-smelling face in the world.

Henry shut the door of his room and crept over to his underwear drawer. It looked just as he'd left it. He felt underneath the loose slat and pulled out his bag of three joints. He unwrapped one, pinched the dried flakes, and threw them into his mouth. They stuck to his tongue and tasted spicy; not that bad.

No way was he going to get caught again. That was really stupid. Bad enough to have the whole school know, but to have to go in every day and be Taylor's boy!

The weekend had been a total shitpile, just as he knew it would be. Dad was so weird. And what was with the scruffy no-shave look? He wanted to yell, "It doesn't make you look younger! Nothing will! No chick is going to look twice at an old guy like you!"

But Mom had looked, hadn't she? She'd invited him in to talk! That hadn't happened in the whole last year. And they had shut the kitchen door. Maybe they were getting back together? Although, no, Dad had looked really kind of bad when he'd left.

Henry chewed and swallowed, staring out at his dark street. Across the way, a tiny blue television light glowed from the third floor of the Clarks' house. He looked up higher and saw that the moon was three-quarters full. A couple of stars were out, and the air smelled wet and grassy. He shut the window and lay down on his bed, tired but the pot was making his thoughts tumble around too much for sleep. He hadn't counted on that when he'd taken it out. He'd just wanted to relax. Instead, his heart was racing and his thoughts kept getting ahead of themselves so that he couldn't concentrate on the beginning or end of a single one. He shut his eyes, but then he felt dizzy. His dinner burned in his stomach and started to rise.

He sat up. "What the—?"

Running across the hall to the bathroom, Henry threw himself down across the toilet and vomited. He lay there for some time, afraid to get up, afraid to move. But he knew he had to before Mom—*Oh, man he should flush it, what if she could tell somehow?* He reached over , flushed it, and crumbled to his knees again.

"Henry?"

Emmy poked her head into the open bathroom. "Oh my God, Henry! Are you sick?" She rushed over to him, then got him a cup of water and knelt down to look at him. "What happened?"

"I don't know. I threw up everything I ate." Henry hoped she wouldn't probe further. His head was still spinning and foggy, but he could think clearly if he shut his eyes.

"Henry, you look very strange. I want you to get right into bed. What, was it something you ate? I'm going to call Dad." Though she didn't know what Eric could do about this.

"No!" Henry hadn't liked the dinner Dad had made (mushy fish sticks and partially frozen French fries), so Dad would tell her that Henry had hardly eaten anything, except, like, a banana and some crackers—hardly barf-inducing food. And he didn't want her getting on his case for not eating, being a growing boy, and all that shit.

"No? Henry—"

Henry groaned and turned toward the toilet again. This time, only dry heaves came. He was completely empty. "Okay, I'm going to bed. Don't make such a big deal, Mom." He rose unsteadily and pushed past her to his room, closing the door behind him. Shutting the door on her usually worked. Mom was into letting Henry be An Adolescent.

But what the hell was it, anyway? Reluctantly, he recalled the detective's words, about how sometimes the dealers put other shit into the pot. Was it the dope, or something else? No, that guy was a total moron. Maybe he was just sick?

He heard Nick talking kind of loudly to himself in his room. He knew that Nick was probably freaked about the puking; he always got really upset when someone was sick or crying. Not upset like, "Oh, are you okay?" But upset like lots of talking to himself in a high-pitched voice and rocking.

Henry used to think he was lucky because he was the only little brother he knew whose big brother never picked on him. He remembered feeling this beaming pride when he was, like, three or four, that his big brother was so different, so nice. *Nice.* Henry shook his head. The loud talking persisted next door, so he decided to go in and maybe reassure Nick.

He let his eyes adjust to the darkness and focused on the shape on Nick's bed. Nick was lying flat on his back. The self-talking stopped when he heard Henry.

"Yes," Nick said softly, in greeting.

"Sorry to upset you, Nick."

"Sorrytupsetyou. Frow up. Feem."

"Yeah, that's right, Nick. I did throw up. I got a little sick. But I'm okay."

"Okay, yes. Feem, whoooom. Frow up, feem."

Henry stood there for a moment, a hot pressure rising up out of nowhere, from his chest, gripping his throat, lacerating his eyes. "Yeah. Sorry, buddy."

"Okay, yes. Henry will go out."

"Okay, Nick. Sleep well."

"Yes, okay, yes."

"No more talking, okay? It's late."

"Okay, yes."

After Henry went out, Nick sat up in his bed. He sniffed the air. The smells were very bad. There was that tiny smell again, a very faraway smell, but it came from Henry. And there was the throw-up; that was a smell that went right down his nose into his stomach. "Frow-up," he said again. He pressed on his mouth, because he didn't want to throw up, too.

His eyes hurt and they felt full of water, which he also hated, the wet on his face. He knew that the word for this was *sad*. That's what Mommy told him. Mommy knew all the words. Nick hated words. Nick hated Mommy's words, but he loved his own words. He let a few come out of his mouth.

He felt something else in his belly now, stretching up to his throat, like when he was hungry, but he wasn't hungry now. He thought of Daddy, and the feeling got worse. But it wasn't because of Daddy. It was because Daddy was not here.

Nick hated the throw-up smell around his nose. He pressed on his mouth some more, watching the shapes of his room come out of the dark. "Dark," he said out loud. Then he remembered Henry telling him, "No more talking." But he had to say one of his words before he stopped. "Feeeem," he said as quietly as he could. Now he could lie down. He pushed his belly into the mattress and burrowed his stuffy, wet nose into the pillow.

Chapter 23

As Eric walked up his stairs, he felt like an old man. His knees, his back, even his hip joints bothered him. All psychosomatic. There was nothing wrong with him, he knew. This went way back, to childhood. When things got bad, he focused on his body. Probably a therapist would say it was because pain was the only sure way to get some positive attention from Mom. She responded to sickness, and nothing else, really. Totally spoiled him on his sick days—even sat on his bed once and kissed him when his fever was especially high. He would never forget the way her eye was shining and how he realized there was actually a tear in it. He only remembered the one eye, but still, a tear was a tear. That had made the whole bout with strep bearable.

The exchange with Emmy had taken the wind out of him, making him so tired that climbing his stairs was a real effort. Well, not a "real" effort, if Dr. Freud were to be believed.

He frowned and threw himself down on the couch, only then realizing how badly he wanted a beer. His throat was practically numb from dryness. But how could he get up now? He was so tired.

He pushed himself up into a sitting position, his head pounding. Still, he was determined to get drunk, so he made his way over to the fridge and pulled out a glistening Sam Adams. The tart wetness soothed his throat, and the alcohol started working almost immediately. It was as if a balloon were filling in his head, carrying Eric aloft to where he could just float.

He took the beer back to the couch, where he slipped out of his shoes and began flipping through one of his vintage Playboys. But of course, like some bad romance novel, all he could see was Emmy. He put down the magazine and closed his eyes.

There was no getting around it. The pleasant bubble-buzz in his head burst. He felt horrible, just ripped apart. Did not want her to flirt with another guy. Could not stand the thought of it. He wanted to kill that guy. He wanted—

What did he want? Here they'd been apart for so long without discussing anything. He'd just left and not tried to come back. All he'd been was humiliated and angry. Mostly at himself. He'd actually knocked his own son over. What kind of a monster did that? Even in self-defense.

He was a long way from done with his marriage and family life, apparently. He swigged a third of the bottle, seeing Emmy's eyes again. How had this happened? She was his. And now some other guy wanted her. And she'd enjoyed his attention.

What was he going to have to do, let her go? How in hell could he do that?

But she was breaking away from him. And he had no idea what to do about it, except drink down this awful, ripping pain that kept resurfacing in his throat, like strep.

Chapter 24

The entire drive over to speech therapy, Emmy felt anxious. She was so worked up about Eric that she couldn't concentrate on her driving, and she went the slow way by mistake, even hitting the pothole again. There had been no further word from him, and by now she was beginning to obsess about the whole thing. What was he thinking? How would this change things between them?

She swung the car into the lot across from Tom Palmer's squat building. "Here we are, darling," she said to Nick.

"Yes." Nick waited for the brake to creak before unsnapping his seat belt. Tom was in the front foyer.

"Hey there, Em. Hey, Nick. Let's go."

After the door closed, Emmy tried to read in earnest. She thumbed through every magazine on the table, even the *Highlights*. Nothing changed. Still the corny Goofus and Gallant, still the bizarre Timbertoes. Finally, she decided to deal with one thing that was bugging her. She took out her cell phone and dialed Eric's work number. He picked up on the first ring, his voice sounding tight and harried.

"Hey, Em."

"Hi, Eric. How are you?" Emmy couldn't tell for sure, but he sounded guarded, yet calm. Maybe he was okay with it all now?

There was silence for a few seconds, and then, in a cold, flat tone, he said, "Emmy. I'm working."

"Eric, I know what you do there. I know you have your own office, and you can close the door."

Eric said slowly, in a serious voice, "Yeah? So why should I do that?" He didn't want to talk to her. Didn't want to deal with what she'd done, and how it made him feel kicked in the knees, or ill. So he hadn't let himself think much more about what she'd told him the other night, about Will. He had closed down, drunk a lot of beer, slept in, and then worked straight through into the next day.

But now he was angry again. He did not want her to have a relationship with another man. Hated the fact. Nor could he believe how much it rankled him. So now he just said it, to get it out there: "I hate this. It changes things." As he said this, he felt some of the pressure that had been in his chest for the last day start to recede; unfortunately, it also made his eyes and nose start to tingle with tears.

Emmy's interest in another man did change things. She was moving away from him. And this hurt like he couldn't believe, but he also knew that he had no idea how to stop it.

Emmy's heart started racing again, and her palm was sweaty where she held the phone. What did he mean? Divorce? "Like?"

"Like . . ."

"Like what?"

"Like, I don't know." He exhaled. Yeah. Okay. He could not deal with this, after all. He just couldn't. This was actually the opposite of what he wanted to do, which was to rage at her. But he fought this impulse, knowing it would push her further away from him. So he didn't know what he could possibly say that would (1) make him feel better; (2) not make him burst out in horrible, embarrassing tears; and (3) not make her hang up on him.

He took another deep breath, and knew from the soft space that had opened up in his ribs that this was the most he could manage right now. He had no clue what else to do; all he knew was that thinking about it only made him want to explode. So he was pushing it away. *Put it in a box, shut the door, and don't think about it anymore*, his mother would say when he was a little kid crying over something. "Okay, I have to go. Do whatever you need to do." He felt as if a part of himself were drying up as he said it, but at least this was something he could tolerate, more than the tears and the bellyache.

"What?" His unexpected reaction left Emmy very confused. Where was all this coming from? He didn't care? He didn't want her back? This thought slammed into her, leaving her breathless for a moment. What did *that* mean? "Why? What are you saying?" But she was afraid to hear his answer. She'd been living this way for so long, where Eric was the obstacle, the enemy. And now? He cared?

"That's all I'm saying. I can't think about this anymore. It's killing me. I'm done talking about it."

Killing him? "Well, I—"

"Emmy, I've got to go. Sorry. Bye." He clicked off.

But when Eric looked around his quiet office, with the hum of a faulty fluorescent light buzzing in his ear like a mosquito, he panicked. And just like that, he knew he'd done the wrong thing. He had let her go.

He stared at the phone and willed it to ring. But she'd never call him back now. Not Lady Black and White.

No. He was going to have to do the calling. He was going to have to do some hard work, relationship work, the kind he absolutely hated. The kind he ran away from a year ago. Emmy always made everything so hard, but that, perhaps, was why he loved her so much. She really made him feel things, bad and good.

And now? "Christ!" he yelled. He didn't know. He just knew he did not want her with that creep. He put his head in his hands, running his fingers through his hair. What a holy mess this had turned into, just because he hadn't paid as much attention to someone as he should have. You'd think he would have learned from his mother's bad example, but that, again, was for the crunchy-granola Birkenstock therapists to figure out.

Emmy's ears were ringing, she was so angry. She wanted to scream. *Goddamn that man!* she thought. How could ever she have cared about someone so idiotic? Emmy flung her phone into her bag, then punched the chair and the cushions, for good measure.

"I was wondering if I should do something with the décor here." Tom's voice, filled with amusement, came from behind.

"Never thought of punching stuff to improve the look." He smoothed the dented pillow next to her. Nick was pacing behind them.

"Oh, it's time. Look at that. I lost track. I was just on the phone." She refused to look at him.

"You know, Emmy, there's a no–cell phone policy here."

She snapped her head up at him. "What? There's no one else here! I wasn't disturbing anyone!"

Tom sat down right next to her on the cramped sofa. The faint piney detergent smell wafted over to her. "Hey," he said softly. "I was only kidding."

She looked down at the carpet. "Yeah. Well. You could use a better color carpet."

He threw his head back and laughed, hand on his chest. It was the sort of gesture her grandfather used to make, kind of Old World and charming. Tom was so warm and easygoing. No wonder Nick liked coming here. "But it's a new carpet! Nick! Come here and say good-bye to me."

Nick came over immediately. "Goodbyetome."

Tom smiled and touched Nick. "G—"

"GoodbyefanksTom."

"You are welcome. Good-bye, Nick."

Emmy was still thinking about what Eric had said, the way he'd just crumpled up. She realized how it was kind of a pattern with him: withdraw without a fight. He let go so easily! She dialed the pizza place without even realizing it, the moment she got in the door. "Henry!" she called with the phone to her ear. "Are you going to eat?"

"Yeah!"

Henry had stayed home from school today because he'd been so sick last night. Emmy had had to force him. He claimed he was fine, but she thought he looked green around the gills, as her mother used to say. Emmy figured he must have picked up a bug at Eric's or reacted to something he'd eaten.

"Nick, will you come in here and help Mommy with the table?"

Nick got up from his spot on the couch and pulled a napkin out of the drawer.

"There's more than one person eating, ya know," came Dan's voice out of nowhere.

"Dan, where are you?"

"In here."

Emmy looked around the kitchen, under the table, but couldn't find him.

"Here."

The voice was coming from the slats in the louvered pantry closet. He couldn't possibly fit—or could he? She pulled the door open, and Dan came tumbling out. "Ow!"

"Well, honey, why were you in there? You're too big for that."

"I like it in there. I can be a spy. And let me tell you: that guy does NOT know how to set a table." He pointed vehemently in Nick's direction.

"Well, why don't you show him?" Emmy asked, a little harshly, because she was running out of patience. Dan walked hurriedly to the napkin cabinet. Emmy got out the juice and the salt.

"Hey, I thought we were doing that!"

We. She liked that. Dan and Nick, doing something together. She smiled and stepped back from the fridge. "Oh, sorry. Didn't mean to get in your way. Go for it, guys!"

"Yes," said Nick, hurrying to pull out one more napkin.

"You need three more!" shouted Dan, practically into Nick's ear.

Nick threw the napkin aside and brought his palm down hard on Dan's head.

"Ow!" Dan flung his hands outward at Nick to get him to stop.

But Nick was too tall for him. He kept hitting Dan in a blind rage, then started biting his own arm as Dan began shrieking and crying.

Emmy came running in from the dining room. "Nick! Nick!

Sit down." She pointed at the floor. "Time-out."

Nick sat down immediately but kept biting his arm.

"Calm hands, Nick. Calm hands."

"That guy is a stupid idiot freak!" Dan was rubbing his head. Tears mixed with snot ran into his mouth. "An idiot freak!! I'll never forgive him for this! Never!" He stomped out of the room.

"Idiotfreak hoooom yelling," said Nick, covering his eyes. "Sorry elled atyou, sorry elled. Yelling."

"Oh, baby," Emmy said, her heart twisting, and started to cry. "Oh God. I can't do this. I can't do this." She balled herself up in the corner by the pantry door and just cried.

Then there was a hollow silence all around her that felt as empty and gnawing as her insides. Her sadness about her boys, her failure to figure out how to help, being alone—all of it just flooded her and carried her away. Then she was completely wrung out. After a while, she became aware of a pair of feet next to her. Nick.

"Cryingwhooom," Nick said. "Mommysad." He was peering down into her face. He put his hands on her cheeks, his touch soft, tentative, as if his fingers were made of air. "War," he said, which was how Nick said *water*.

"That's right, Nick," Emmy said, sniffling and wiping her nose, her heart squeezing at his tender touch. "Good talking." She stood up slowly. "And you know what, though? I think Dan's sad, too." She left the kitchen to go to Dan.

Emmy finally put her book away and took out her laptop at 10:30 p.m. Still no e-mail from Will. Suddenly, a tiny blue mail bubble materialized—tpalmer@comcast.net: "Heard a friend of mine is buying a house from you. —T."

She typed back: "Who's your friend?"

She watched the clock in the upper-right-hand corner change from 10:32 p.m. to 10:34, when, suddenly, tpalmer@comcast.net was back.

"Sally Frye."

Whoa! Tom knew Sally? She typed back quickly, "I didn't know she was your friend!"

This time it was five minutes before she had her response: "I referred her to you, for her house hunt. She's a therapist, too. Child psychologist. She was supposed to tell your office about the referral. She never mentioned it?"

Emmy thought back to the first appointment. Maybe her secretary had said something about a referral, but she never paid attention to stuff like that. Not much of a salesperson, she thought. See, Eric was right!

But at that first appointment, they'd only looked at a few rooms when Emmy had gotten the call from Ben Taylor and the whole showing had been totally disrupted. So maybe Sally would have tried to tell her later on but hadn't had the chance.

She typed back: "My office may have told me, but I didn't put it together. Wow! Thanks!"

Tom wrote: "Sally is great."

Emmy wrote: "Sally's coming in this week to make an offer. I really hope it works out. What kind of therapist?"

Tom: "She's a psychotherapist, single mom (husband a total bastard, long story). It should work out. She knows what she wants."

Emmy: "That's good to know. We all have our long stories, I guess."

Tom: "Yes, we do."

The phone rang, interrupting their pleasant back-and-forth. Emmy quickly typed, "GTG," hoping Tom would understand the abbreviation for "Got to go."

It was Eric. "Hey," he said.

"Yeah. Hi, Eric."

A pause. "Well, I was thinking about before."

"Yeah," Emmy said dully, too tired emotionally to hear what he had to say. *Why now*, she thought, *when my reserves are so low?*

"Well, I know I was abrupt with you. And angry."

"Eric, it's okay. Tell me what I should do," she said. "I know this is my fault."

"Yeah."

"Yeah. I mean, I don't blame you. I know I kind of surprised you with my—my news. Hurt you. But I don't know if that's it. What are you feeling about all this?" She said this last bit gently. She did not want Eric to feel bad because of her. She'd assumed he was pretty much over her. He had just walked out on them, after all, and never once talked about it, or about coming back. This had hurt so much, she now realized: a huge abandonment. But now she was trying to get past it. That was all.

"How do I feel? How should I know? You always have to talk everything to death, don't you?" he said, albeit not unpleasantly. She could tell from the way his voice lifted that he was even smiling a little, and this completely threw her off. She'd expected anger, not resignation. Not sad smiles.

Emmy felt her cheeks get red, the way they always did when she was uncertain of herself. "Uh . . ."

"Ah, at a loss for words. Very unusual."

His joke made her relax. They were now on familiar ground again. "So what are you calling about, asshole?"

"Nice language. Okay, here's something: how about dinner?" This thought had only just occurred to him. But it felt good, because it would take her by surprise and give him some power over the situation, which he needed to feel right now.

"Dinner? With you?" Emmy was intrigued, but it also made her feel uncertain about him. The memory of the time he asked her for coffee flew treacherously into her head.

"You got someone else? Oh, never mind. I know the answer to that." Now that he'd asserted himself like this, Eric felt much better—good, in fact. He felt on top of this whole thing, as if he were some kind of smooth guy instead of the nerd he really was. Or maybe he was just relieved to be taking action.

Emmy considered this for a moment, then thought, *What the heck? Why not?* They were adults. They could work out their differences over dinner. Maybe it would help smooth things out a little. "Sure."

"Really?" He sounded like an eager boy.

"Really." Emmy couldn't help laughing at his enthusiasm. She realized, to her surprise, that she was happy—flattered that he'd asked her out. She had that little rush people get when a crush suddenly becomes real. She also realized that she hadn't felt this happy talking to Eric in a very, very long time.

Chapter 25

After the boys were shipped off to school, Emmy threw on her clothing from the day before and ran outside to inspect the yard. She'd just picked up a Jacob's ladder at Stop & Shop to plant near the wall.

Overnight it had rained, and the grass now had a bluish undertone to the rich green. She would have to mow it this weekend. Or better yet, have Nick do it, since the yard was small enough that they could get away with using a mechanical push mower rather than gas or electric, and he seemed to enjoy the back-and-forth motion of mowing.

The dogwoods were starting next door, where a border of them in alternating white and pink separated their two yards. Over at the Clarks', the magnolia was almost shaken bare from yesterday's strong winds, its white blossoms scattered like snow across their yard. Emmy went over to her part-sun garden by the stone wall, where the red tulips were going strong and the phlox spread across the wall like an overturned strawberry milkshake. She saw some fat bunches of green growth, like half heads of lettuce poking up in clusters, and peered closely to identify them: the starry, purple-edged leaves of the lupines; the chubby, fuzzy mounds of catmint; the welcome surprise of a returning finicky delphinium.

"Flowers are just ads for bees," Eric used to say, in that typical overly rational way of his. She considered this, unsmiling. How could two people be so different? And why hadn't it mattered before?

Because then it was fun, until it became polarizing—when all the difficulties with the boys started happening. Her spade hit something hard and rang out like a bell. She reached down and pulled out a rock the size of her fist. It was as if they grew there, like potatoes. You never could get rid of all the rocks here.

That's why there were so many quarries and stone walls in New England: people (frustrated would-be farmers) had to do something with all the rocks. Her father used to take his rocks and line every single garden bed with them. No walls for him: "Some*one* there is that doesn't love a wall," he would say with a wink, punning on the Frost poem. But he sure loved to line his gardens. And so his property was littered with all these miniature tacky Stonehenges.

Her father had loved his dumb little jokes—much like her husband. Sighing, she tossed the rock into a thick area of underbrush. Her cell buzzed. She looked and saw Will's number. "Argh," she said, not wanting to deal with whatever it was, good or bad, just then. She let it go to voice mail and clawed the plant out of its plastic pot, breaking the root ball. "Oh, man," she muttered, attempting to rescue the rest of it and stuffing the whole mess into the hole, which she now saw was not big enough. Part of the root ball stood above ground level. "Grrrr," she said, and dug around the plant, which was now drooping unhappily.

She crouched next to it, hoping she hadn't killed it. Seeing Will there on her phone had taken the stuffing right out of her. But she knew she had to listen to his message; she was still his realtor, after all. Unable to concentrate on planting any longer, she wiped her brown fingers on her pants and pressed the voice mail speed dial, feeling pissed off.

"Hey. Sorry I've been out of touch."

Out of touch? But they'd already closed on the house! There was no longer any reason to be *in* touch!

" . . . A big deal just went through, and I was in California. Just got back. Miss you. But I'm not asking for anything, baby. Would've been nice, though. Anyway. Bye."

A deep breath escaped from her. He was not pushing another get-together. She sank back onto the garden bed, relieved. Now her life could move forward. But toward what?

Henry shut his locker and hefted his backpack over his shoulder.

He was headed for the principal's office to report for duty.

As Henry walked up, Mr. Taylor opened his door. "Henry! Just the kid I was looking for. Mr. Daniels needs help setting up chairs in the auditorium for a PTO event tonight. Is your mother coming to it?"

"I doubt it. She's always got something going on at night these days, with my brothers or work."

"Oh." Henry ventured a glance at Mr. Taylor's face. He looked disappointed, but Henry couldn't be sure. Was this going to count against him somehow? Did PTO events matter? *Who cared about that shit?* he thought.

"Okay, I'll go find Mr. Daniels."

"Try the boys' bathroom. There's some graffiti there he's trying to remove first."

Henry knew who'd done that, but he didn't volunteer anything and was glad Taylor didn't ask. Taylor was cool that way. He understood the code. And Henry was no squealer. Besides, that kid was his connection. Which reminded him, he'd better find out if there was something in that pot or what, because he didn't want to get sick like that again. It had laid him out for an entire day, with Mom hovering like a mother bird, reminding him of that joke of Dad's: "There's a reason why the words *mother* and *smother* are just one letter apart."

Emmy and Dan crossed the cement steps that led past the school playground. The May sun was warm, without a hint of chill, and the play structure thrummed with activity.

"Mom, I want to go to the playground, okay?" Dan tugged at her arm. One thing that Emmy had forgotten about when Henry got into trouble and had to do his community service was that she would have to go get Dan every day from school, because Henry wouldn't be able to walk him home.

Emmy looked to see what it was—or who, rather—that beckoned him to come play. Her eyes passed over the shiny green metal bars of the play structure, every few rungs occupied by a child roughly Dan's size. She couldn't pick out anyone in particular whom they knew. But if Dan felt like hanging out with kids he barely knew, who was she to judge? Whatever made him happy, which she found had been kind of a hard thing this past year, with Eric gone. She let Dan lead her into the play area.

The mothers formed a tight L around the outer perimeter, between the structure and the field. They stood with arms folded or with hands in back pockets, handbags and backpacks piled at their feet. In a quick glance, Emmy couldn't see anyone she knew well enough to stand with. A packed playground and not a real friend in sight, with an hour to kill. This was probably one of the harder things she had to do as a mother. She was not good at small talk and felt lost in the sea of school politics, birthday party plans, and softball sign-up sheets.

"Dan, I don't know if I—"

"C'mon, Mom! I really wanna stay."

"Okay," she said, shuffling slowly over to the women. They were mostly in twos and threes. No sign of Beth, her only real friend at Jefferson. For all her joking around, Beth really knew how to connect with Emmy.

As Emmy approached the group, she studied each face, sizing them up to see whom she knew at all and who looked approachable. She spotted Maureen, a down-to-earth young mother of two, the older of whom had been in kindergarten with Dan four years ago. Maureen was always friendly and easy enough to talk to, so Emmy walked up to her and greeted her in a way she hoped was warmer and more relaxed than she felt. She wondered fleetingly if Maureen knew about Henry and the pot, or the cheating, and if she'd somehow have to explain that, but then she figured Maureen wouldn't have heard because her kids were too young. None of the older mothers were there, which was a relief. She couldn't bear having to discuss the changes in Henry, which she scarcely understood herself. Together, they watched the children in companionable silence, then started to talk about Ben Taylor, who was fairly new but doing really well, they agreed. Maureen had been on the search committee for the new principal, so she seemed personally pleased that Emmy liked him. She didn't know the half of it, Emmy thought, remembering how kind he'd been about the pot.

Soon Emmy did a Dan check. He wasn't on the structure. She couldn't see him. "Dan!" she called, scanning the playground and beyond. She felt a tiny ping of anxiety, but it was too soon for it to blossom into full-blown panic. Then she caught sight of a red shirt over in the big shrub and tuned her listening toward that area. Sure enough, she heard a deep voice talking very fast. She walked over to the bushes and saw Dan in there, talking to a group of smaller kids, who were listening, raptly.

Satisfied, she headed back over to Maureen, who was turned toward the field, talking to Carol, a mom Emmy didn't know that well. Emmy could see a bunch of kids down there, and they all seemed to be wearing the same green shirt. As she watched the kids running and laughing, she realized it was baseball practice. She hadn't signed Dan up in time.

Dan looked out from the shrubs, making sure he was concealed. He loved being hidden and spying on everyone. The boys who had been in there with him had gone on to do something else, and Dan was glad. *Stupid little kids*, he thought. Now that he was in third grade, he was no longer a little kid, and so he could see exactly how idiotic they were.

Dan loved the sharp smells of the bushes, and he loved the way they gave him cover. "Cover" was how they said it in the army, and when you were a spy. Also policemen. One guy would cover the other while the first guy went in with the gun. That's what he wanted to do. But he knew he couldn't convince those kids to play that with him; they were too little and just wanted to play hide-and-seek, which was a boring baby game. Cover was what he played with Mark, who wasn't here.

But he had stayed where the little kids were so that could he watch the other, bigger kids on the structure, and see if any of those mean ones came back. Last time, they'd called Nick a retard and laughed. Dan balled his hands into fists, the way his favorite cartoon character, Ben 10, did when he was mad. Ben 10 could beat guys like that because he had superpowers. He and Mark acted like they had superpowers, too, and one time it really seemed like he did, because Dan had jumped off his swing and actually flown a little bit. Mark had seen it, too, so it was true. Mark wanted invisibility for a superpower, but Dan thought that was dumb. You couldn't really beat anyone with invisibility; you could only trick them. And he wanted to beat those mean guys. Even if it was true that Nick was a retard, which it was.

He stood up, trying to get Nick out of his brain. *Bzzzap*, he thought, imagining a memory-erasing laser gun aimed at all his thoughts of Nick. He hated thinking about Nick. He wanted to be like Ben 10. Ben 10 would never have a retard brother.

Several more of the newest moms had come over because they knew Maureen, who had a little one in the preschool. Carol was a pretty blonde who looked as if she'd never had children, except somehow she'd had four, just as pretty and blonde as she was. Emmy listened to Carol and Maureen's comfortable chatter, but, as she'd predicted, she couldn't join in. Girl problems. Barbie. Early girlhood bitchiness. Emmy stepped back. She didn't know how to talk to them when the subject was girls' stuff. Been too long since she was a girl, and all she could produce, it seemed, were very complicated boys.

And where was her boy now? Emmy searched for Dan's voice again, locating him on the play structure now. He was at the top, calling down to Maureen's and Carol's daughters, his classmates—the girls who just weeks before had been mesmerized by his soccer skills. They looked at Dan but didn't respond to him because they were engrossed in their own game. Dan went right on shouting to them, and also began directing his loud, running commentary at the entire playground of kids, none of whom paid him any attention at all. He smiled, though, his brown eyes shining. That smile. It always had the same effect on Emmy—one similar to his father's smile, way back when. She got all watery inside.

Every now and then, different children would glance at Dan and try to follow the elaborate loop of what he was saying, but they couldn't. He kept right on yelling. She'd had enough, and since he hadn't found anyone specific to play with, she felt justified in ending this.

"Dan," she said, tired. "Let's go home."

"Aw, Mom."

"You're not even playing with anyone!" Emmy said.

He was quiet. "Well, I just finished hide-and-seek."

"Okay, sweetie, but I really should be getting us home."

Dan shrugged and started walking to the car. "Okay, but don't talk to me because now I'm a robot."

Affirmative, she thought, grinning as she watched him lumber along with stiffened arms and legs.

Chapter 26

It was late in the afternoon, and Nick's classroom shone with soft, 3:00 p.m. light. Special window shades further muted the sun's brightness, so that Nick and his classmates wouldn't be distracted or bothered by sharp light. Similarly, there were white drapes covering many of the bookshelves, to minimize distraction while the students worked on other things.

Each student worked at a desk with his or her own teacher. One boy, closest to Nick, periodically screeched, and the teacher would redirect him by gently pushing his head in the direction of his work, small multicolored cubes that fit into one another in stacks. Invariably, Jack would scream, and Laura, the teacher, would press her lips together and remind him about work.

Nick couldn't think when he was next to Jack. He giggled every time he heard Jack's screech. It was not because he liked the sound; it was because he liked the heated energy that the teacher exuded in trying to control Jack. Nick could smell her because of the heated air around her, and the smell was good, like lemons and sugar.

Art was next on the schedule. Nick was breathing easily because art did not have words in it, or numbers. Or people. Margaret, Nick's teacher, put the brush into Nick's hands and gave him a color choice. He liked that: "Do you want red or orange?" And not, "What is your favorite color?" He did not know how to answer that. *What* was a bad word. Not as bad as *why*, or *how*, but bad. He knew that there was a right answer to every question but that most of the time he did not know it. He hated words and the way they lumped together in his head, or hid behind other noise.

The brush in the orange paint was smooth and beautiful. The paint was wet and glided slickly all over the paper, turning white into orange. Nick dipped and stroked over and over, watching the tiny drips of orange dry and harden on the paper, watching the orange grow bigger. Good prickles crept up his neck, like when he was holding a ribbon. Or playing with water. He wanted to do more with it, so much more, but soon the timer went off and he had to go to the next thing on his schedule. The hard knot in his stomach came back, and he felt his hands squeezing. Nick saw an arm nearby, smooth and soft and close, and pinched it hard. Then there was a little yelling, which made him want to cry, but then he had to sit by himself for a while, which was very good. While he sat there, he thought about orange. When Margaret came back, she talked about the painting. She had ugly Band-Aids on her smooth arm, and her eyes looked at him too hard.

"I know you liked the painting, Nick, but we have to do other work now. If you do a good job, we can do more painting, okay?" As she spoke, the hardness left her eyes and he could breathe again. He had heard what she had said, about the orange paint, and he was able to say the right thing back: "Okay, yes." He rocked a little and squeezed the air, and waited for Margaret to give him his work.

Emmy had finished dressing and was getting ready to go to work when the phone rang, startling her. She waited for the caller ID to come up. "Ford School," Nick's teacher. She picked up. "Hello?"

"Hi, Emmy? It's Margaret from Nick's classroom."

"Oh, hi!" Her anxiety level jumped. A call this time of day from the school was never good, no matter which of her sons it was about.

"Hi. Nothing's wrong. Just wanted to let you know there was an incident today."

An "incident": Nick hurt someone. This was the school's banal way of discussing difficulties that arose with the students, thus maintaining a professional, neutral distance from these episodes. The school was big into unbiased observation, analysis, and scrupulous note-taking. Sometimes the science-heavy attitude of the place really irritated Emmy, but she did think the staff's crisp, clear, no-nonsense style worked well for Nick. "Oh?"

"Yeah, it happened just as he was finishing one thing and was asked to transition to another part of his schedule. He aggressed with a teacher."

"Who was it? Did he hurt anyone?"

Margaret hesitated. "Just a staff person. No, it's fine."

Emmy suspected that it was Margaret herself who'd been hurt. She always wished they would tell her this, and make Nick apologize, make him have normal consequences rather than neutral ones—instead of treating him like a set of behaviors to be normalized or discouraged. Emmy also wanted to know which activities he'd been doing at the time; was there a reason behind his aggression, other than what the school saw as autistic stubbornness? Maybe he had merely liked what he'd been doing. Whatever it had been. And if there was something Nick liked that much, she wanted to know what it was! "Can you tell me what he was doing just before he aggressed?" *Aggressed*—she also hated the jargon the school used, the pseudo-science of it, making all of them seem that much more distant from the students.

"Painting."

"Oh? Did he like it? Maybe he did it because he didn't want to stop?"

"Um, I guess so. Let me say, though, that before the outburst, he performed his painting task admirably. Covered an entire sheet of paper with orange." Margaret's voice swelled with pride. Emmy teared up. This was the reason she kept Nick at Ford. The teachers, just about every one of them, loved their kids. Everything about them.

"So he likes orange?" Emmy had not known this and felt a little light-headed with the news.

"Yeah. He even chose it. He was offered a choice of orange or red. He picked orange right away, like he meant it. He's actually never done that before. I guess maybe we've always just picked random colors for him, because it didn't seem to matter. Anyway, the word *orange* rolled right off his tongue."

That was a first! The right word, coming right out? And letting them know something he liked? She wondered, was this from Tom's work? She felt a familiar, very old, surge of hope, a sweet but sad melody rising from a worn groove in her heart.

"Okay. Well, that is all really good to know!" Emmy said happily. "Anyway, I hope the rest of the day goes better."

"I'm sure it will," Margaret said warmly.

As Emmy hung up, she told herself to remember to buy some orange paint this afternoon.

She zipped up her boots and decided she would call Eric a little later and tell him about it. Right now she had to get to a showing—the Pearls again.

The condo they'd be seeing was in The Farm, a historic section of town that was extremely desirable and difficult for most middle-class people to afford. But, she figured, maybe the Pearls had some undisclosed source of income, so who was she to judge?

As soon as they pulled up, Emmy knew she had a sale. The look on Mrs. Pearl's face gave it away. The neighborhood had all the signs of pedigree that Mrs. Pearl craved: tasteful black or silver Mercedes, Audis, and Volvos were parked outside on granite-block driveways. The gardens in front were small but well tended, with neat gravel or winding brick paths. Black wrought iron or stone balustrades edged properties and terraces. It was a 1.5-million-dollar barely two-bedroom, but every square foot was polished and perfect. Mrs. Pearl tried to restrain her Cheshire cat grin—she was already trying hard to fit in here—but every few feet, she let out an "ooh" or "aah." Emmy didn't like her, but she couldn't blame her, either. This was a pristine, beautiful showplace.

The Pearls walked through it and within fifteen minutes told Emmy they wanted to make an offer, before anyone else did. Emmy smiled. "Sure, let's go back to the office." *Ha, Eric, see?* she thought. *I may not be a real estate wiz, but I do know people.*

Nick settled himself into the middle of the white couch. He was alone in the living room, because Dan was upstairs in his room; Dan rarely went into the living room when Nick was there. So Nick usually claimed the room for himself, especially in the late afternoon, because it was quiet and the light in there was often soft and gray. Nick preferred this subdued, opalescent light; most other lights caused what felt like a flickering in his eyes, and a sickening throbbing in his head.

Nick listened carefully, moving his hands very lightly through the air. Mommy was nearby, so he crouched over, covering his face with his hands so that he would not have to look at her. Most people's eyes scared him. They glowed outward from faces and pressed into him like hot fingers, making all the words in his head whirl around, clump together, or disappear.

Mommy moved into the playroom. He heard rustling in there, but no talking. He felt the breath come out of his throat again, open again. He opened and closed his hand, and felt the air stir around his fingers.

He thought over and over about the orange paint at school. The orange had filled up his head and twinkled in front of his eyes, like music. He had wanted to sing while he painted, but he knew that he couldn't do that in school. Someone was always saying "Quiet" to him, except when they wanted him to talk. He did not understand those rules, either.

But the painting had no rules. There was just the liquid softness on the soft page. The perfect furry black brush, soaked exactly right with wet, glowing orange. He almost cried remembering the orange, like the way he almost cried when Mommy made fudge. The taste filled him up, blocked out all noise. This was what orange did.

"NickIhavesomepaintforyou!" Mommy came crashing into the living room spouting loud words. Nick pressed down on his eyes, hard.

"Oh. Sorry. Nick," Mommy said quietly and slowly, "I have some paint for you. Like at school."

Nick popped up his head. "Yes." He stood from the couch.

Emmy pulled out a rustly white bag and dug around. She produced five brushes of differing thickness, and five fat jars of bright paint, all in various shades of orange. Nick looked at them and felt the color glide over his eyes, like sunshine. He shut them, because they were now full. He smiled and turned away, tucking his chin into his shoulder.

The hairs on Emmy's neck stood up, seeing this gesture from so long ago. "Oh, Baby Delight," Emmy whispered. It had been a long time since she'd seen "Baby Delight." This was the very first nickname that she and Eric had given Nick, because of the way he would turn away from them as a baby when he was especially happy. It was how he'd showed his delight, which was too much for him to handle, along with their full eyes. It was also, most likely, the first sign of his autism. She knew that now; she had not, then, but she had felt it. "Too much joy" was how she explained it, understanding in a silent maternal way that her little son experienced the world in some very intense ways, so different from how she did, and sometimes he simply had to shut it out.

Too much joy. It had really worried Emmy once she realized what it all meant. Not anymore. Now she understood Nick and took the tiny, radiant gifts he occasionally gave her, like this show of delight, and she just ran with them. She handed him the bag and watched him race upstairs to his room, a tearful joy on her face, knowing that for the first time ever, she'd actually given him something that he wanted, that he loved.

Emmy let the hostess lead her to the corner black leather banquette in The Park, a trendy restaurant in Boston's South End. Eric was already there, with a half-finished beer.

"Oh, been here long?" she asked.

"Hi to you, too," he said, standing while she sat. He was wearing a dark blue jacket, red silk tie, and khakis. She'd bought him that tie for a Christmas party three years ago. *Overgrown prep schoolboy*, she thought, always susceptible to that look in a man.

"Want something to drink?"

"Yeah, definitely some kind of dry white wine," she said, reluctantly remembering Will's assessment of her and her Pinot Grigio.

"Okay," Eric said, and she smiled, because he probably wouldn't even know a Pinot Grigio from a Merlot, nor would he care. He raised his hand to signal the waiter, a slim, bald black man with hoop earrings. He looked over at Emmy, and she told him what she wanted; Eric reiterated it as if she'd spoken in a foreign language. She was irritated and yet touched by this. After the waiter left, Eric looked at her with his Rhett Butler smile.

"Something wrong?"

"No. Yes, actually," she said, her voice a little hard to cover the emotion she was feeling. "You don't have to order for me, you know. Since when do you do that? I'm perfectly capable of dealing with a waiter."

"'I'm perfectly capable of dealing with a waiter,'" Eric mimicked. "Who said you weren't? Relax," he said, a little gruffly, and studied the menu, leaning back and stretching out his long legs until they bumped hers. He did not say, "Excuse me."

"I'll relax when I feel relaxed," she said pointedly, crossing her legs and knocking into his again.

Eric tried to improve the mood by inquiring about the boys. "So, did you ask Margaret to sit?"

Emmy was surprised he remembered the name of Nick's teacher. Even she sometimes had trouble keeping track because there were always so many adults who came in and out of Nick's classroom, mostly cheerful young women named Jen or Megan. "Yes. Margaret is a real gem," she said. It was true: Margaret had figured Nick out quicker than most of his teachers, and so when he had transitioned into her classroom six months ago, there had been very few episodes of aggression. In previous years, the school had had to resort to using the time-out room to give Nick a moment away from whatever had caused his outburst, and to keep others from being injured or using protective holds on him.

"I'm glad," Eric said, sounding serious. "I like Margaret."

This pleased her even more. She wanted to tell him about the paint, but just then the waiter grabbed her glass and refilled it.

As she sipped her wine, she looked at Eric over the rim. She felt wary; these new, warm emotions toward Eric scared her. They made it harder for her to maintain her hard-won defenses. If she didn't have her straightforward anger to hold her up anymore, where, exactly, could she stand? She almost wished she could go back to seeing Eric as this dorky guy, kind of rumpled, sloppy, and a little snarky. Someone she didn't want in her house, in her bed. But now that was impossible. She felt that something had changed inside her, or between them, ever since she'd told him about Will. Or maybe something had been changing for her for some time now—a softening, a longing for an indefinable More. Whatever it was, a window into her own life had opened, through which she could see not only others' flawed actions, but her own, too. She could see how she'd been closed to Eric, using self-righteous anger to keep him at bay—excluding him without even giving him a chance. And wrapped so tightly in her moral superiority, she'd been blind to Henry's downward spiral.

But she didn't mention any of this, because it was too new. She needed to allow these feelings to shape themselves into concepts before she brought them out into the open—especially with Eric.

Eric kept his eyes on her for the entire meal, until she began to feel very uncomfortable. Finally she asked, "What?"

"What?" he mimicked.

Emmy rolled her eyes.

"If you keep doing that, your eyes will stay like that," said Eric, in perfect imitation of Dan's nasal voice.

Emmy smirked. "Pretty good."

"Dessert?" The waiter asked, appearing out of nowhere.

"No thanks," they said simultaneously. Well, at least they both felt the same about wanting to get out of here, Emmy thought while Eric paid. Then he helped her on with her shawl. "Thanks. This was nice," she muttered, hoping she sounded a little sincere.

"Yeah, wasn't it? Kind of gives you a warm fizzy feeling inside."

"Don't you mean, 'warm fuzzy feeling'?"

"Do I?" He laughed a little.

They'd reached her car. "You okay?" he asked.

These two words, more than anything—the dinner, Eric being charming—made Emmy smile.

Then he kissed her on the cheek, out of the blue, but also the most natural thing in the world. "Well, well," Emmy murmured in a low voice, hoping to hide her immense pleasure. This sudden tiny act of tenderness left her almost breathless, nakedly vulnerable.

Eric laughed softly, because he'd surprised both of them. But it did feel good, and he just wanted to go with that. He kissed her again.

They heard footsteps and loud, laughing voices approaching. Suddenly a little embarrassed by their nascent friendliness, and fearful of its fragility, Emmy gathered her shawl around her and started an agitated hunt for her keys. She could hear the jingling but couldn't find them.

Out of nowhere, she remembered Will's hot eyes moving languidly over her in the hazy golden light of the Oak Room. The delight in his attention flashed through her like a lurid movie trailer. Emmy stopped ferreting around in her bag and looked at Eric, her eyes bracketed by lines of guilt.

Eric could feel Emmy receding from him, with her cloudy eyes and nervous hands. He had a feeling she was thinking about that jerk, Will. Did she still want him? But the way she'd blushed when he'd kissed her cheek just now: that had been beautiful. Those softened eyes of hers had told him all he'd needed to know; they'd made him want to forgive her for everything, and ask her to forgive him for everything, too. But now she sat there chewing the inside of her cheek, a total stranger, just like that. Lights on, nobody home. Nothing had changed. He sat still for a few moments, then turned on the ignition. "Okay, well, see ya," he said, and left without waiting for her to say goodbye.

Chapter 27

The next morning, Eric got to the house early to take the boys for the weekend. Even though last night had ended on a slightly sour note, he didn't want to give up so easily. He felt sure he could recoup the good feelings by being cheerful and positive. So he knocked and walked right in when Henry called out, "S'open, Dad."

Emmy smiled at him as she came into the foyer. "Hi there. Want some coffee?"

Eric grinned. "I always like your coffee, Emmy."

Knowing he was referring to how they met, she blushed, but felt annoyed by his constant need to joke. Yet she was pleased as well, seeing that he was okay from the weird way last night had ended.

Eric was already following her into the kitchen. He closed the door behind them.

"So, what is it? Want another date?"

Emmy took a deep breath to steady herself, and decided that the best defense was a good offense. "You know, Eric, I just want things to be okay between us." She turned her back and busied herself with scooping coffee. "I really am so sorry I hurt you." She was actually referring not to Will but to that day she kicked Eric out.

Eric knew what she meant. With Em, there was always something deeper going on; it was always the bigger thing that she was referring to, not the obvious thing. "So—why, Em?" He looked at her back and suddenly sensed all those unwanted feelings coming to life again. He wanted her for himself. Goddamn it, he did. And how could he ever get into Em's life again, other than as the Fuck-Up Weekend Dad?

As she began to cry, he just wanted to pull her to him. He was suddenly filled with an aching love like when he had first met her.

How could they be living apart the way they were? Eric looked at her, realizing she was not going to answer him. Finally, he said, "Because of . . . what I did to Nick?" he stammered, and looked down.

"That and—well, the problems with Nick before that, and also because you just left," she said, quietly, even though her blood was pounding because she was saying it, at last. Finally. They were actually going to talk about that day.

She didn't trust herself to meet his eyes. Her words came out in a rush. "You did. You hurt him—and then you left. Us. Me." As she said it, she felt again how much this had hurt her, how much it still hurt her. The words tore out of her and then just hung like smog in the air between them. Neither knew what to say or do. They stared at each other, thinking about what they were saying. They'd never talked about any of this before, for an entire year. It felt freeing, and terrifying.

Eric reached for her hand and grabbed it hard. "Emmy, I'm sorry. I mean it. I'm sorry I hurt him." Her eyes were wide and pleading. "Oh God, I'm so sorry. If I could ever take back a moment in my life—I just didn't know how to make him stop." He was sobbing.

Eric turned away from her, but they didn't let go of each other's hand. "Oh, Eric," she whispered. She leaned her head on his back. He didn't shove her away, as mixed-up as he was. It felt warm where her head touched his shirt. "Eric, I don't know. I don't know what to say, what any of this means."

His head was a stew: he couldn't think clearly or say anything. He just knew he didn't want her to say anything else. Maybe she was forgiving him. But maybe she was also letting him go.

There was silence for a few minutes. Then Eric turned and pulled her close. It felt so good to her—familiar, like falling into bed. It was as if their bodies had a memory all their own.

But. It was not enough. It was not enough because she still didn't know if Eric was up to the task of parenting Nick the way she needed him to. Emmy felt so much confusion mixed in with the comfort, or because of it, that she had to step back, get a little space, and look at him.

Then she realized that for the last year, Eric had been doing just that. Parenting Nick. He'd taken care of him without any incidents, by himself, every weekend. And he'd successfully balanced Henry and Dan as well.

A flood of incongruous memories washed over Emmy. Their first time, in his studio apartment in Cambridge. Milk crates for furniture. His endless, unquenchable, almost embarrassing fascination with her body, while they made love on a mattress on the floor, covered with Indian print blankets bought at the university bookstore. Even when she was hugely pregnant, Eric had been so excited by her, physically and emotionally. Then her mind flashed to him hefting Dan with one hand, as if he were a free weight, Henry screaming with delight. Then, Eric holding her in his arms while she breast-fed Dan (successfully, at last), and how he'd tasted the milk and said it was like the milk at the bottom of the cereal bowl.

Emmy had a strange look on her face that Eric couldn't pinpoint. Fear plucked at his heart; he suddenly felt as if he'd just lost something he had meant to keep. Whatever would happen next felt very important in terms of their future, but he had no idea what that should be. He didn't want to make any mistakes, so he did nothing.

"Bye, you," he said in a hoarse voice. Then he quietly walked out.

Emmy sat down shakily and shook her head. She sipped her coffee, which was now lukewarm and cloying, from too much Splenda. The feeling of having made the wrong decision throbbed in her head like a migraine. She dumped the coffee in the sink, along with Eric's cup, and turned on the faucet hard, shattering the brown drops with the spray.

Emmy spent the next morning at the only place that could soothe her tumultuous thoughts: Mahoney's Nursery. She got a cart and wandered aimlessly through the perennials, her goal to add colors other than the predominant purple or white. Color brought her back to life, the same way she now knew it did for Nick. For Emmy, color had always been something that had a shape, a taste, a sound. And the way Nick responded to orange made her think he was that way, too. Emmy knew there was a clinical name for this: *synesthesia*. But that was neither here nor there to her; the important thing, she knew, was that color was a real entity to Nick and to her. And the word for that was *miracle*.

Suddenly, she knew what color she was looking for: orange. For Nick.

This discovery of orange took her breath away every time she thought about it. Her son now had a hobby, a passion that other people could relate to. She could do orange things with him. Surround him with orange.

She'd forgotten to tell Eric! He'd left too quickly, and in too much of an emotional thunderstorm. *"Bye, you,"* he'd said. The words sounded so intimate. As if they were in on something together. *Bye, you* was what you said to a lover: *Bye, you*. It made Emmy think of the word *bayou* and the song "Blue Bayou." Lifting some tiger lilies into her cart, she sang it softly to herself. She headed over to the roses and found two different orange varieties. Then she pushed her cart over to the annuals, which were full of orange choices, like zinnias, nasturtium, and lantana.

Back home, Emmy piled the shovel, the trowel, the manure, the mulch, and the plants on her wheelbarrow, and pushed it all to the backyard. The wheelbarrow was too full, as always, because she hated making more than one trip with it. It wobbled on its delicate, rusty legs, careening over onto the grass. She bent to lift the thorny rose back in, and scooped up whatever mulch had slipped out. After wiping her forehead with the hem of her T-shirt, she pushed the load successfully to her garden areas.

Emmy dug several good holes for her orange acquisitions and threw in handfuls of the manure mix. She imagined—as she often did while gardening—what it would be like to set up Gardens of Eden, her little garden design business. Drafting tools, digging tools. She'd have to establish contacts at like-minded nurseries, to get the stuff wholesale. She had no idea how to do that. Also, there'd be the cost of advertising. Spreading the word to her friends and to their friends. The fielding of phone calls; determining what to charge and how to subcontract, and to whom. She'd kept an eye on the different trucks that came to her neighborhood, the reliable old lawn services that lasted over the years but were probably completely booked, or the newer trendy ones that were probably hungrier for business but perhaps charged more, being more upscale in look.

She hadn't spoken to Eric much about this particular dream in a while because by the time it had taken real shape, he already seemed lost to her. The one time she had talked about it, his eyes had glazed over pretty quickly and his tone shifted from impatient to annoyed in seconds. She stopped and furrowed her brow. Would that kind of thing between them ever stop hurting?

She hauled the hose over to the holes, thinking of how Nick loved water. Maybe now he'd like to water for her; maybe she could teach him even more than that. She wondered again why she'd never gotten any of her boys into gardening. All those books of hers contained pictures of Laura Ashley pinafore-clad earth mothers with their matching, charmingly messy, happy towheaded children gardening together, with equally alluring chapter headings: "Seeds for Children," "Edible Gardens," "Easy-to-Grow Perennials." But her kids treated gardening like a chore. Well, she had, too, when she was younger, because Dad had been so driven to perfection that nothing was ever good enough, so it wasn't until she was an adult with her own house and a husband who felt as she did that she realized she could garden her own intuitive, less-than-perfect way. Nothing in her garden was orderly, exactly, but all of it fit well together. It was beautiful naturally, and utterly comforting. Exactly the way she wanted to live.

Which brought her back to Eric. How had things gotten to this point, where it was all such an ugly jumble? No matter how much she tried to answer and resolve, new messes appeared.

She tried to wipe the sweat from her forehead and upper lip

without letting her dirty hands make her face muddy. Her cell
phone rang. It was Will. She let it go to voice mail, then deleted
the message without listening to it. Whatever it was, she had no
interest in it. Despite her annoyance, she didn't let the intrusion
dampen her spirits, because she was also happy to realize that she
had enough going on, right here—Nick and orange, things opening up with Eric, her garden dreams—and that she wanted to
keep it that way. Watch it all grow.

Chapter 28

Monday afternoon, when Emmy opened the waiting room door, Tom was standing behind the desk, sorting mail. He looked up at her. "Hey," he said.

"Hi. Go ahead, Nick, hang up your sweatshirt. I got some new Play-Doh. Lots of bright colors. Go take a look!"

"Yes," said Nick, staying where he was.

"Seems happy," Tom remarked to Emmy.

"Yeah, sure. I think he likes coming here," Emmy said, taking a seat. She glanced at the magazines, but they were all the same as last time. She really should have brought a book.

"You okay?"

Her experience with Eric had left her feeling very mixed-up and shaky. "I'm fine," she said, struggling to smile.

"I don't think so," Tom persisted. Nick was pacing in a circle around the waiting room. "Nick, go in and play with the Play-Doh for five minutes while I talk to your mom."

"Play-Doh, yes." Nick ran into the therapy room.

"I hope he doesn't eat it," said Emmy. Nick had always loved the salty flavor of Play-Doh.

"It's nontoxic, anyway. What kid doesn't eat Play-Doh?" He came over and sat right next to her again. Just smelling his piney soap smell made Emmy want to bury her head in his big, bearlike shoulder. "You seem so forlorn. What is it?"

"Tom, it's hardly the time for a heart-to-heart."

He gave a self-conscious cough, slapped his knees, and stood up. "I think it's the perfect time."

"It's just—"

"Stuff at home?"

"Yeah. My husband." She rolled her eyes but then started to blush.

"I thought so. You guys divorced? I've never met him."

"Yeah, well, no. We're separated. He doesn't do *therapy*." She used air quotes. "He doesn't—" She was going to say, "He doesn't do much with Nick at all," but she stopped, feeling like a heel. It wasn't really true, was it? Even though it sure was an easy explanation for things. Blame indifferent Eric. The phone-it-in-dad. But that was all changing, wasn't it? He did plenty with Nick; maybe not the way she did, but every single weekend, he made a family for his sons. She smiled sadly at Tom. "Really. I'm okay. Just a weird week."

"Okay. I'll let it go for now. But if you ever want to talk . . ." One hand extended toward her, he walked away, into the therapy room. As the door swung shut, she heard him exclaim: "Nick! Whoa! That's a lot of orange Play-Doh you got there! And it's all over the table! Whoa, whoa, stop!" She couldn't help laughing.

Tom took down the *Beginning Drawing* book, which he'd brought to the office on a whim, as something to help fill the vast book-case that took up one wall. He had found all but the very first lessons to be elusive; his skill was definitely in the oral and verbal rather than the tactile or artistic realms.

But something about the way that Nick had opened every can of orange Play-Doh—and only orange—and pressed his finger-nails into the flattened mushy discs, the same pattern every time, gave Tom an idea.

"Nick. No LEGOs today. Today, art."

Nick did not respond, but kept indenting the Play-Doh with his thumb and then index fingernails.

Tom leaned over and put his hand on Nick's, to stop him so that he would attend to him. "Nick."

Nick looked up and then away. "Yes. Art. Okay, yes. Hooooom, heeeem, art."

"Good. I think you like art."

"You like art."

Aha, thought Tom. He knew Nick well enough by now to know that an immediate response, though echolalic, indicated some passion. "So we can work with the Play-Doh for a while and then maybe take a look at this drawing book and get out the paints."

Nick snapped his head up from the Play-Doh. "Paints, yes. Yes."

"You like paint?"

"You like paint."

"Then let's paint."

Tom brought out large sheets of white paper, brushes, and paints. He opened the *Beginning Drawing* book, and pointed out the steps of forming basic bodies with the most basic shapes. Pointing to a shape, he would ask Nick to tell him what shape it was and then have Nick first draw it with a pencil. Then he got to draw it with the brush in the color of his choice. Nick had no problem doing everything Tom requested, and had a remarkably steady grasp of the pencil and the brush, far better than his shaky handwriting would suggest.

By the end of the session, Nick had drawn and painted a house, a snowman, a cat, and a clown, using basic shapes and naming them all clearly. His lines were crisp and true, and he chose fiery colors—always in the same pattern: orange, red, yellow, orange, orange; orange, red, yellow, orange, orange. Tom was impressed that Nick was interested in patterns and could create them with paint.

"Let's hang them here to dry, Nick. It's just about time to go home."

Nick jumped up from his chair. "Yes. Go home."

Outside in the waiting room, Tom walked over to Emmy, beaming. "A fantastic session today," he said. "Does he paint much at home?"

"Actually, only just now, because we tried it when he was little, you know, when they're like three or four and you get them finger paints—"

"A lot of neurologically atypical kids are squeamish about messy, wet stuff like finger paints. Actually, a lot of kids are, period."

Emmy nodded. "That's what I discovered. I tried brushes with him, too, but he just looked right through them. After a while, I gave up, you know?"

"A hazard of the disability. Sometimes these kids aren't into things developmentally until years past the typical time. You know, the guy who didn't talk until he was thirty. The teenager who suddenly liked being around other kids."

"Yeah. And Einstein not talking until he was four. I never believed those stories—or thought they had any relevance to Nick. But I found out the other day kind of by accident that at school he'd been thrilled with painting, particularly using orange paint. So I bought him some, right away, and he's been painting in his room every day after school."

"Really? Independently?"

Emmy nodded, smiling as she thought about it. "It's the first thing he's ever liked that I can understand. You know, there's not much I can do with wiggling string or squeezing air with my hand. But I can paint."

"I know what you mean. This is fantastic. We can really do a lot with this."

Emmy smiled, feeling hope fluttering again, a paintbrush gliding over her heart.

Chapter 29

Eric couldn't concentrate on his work. Drawing shapes was always his first love, but sometimes that just didn't cut it. There had been only one thing that had ever displaced his obsession with computers, and that's what was commanding his attention now: Emmy. Now, always, Emmy. *Goddamn her*, he thought angrily. From the moment he first saw her, with her wild hair and green eyes, at a party during grad school, a modern-day Scarlett O'Hara, surrounded by, like, six other guys, he knew he wanted her, and only her. He'd hardly ever dated before Emmy. But once they became friends, it had been only a matter of time.

They were inseparable—total opposites who had somehow found each other appealing. Emmy had been getting her master's in botany, but she was a total humanities type; she'd majored in English, after all. The master's was to learn more about plants, which she loved, she had said. But of course, in the final analysis, she hadn't done anything with it; she'd ended up becoming a second-rate realtor. It occurred to him just now that he'd never figured out why. Because she had no business sense? Or because he'd always *told* her she had no business sense?

Eric stood up, walked to the bookcase, and pulled down the photo album. A piece of paper fell out; looked like a receipt. He turned it over: "Barmakian Brothers." The jeweler where he'd bought Emmy's engagement ring. He smoothed it carefully and slipped it back inside the album.

He leafed through the rest of it: the funny grad school shots, so oddly poignant with their out-of-style hair and clothes. Even a geek like him could tell that these pics were about twenty years old.

There was Emmy in her wedding dress, and him in that monkey suit, looking really thin and scared, with way too much hair. And happy. He remembered feeling as if he'd won the jackpot.

He kept thinking that people weren't supposed to be this lucky. Why had she picked him? Why were they together? Why did she love him?

He kept asking himself until he got too busy. First with work, and then with the boys.

Then, autism. Everything was autism. Emmy nearly lost her mind over Nick back then. His thoughts flashed to the day in that doctor's office. That stupid, clueless man. "He'll probably never marry, never go to college. He may be mentally retarded." Emmy—that firebrand—had looked him in the eye and said, "No. Autism, maybe. Delayed, maybe. All the other stuff—you go to hell." She'd picked up Nick and her pocketbook, then walked out, slamming the door. It wasn't until they were in the car that she'd lost it. She had cried all the way home, and for days after, it seemed. She'd been a zombie. Just barely functioning, taking Nick to the playground and letting him sit in the sandbox, eating sand while she simply stared. Her playgroup dumped her. They stopped telling her where they were meeting, and she'd run into them by accident. Her parents didn't seem to get it, either, acting as if the doctor were totally wrong.

All Eric had felt back then was numb, or angry. He solved it by going to work. But Emmy could think of nothing else, talk about nothing else, except what was wrong with Nick. What should they do? Then, where should he go to school? Were they doing enough? And once in a while, she'd pay attention to Henry.

Well, that wasn't fair. She paid a lot of attention to Henry, because he was normal, and a knockout baby. He made her laugh again, after so much crying.

Their whole life, though, had really become autism. Their vacations became few and far between, and extremely difficult. Then Dan came along, and Emmy couldn't get enough of him. But because of Nick's autism, as well as Dan's fiery stubbornness, they were both terribly worried that he'd be autistic, too. When it turned out he wasn't, Emmy was so relieved, but Eric was wondering what they would do with such a difficult kid, regardless of his label. She kind of spoiled him, and Eric had to admit that he did, too. Dan was easy to spoil because he was charming, witty, tough, and yet somehow vulnerable.

With her three little boys, Emmy became the total earth mother that she'd always threatened to be, completely absorbed in her children and her garden. Nothing else mattered. Certainly not Eric. He was like part of the furniture. The main breadwinner. At first, he would pick fights with her to get her to notice him. Or be really nice, really thoughtful. Nothing worked. Nothing. She was too far gone into the kids. Suffering over Nick, taking painstaking notice of his every triumph, no matter how small (and they usually were pretty small; how excited could a person get over a fifteen-year-old who could finally read on first-grade level?). Exulting over Henry's Golden Boy aura, and Dan's intense passion. The three boys filled her up completely.

Eric felt horrible thinking this. But it was the truth. And even though he felt the same, he loved them, too, it was as if there were no room left for him in their family. So when Emmy asked him to leave at last, he was only too willing. The fight with Nick had been merely the catalyst, he saw that now. He had been leaving for a long time.

Except he hadn't known how hard the reality of leaving would be, of being apart from all of them like this, including Emmy. Even with the challenges and difficulties the boys brought, he wanted to be with them so much more than this living situation allowed.

Not really sure what he'd hoped to accomplish by stirring up painful memories, he put the photo album away and sat down at his computer, determined to make some drawings that would bring him back to life again.

The phone rang before he could start. It was Emmy. Creepy, because of how he'd just been thinking about her. But actually, he often thought about her. "Hey," he said. He never bothered pretending he didn't have caller ID. What was the point? Pretending was hard, and technology was supposed to make your life easier.

"Eric. I wanted to tell you something good for a change. I've been meaning to tell you for a while!"

Eric smiled just hearing her happy voice. "Okay," he said. "I wasn't really working, anyway."

Emmy laughed as if he were joking, because in her experience, Eric was always working. Whether it was on his open laptop or with a small index card shoved into his pocket on which he scribbled passing ideas. "It's Nick," she said. "He's doing really well!"

At that, Eric felt light and airy inside. "Oh?" he asked carefully, aware that he was holding his breath. Good news about Nick was so often a house of cards: it didn't take much to topple it.

"Well, I mean, it's just really nice. Sweet. He's started painting."

Eric exhaled, rusty, familiar disappointment cutting through him. "Painting?" *This* was the big news flash?

"Don't sound like that! It's really good. He's very into it. And he's good at it, too."

"Good at it? As in, he might have a savant skill as an artist and will possibly be able to earn his living, or as in, he painted a few circles with a fat brush dipped in tempera?" He instantly regretted it.

"Jesus, you piece of shit," Emmy whispered.

He could tell by the way her voice caught that she was crying. "Emmy, wait! I'm—"

But Emmy slammed the phone down.

"Sorry," he said to the silent receiver. He hung it up and thought, *Paint.* Fucking paint. Paint. Sighing, he pictured Nick, concentrating with a fat paintbrush, stirring sauce-like paint, wetting page after page with it. His sharp, out-of-control emotions slowed down, coming closer to him, softer now. He sighed again. Well, it apparently made Nick happy. That was something. And it made Emmy happy.

He liked it when she was happy. Why wouldn't he? He'd fallen in love with that girl who was the belle of the ball back in grad school. Vivacious, flirtatious, *happy* Emmy.

Eric felt bad about what he'd blurted out. He hadn't meant it. But once again, his sarcasm, his bitterness, had knocked the stuffing out of her.

Well, Goddamn it, that could stop right now. He was no saint, but he could work at being a father to his oldest son. Maybe to all of them. That would make Emmy happy. And *that* would make him happy. He had to admit he still cared how she felt. It was just that he didn't know how to live with her anymore, but maybe if he changed just one thing here, he'd be a little closer to that.

Eric's decision sparked some new energy. Suddenly, he found himself no longer spinning his wheels in anger but eager to take action. He would buy some paint for Nick. Next time they came, they would all paint. And he was going to meet with Tom, Mr. Annie Sullivan, and figure out what to say to his kid.

Emmy sat fuming, trying to shake off her anger and disappointment. What was that saying? You could take the boy out of the shit, but you couldn't take the shit out of the boy? Something like that. Why was Eric so quick to jab? Especially when it came to Nick? Just when she'd needed to share this amazing thing, he'd kicked her right in the ass.

She dragged herself downstairs and poured a glass of cold white wine that she had recorked a while back. It was hard to finish bottles now that she lived alone. The wine was old and almost vinegar, but she didn't care. It hadn't been that good when fresh: $4.99 Trader Joe's bargain brand. Oh well, she needed the buzz, not the taste.

The next morning, probably because of the wine—which these days always either upset her stomach or gave her a headache— Emmy was running late. She snapped at the kids several times trying to get them going. "You mean you haven't showered yet?" she yelled at Henry, who seemed to be daydreaming in his bed.

Daydreaming! At 7:30 a.m. on Tuesday! She stormed downstairs, where Dan was supposed to be getting the cereal out. He was sitting in front of a full bowl of Cocoa Krispies, reading the back of the box. "Mom, can you find all the hidden 'Cocoas' in this picture? I got ten."

"Dan, where's your milk? Why aren't you eating? You can't just play in the morning!"

"Can you get it?" Dan asked, as if she hadn't said anything.

"Honey, why do I have to get it every day? What's with that?"

Dan sighed and looked at her, pouting. "Okay, I'll do it." He started to slide off the chair. Red spots burned in his cheeks at his mother's words. He felt his mood flip over, right to anger. *Meanie. I haven't even done anything,* he thought.

"Oh, never mind, I'll get it!" Emmy said, exasperated. She bent to the low refrigerator shelf and pulled out the gallon, already halfway done. She slammed the milk onto the table. Then she looked for the telltale signs of Nick: crumbs, scattered bits of cereal, a ghostly wax-paper cereal box lining floating lightly on table, the empty brown box sticking out of the trash. Nothing. "Nick!"

A muffled "Yes, okay, yes" came from upstairs.

"What, did everyone forget that it's a school day?"

"Why are you mad?" asked Dan.

She looked at Dan. "Argh, I'm sorry. I don't know, I just am. It's not you. I'm stressed."

"Is it Dad?"

She sighed. "I don't know, Dan."

"That means yes."

"Dan, no. It means I don't know."

"Can you get me juice, too?"

Henry slunk in, wet, stringy hair clinging to his emerging man's face. Emmy stared in surprise: would she ever get used to that strong chin, those all-seeing eyes, that bit of mustache? He said, "Is there any more OJ?"

"Oh, I don't know. Did you check downstairs?"

He shuffled off to the spare fridge in the basement. She knew there was probably either no OJ or just one more. She'd have to go food shopping today. And she'd just gone yesterday.

"There isn't any after this," he said tonelessly.

"I'm sorry, honey. I'll get some today. There's a lot of apple."

"No thanks," Henry said, light and polite. Emmy grimaced.

"Mom! You said you'd get me orange juice," yelled Dan.

"Orange, yes," said Nick. "Orange."

"Not 'orange'; orange *juice*!" shouted Dan.

Nick clapped his hands over his ears.

Emmy came back into the room and saw Nick covering his ears. "Dan, why is he upset? Did you do something mean?" she asked, just knowing it was Dan. *Why can't he just—?* She set down the cup with a loud bump. Henry returned with the last orange juice container in his hand. After pouring himself a cup, he slid the container across the table to Emmy.

"I don't know," Dan said, not looking at her.

"Oh, Dan!"

"Well, I only told him it wasn't just 'orange,' it was orange *juice*. He kept calling it just 'orange.' Can't he even *listen*?!"

Emmy looked at Dan, trying to take it all in. "Nick said 'orange'?"

"Yeah." Dan poured his juice to the brim of his cup.

"You don't have to take that much, you know," said Henry. "He never finishes it," he added to Emmy in disgust.

"It's okay, Henry, never mind," said Emmy quickly, wanting to grab hold of something she felt was flying away from her. "Dan, Nick said 'orange'?"

"Yeah. What's the big deal? I say it every day." He picked up his cup and spilled a third of it onto the table.

"You're not Nick, though, are you, dorkus?" asked Henry, pouring more juice for himself. They both stared at Dan's juice puddle.

"Don't call him that, Henry," Emmy said. Henry looked at her, annoyed, but she ignored him. "I think it may be a very big deal, Dan," Emmy continued, getting up for the sponge. "It means he's found something he likes and he can tell us."

Dan was looking at her intently, waiting for her to finish. He could see that she was no longer mad at him; she was happy, in fact, which was a quick mood change, even for his mother.

Why is it so good? Dan wondered, near to tears. He was always getting yelled at—because of stupid Nick. But even as he thought it, he realized how strange it was that in all this time, Nick had never told him about anything he liked. Dan didn't even know that Nick *did* like things. He felt something weird in his tummy, like the first day of school. Only not bad.

Emmy noticed Dan's curious expression, and her heart squeezed with love for him. *My poor darling, so much pain in his young life.* "It's a big deal," she repeated softly, in a whisper, and stroked his black curls, "It's good." She kissed him. "And so are you."

Dan didn't pull away from her. Her hand in his hair felt warm. He was happy and didn't really know why. He just wanted her to keep her hand in his hair, even if it was a baby thing. And she did. They all sat without saying anything for a while, except Nick, who said, "Feem, ssh, juice. Sssh, juice."

Chapter 30

"I'm really glad to meet you," Tom said, holding out his beefy hand.

"Yeah, same," said Eric, though it was only half-true. He was nervous about the guy, Emmy's guru. Grasping Tom's hand firmly, overly bright grin, he said, "Finally, right?"

They were standing in the therapy room, with floor-to-ceiling games, puzzles, books, art supplies, stacked messily on all the shelves. Instead of the customary fluorescent lighting trays that flickered with strobe-like consistency in most offices, there were sturdy stainless steel floor lamps placed at regular intervals throughout, around the perimeter of the room. Eric had heard that recessed overhead lighting was sometimes too intense for hypersensitive autistics—it had certainly been true for Nick—so he was impressed with Tom's lighting. New jade-green carpeting whispered underfoot; Eric could tell it was that expensive hypo-allergenic stuff, because he remembered way back when he'd had to help Merle buy rugs like that when she'd learned one of her girls was allergic to dust.

There were sheets of paper masking-taped up on the wall behind Tom's head, obviously done by kids, with the predominant theme being orange houses. Eric smiled graciously, trying to show Tom that he could appreciate the things kids did. God knew what Emmy had told this guy about him, so he wanted to present himself at his best.

Tom saw where Eric was looking; narrowing his eyes just the slightest bit, he said, "Nick's work." His voice dipped low, full of pride.

Eric's eyebrows shot up. "Really!" He walked over to have a closer look. Bold brushstrokes, slanted, thick lines. So much orange. "Orange," he murmured.

"Yes, he loves orange."

"Never knew that," Eric said, thinking, *Never knew Nick liked anything beyond those damned ribbons and spices.* He immediately felt ashamed at these thoughts—ashamed, too, that this stranger knew more about what interested his son than he did. His face reddened. "But I suppose . . . Emmy's told you all about me." He didn't look at Tom but continued to take in Nick's work: sheet after sheet of painstaking attempts to capture the most basic shapes: houses, stick-figure people, a cat. All in orange. It made him sad looking at the labored efforts of his fifteen-year-old son. He remembered, now, Emmy's trying to tell him about Nick's painting. She'd hung up on him after he made some stupid remark about it.

"Not really, no," Tom said. "We just talk about the boys, if we talk at all."

"All of them?" Eric turned to look at Tom, to get a read on him. Warm brown eyes met his with self-assurance, curiosity, but also kindness.

"Well, yes. Treat one kid, you kind of end up treating the whole family, you know?"

"I guess." Eric shrugged. He hadn't thought of this before and was surprised at himself for not feeling threatened by it. He'd never been in therapy himself—it seemed as if it would be embarrassing and intrusive, with uncertain results. And the idea of paying to talk to someone was beyond pathetic.

Certainly he'd never had anything like this conversation with any of Nick's former therapists. He couldn't imagine hapless Jackie, the last speech therapist they'd endured, "treating the whole family," however, and this image made him smile.

"You've got great kids," Tom was saying. "All so different. Want to sit down?" He motioned toward the chairs and the worktable.

They sat. The chairs were surprisingly comfortable, yet supportive of your back. Tom waited for Eric to begin; it was his hour, after all.

"So, what do you do with Nick for that hour? Or fifty minutes," Eric added under his breath with a smirk. He knew all about the abbreviated therapy hour from when Emmy had gone to therapy, back when Nick was first diagnosed. Eric hadn't gone, of course, but Em had told him everything, to try to bring him into it, he supposed. But the only thing that had done was make him feel more disconnected from the whole situation: Nick, therapy, autism, Emmy.

He thought now that maybe if he'd gone with her occasionally—even though Nick freaked out at times—it wouldn't have all seemed so alien and weird. The idea made him feel wistful. Maybe a little regretful. Maybe a lot regretful.

"Actually, I do go the whole hour," said Tom. "I just schedule my clients with good-size breaks in between. Works out better for everyone." Tom sat back and folded his arms behind his head, showing two yellow sweat circles in his armpits.

Eric raised an eyebrow. This guy clearly did his own laundry—and was okay with the crappy results. Eric felt himself warming to Tom. "So, what do you guys do? Besides paint?"

"These days," Tom said, "not much else!" They both laughed. "I think Nick has finally found a hobby others can relate to."

"You mean other than twiddling string?" It just slipped out. Eric grimaced and felt his face reddening.

But Tom waved a hand dismissively. "Of course, twiddling string is highly underrated in these parts. Don't knock it till you've tried it." Then he added, "Not my cup of tea, though."

Eric grinned. He suddenly felt his body soften and settle into the chair, and a sigh escaped before he knew it. "I guess . . . ," he ventured, a little at a loss. "I guess I came here to find out more about what I can do. You know, for Nick. Living apart from him, and all."

Tom thought for a while. The pause went on for so long that Eric began to think he wasn't even going to answer him. Finally, Tom said, dropping his hands down to his lap, "That's a tough one. For all of you. I guess the main thing is, don't try to do too much, but try to make it good, whatever you do. You know, you don't have to take them to the circus and museums for it to be a good thing. Think common denominators. Sometimes just sitting, guy time."

"Are we still talking about Nick?" *Guy time?*

"Yeah, but actually I think this applies to all your boys. They just need to enjoy you, don't you think? They probably miss that, in your situation."

Eric nodded. This made sense. It also made him feel better, and wistful again. "My situation, yes."

Tom shook his head, holding up his hands. "Not a judgment. Just an observation. The truth. It *is* a situation, and it can't be easy. So you've got to try to connect with them. And that's really it. Nick is probably the easiest of the three of them right now, in terms of connecting."

Eric's eyes widened in surprise. "Nick!?" He never would have put the words *Nick* and *connecting* together in the same sentence.

Tom went on, "Because you can do the painting with him and make him so happy, so easily. You'll see, when you try it. But the other two—well, especially Henry. He's at a tough age."

Eric thought, *Nick is at nearly the same age, but no one ever remembers that.* Nick was forever a little guy, or so it seemed. He leaned forward and said, "I think I see what you mean."

"Not that Nick's at an easy age, either, but, well, I'm guessing that it's a little harder to focus on Henry, because of who he is. So quiet, you know?"

"I know. I was—I am like that, too."

They talked more about all three boys. Eric was amazed at how, for a nontalker, his words just flowed out. He liked this. He felt comfortable with Tom, even though he was a stranger, because he had such an easygoing way about him. He was no wimp, not with all that beef on him, but it was more than that. He listened. He just listened—and gave Eric ideas. A lot of them. Where Eric always thought of everything involving Nick and the boys as hard, Tom made things seem possible. Natural.

Also, Eric appreciated that Tom spoke only in terms of concrete tasks. Nothing abstract, no theories. Just nuts and bolts. Arts and crafts. Rewards for trying something new. Five-minute warnings for any transition to a new activity. First-then lists.

"'First-then'?" asked Eric.

"All it is, is you say to Nick, 'First we read a book, then you can watch a video.' You make him try a new thing by enticing him with when it's over. 'Set the table and then you can have your salsa.' It gives him a sense of beginning and end, and really, structure. Structure is so much of the key to anything with Nick. And simplicity. Also, being direct." Tom laughed. "Like most guys, actually. Or so women say."

"Amen," said Eric. Tom also surprised him by talking about how Nick liked making up his work schedule, using choices stuck onto a blank schedule chart with Velcro. Again: "Nick liked this," "Nick was good at that." The Nick that Tom described seemed so opinionated, so definite. So real. It made Eric feel like trying it all out.

This was all stuff the school had tried to tell Eric about, everyone had tried to tell him, but it had always seemed so contrived. With Tom, he could believe it. It seemed real. It was small, but real. And it seemed as if maybe he could do this stuff with Nick. It helped that, right then and there, Tom gave Eric a laminated schedule board. The board had lots of Velcro-backed activity choices stuck all over it, like painting, reading, listening to music, and a copy of the list of rewards Nick responded to. He also gave Eric a few ideas about how to set things up in his apartment for painting, and talked about Nick's sensory issues, tactile and odor sensitivities, noise hyperawareness. So many things Eric had known about but had never really attended to before. But now—he had a definite task to go with his new knowledge, and that felt good.

For the first time ever, Eric felt as if he had a plan for dealing with Nick. He had a little control. This gave him a big sense of comfort—not something he was used to feeling when it came to Nick. Usually, thoughts of Nick evoked feelings of the ground opening underfoot, big black cracks that came out of nowhere. But now Eric thought, *I don't have to fix anything, or solve anything.* He would just have a few fun things to do with Nick, that was all. Could it really be so uncomplicated?

When he walked out of Tom's building, Eric was whistling Queen again, and headed right over to Pearl Paint Store in Cambridge, tapping happily to "I'm in Love with My Car" on the steering wheel as he drove.

On Saturday, Emmy woke up to a hot, sunny late May day and figured she'd mow the lawn for her exercise. Usually, she'd ask Nick to do it, but he was with Eric. Emmy liked using a push mower so that she wouldn't have to bother with gas. After an uneventful breakfast and send-off of the boys, she hauled the clumsy green mower out of the shed and started pushing listlessly. Mowing the lawn was always so boring at first, until she started to get into the Zen of it, until the paths started to show, the light-and-dark green striped pattern that formed on the lawn. Also, she loved the *click-click-click* of the blade and the sweet oniony smell of the grass as it was clipped. Sometimes she got a little wheezy, but most of the time, all she felt was a pleasant light sweat.

Webs of chamomile had sprung up across every empty space in her gardens overnight. The good thing about the chamomile was that it had tiny roots that didn't hold very tight, unlike the crabgrass, which sent solid carrot-like roots down deep within days of popping up. Emmy often wondered about the secret lives of plants. She marveled at how there could be absolutely nothing one day and then a three-inch growth of green the next. What happened? When was the exact moment that life began?

That was the question of the century, she thought, the whole debate over abortion. Since having Nick, Emmy was not nearly as staunchly okay about abortions as she'd been before. Not that she wanted to decide for others, but she wondered how many people aborted disabled babies and regretted it. Or would regret it, if they knew Nick or someone like Nick. People assumed she was more pro-choice than ever because of the autism, but actually, she was horrified to think that if there'd been a prenatal test for autism, she might have aborted Nick, never knowing him.

Some of her friends thought that now especially she would want to know, but when she was pregnant with Henry and Dan, she did not want to know anything. She just wanted everything to be all right, whatever that meant. Now she knew what it meant: happy. "If he's autistic," she told Eric with a bravery she didn't really feel, "I just want to be able to deal with it and be happy. No more suffering!"

"No more suffering. Got it," said Eric, rolling his eyes.

"Got it, baby?" Fetal Dan had kicked her hard in response. *Typical*, she thought now.

Chapter 31

Henry knew that he had a few more minutes until Mom came back with Nick from therapy. Little Thing 2 was watching *Dinotopia*, a really bizarre long movie, so he'd be okay and would leave Henry alone for a while. He deserved a short break. He'd worked all day in school, aced his math test, did okay in French, and even got out of breath in gym. Then, on to Taylor's office, to Xerox, like, a million things and staple them. Then, home to watch Thing 2. Yeah, now it was his time. He dug out a joint and lit up, with his window cracked a little bit.

He coughed and felt the slow heaviness settle on his brain, stroking his thoughts until each one stood separately like a shining, beautiful thing. He thought about Sylvie, now in the privacy of his room, and how she'd stood up in front of the class today presenting her report on a figure in twentieth-century American history. Sylvie had picked Amelia Earhart. Not too original, but he knew that Sylvie had wanted to choose a woman. Who could blame her? She'd looked luminous; he had just learned that WordMasters word. Usually, he hated spelling, but *luminous* reminded him of pearls, flower petals, ice on a lake in the cold sunshine. Sylvie.

He closed his eyes, seeing Sylvie, and dragged on the joint a bit more, until his thoughts were too muddy to consider anything clearly. He could hear the noise from the movie coming up through the floor and could practically see the dinosaurs marching in front of him.

Suddenly, his head started hurting like a hammer had come down on his skull. He stood up, clutching his forehead. As soon as his feet hit the floor, his digested lunch of peanut butter and Ritz crackers traveled upward, seizing him by the throat. Covering his mouth, but knowing it was futile, he tried to run to the bathroom. But he couldn't move his feet quickly enough; it was like they'd fallen asleep. Panicking, he reached for the desk chair to pull himself along, but the chair flipped over and he fell on his back, hitting his head on the floor. The vomit started coming out of his mouth, all over his shirt and the floor. He closed his eyes to all the pain and disgusting odor around him. Maybe he could rest for just a minute.

The joint fell from between Henry's fingers and landed next to his bedspread, which dragged on the floor. The end of the joint glowed, a tiny dot of orange, a miniscule sun setting into the hem of the bedspread. Its lumpy cloth turned slowly gray, then a shrinking black, as its heat spread across the white cotton.

The drive home from therapy had been smooth and quick. Emmy was thankful about that because she didn't like leaving Henry and Dan for too long. But they really hated going along to Nick's therapy, so she did it this once. When she walked into the house behind Nick, she yelled, "Boys! We're back." No one answered. She dropped her bag in the corner and headed toward the music coming from the playroom. She saw a small pile of black hair flopped over the side of the overstuffed armchair, and she could see the colorful creatures and costumes of *Dinotopia* on the television. Dan watched it at least once a week. "Where's Henry?" she asked.

"I don't know," Dan replied without looking at her.

Nick started sniffing deeply, as he often did when he first came into a house, puffing little inhaling-exhaling as if he were about to hyperventilate.

Emmy didn't try to stop him this time, even though the school considered this an undesirable behavior, because at least it wasn't noisy, and he never did actually hyperventilate. Dan didn't notice, either. Emmy's gaze focused on the movie for a moment, and then she decided to start dinner. Henry was in his room, no doubt listening to his music and (hopefully) reading or doing something productive.

Nick's nose was tickly with the bad smell, and it made his tummy feel tight. He did not like it. It was not a home smell, a car smell, a school smell, or a Daddy's house smell. Breathing it quickly through his nose made the tickling go away a little, but there was still a pinching feeling in his stomach. "Ssshhmelll," he whispered, trying to turn the bad-smell feeling into a quiet sound in his head. But the smell was too big for that. He tried to squeeze some air, but even that didn't work. He started to walk back and forth a lot, because sometimes fast walking stirred up the air around him like a blanket of steam. After a few circles from living room to dining room, he only felt more squeezing in his stomach. The smell was even bigger than before. "Smmmmmelll," he said again, because maybe saying the word would feel better. He widened his pacing, and walked into the kitchen. He wanted to be near Mommy, who was running the water, so he knew she'd be looking out the window and there'd be a soapy smell. Bubbles, too.

Emmy was washing her hands at the kitchen sink. The hot water felt good. She had such a strong sense of longing all of a sudden, for her boys when they were small and less complicated. When Henry was a fat, happy toddler who smiled up at her with wide eyes and called every brunette he saw "Ma!" Feeding him. Giving him a bath. Picking him up whenever she felt like it, which was very often. Baby Henry had been special to her in a secret way, something she didn't tell anyone, ever. But the way she thought of Henry, almost right away, was, he was her baby for the world. This boy, everyone was going to want and he was going to want them. This baby was easy—smiled easily, was easy to understand, easily birthed, easy to love. He had loved her back. He was the baby who had made her happy again. After all that time with Nick, not understanding, not realizing, just trying so hard, hoping, looking endlessly for certain responses, anything. Worrying while making such an effort to enjoy him, her firstborn. A beautiful baby who had come from her body but was sometimes a stranger.

Henry created a duality in how she experienced her children, a balance. Whatever Nick was not, Henry was. One looked at her, the other did not. One was fascinated with everything people did, the other was fascinated only with what was in his head. True though it was, she hated herself for feeling this way, for seeing her children only in terms of each other. Before she'd had children, she would never have dreamed of such a horrible dynamic. But that was what her life was. Or had been, way back then. At least now she knew her children as the individuals they were, and held each one separately within the soft walls of her heart.

When Henry had come along, she'd almost given up hoping for connection, though she hadn't known this at the time. But the moment he had pushed his way out of her body, she reached for him and her heart opened up again in hungry, gaping want. She had stared at his unfamiliar face, so different from Nick's, the only baby she'd ever really known as an adult. This face was wider, larger-boned. The eyes were deep-set, the chin, square. "Who are you?" she'd asked Henry out loud, laughing. He had looked at her with blurry newborn eyes as if asking her the same thing, and she'd felt like laughing more, even though her body hurt so much.

As she turned to dry her hands, she crashed right into Nick, who had no sense of socially appropriate distances and so was standing just inches behind her. "Oh! Sorry!" she said, feeling her belly knock into his sharp elbow. But whatever small pain she was experiencing, she knew that the shock of colliding was far worse for Nick. He shrieked and bit his arm, raised his other arm with his hand curved like a claw.

"Nick! NO!" she cried out, putting her arms up as a shield and bracing for the pain. Argh, it had been so long since he'd been violent at home—well, other than that episode with Dan and setting the table. "No," she said, more sad than afraid. She looked at him through his hands and saw the expanded black irises of his eyes, just as Tom had observed. She watched as they shrank back to small dots bobbing in a sea of blue.

Nick lowered his arm and looked right at her.

"Nick!" she said. "What. Is. Wrong?"

He opened his mouth but nothing came out. The screams were gone. But he wanted—something. He felt as if he were stretching, but downward, reaching into a deep part of himself, trying to find something. He'd just had it, but now it was foggy.

A word. He closed his eyes. The air settled around him. Blissful silence caressed him. And then his mouth felt soft, and it came right out. He said, "Smell."

Emmy blinked at the surprising clarity of Nick's voice. *Smell?* Without thinking, she inhaled deeply. And then she caught it: underneath the cloying fruity soap bubbles, the sweet leafy scent of smoke.

"Jesus, God!" She took the stairs almost three at a time. She threw Henry's door open, and jerked her hand back because the doorknob was hot to the touch. Smoke met her eyes, and she could just make out Henry's black hightops on the floor.

"Henry! Oh God!" She dove through the smoke to find Henry, lying by his bed, with what looked like blobs of vomit all around him. The bedspread was in flames right near Henry's head. "Henry! Henry, get up!" she cried, pulling on his arms, then dragging his legs. He stirred a little bit but couldn't move. Puffing and sweating with the smoke and the effort, Emmy continued to drag him out through the open door. *The fire. I gotta stop the fire,* she thought. She left Henry in the hallway, safely out of the way of the smoke and flames. Gasping and coughing from the effort, she stopped momentarily, feeling confused, and ran back into the bedroom to the fire. "Jesus Christ, where is it?" she heard herself yelling while she squinted, looking for the source of the flames. She realized it made her feel a little better, and stronger, to hear her loud, angry voice. "Goddamn it!" she kept yelling as she lifted the burning bedspread and dragged it to the floor. Coughing and sputtering while swearing at the top of her lungs, she grabbed Henry's pillow and threw it down on the bedspread, then the sheets, too, hoping all the weight would smother the fire.

It seemed to die down after a few seconds of being under the bedding, so she now ran to the bedroom and dialed 911, reporting a fire that seemed to be out and a boy who was breathing but unconscious.

Dropping the phone, she ran to the bathroom and threw two bath towels into the tub, turning on the water full blast. She quickly soaked the towels and ran back with the heavy, sodden mess in her arms. She spread the wet towels all over the smoking mound of bedclothes and watched, satisfied that the fire was now out.

Henry. She took a washcloth from the bathroom, soaked it with cold water, and went over to where he lay. She could hear him breathing, and she could smell the overpowering cheese-like smell of vomit emanating from him, along with the remnants of smoke. Her hands shook as she put the cloth on Henry's face and washed off some of the vomit that clung to his skin. She could see that he was, thank God, unharmed by the fire, just sooty from having been so close to it. But why was he unconscious? What had he taken?

Downstairs, Emmy could hear the sounds of *Dinotopia* finishing. Dan had no clue what had been going on upstairs. He'd almost lost their home. Maybe his brother.

She heard Nick's whisper before she saw him. "Yelling, hooom," came his voice as he emerged from his room. He was snorting, exhaling, coughing from all the smells. How long had he been there? She hadn't seen him come up. He looked down at Henry, then sniffed the air as if he were eating it. He squeezed air with both hands and kept looking at Henry. His left arm was covered with bite marks, some bloody.

"Henry is sleeping," Emmy said quietly to him, noting the tiny red indentations in Nick's skin, and pretending to be calm for his sake. Then she remembered her 911 call. "Sirens will be coming," she said. "But it's okay. Just a loud noise. Some men will come in and make sure Henry is not sick. Daddy will come, too."

She spoke as slowly as she could so that Nick would absorb it, at the same time she was trying to swallow down her mounting fear for Henry. Just then the harsh whining from the ambulance could be heard in the distance, getting louder by the second. Nick covered his ears and shrieked. Emmy braced for a tantrum, for more violence. She felt herself sinking, getting smaller, weaker, trying desperately to figure out how to head him off: how to help him while also helping Henry—and without getting hurt by him. She looked at him and felt herself almost crushed by love and fear for her sons. All she could think of to say was, "It's okay."

But Nick stopped, as if he suddenly remembered what was going on around him, and stood very still, watching Henry, hands on ears. She knew that Nick knew this wasn't right, but she didn't know what else to say to him. It *wasn't* right, after all. "Henry is okay," she said.

"No okay," Nick said. "No." He turned and started walking a circuit from Henry's room into the hallway and back.

Emmy knew he was right. It was not okay. But she had to be strong for her boys, so she had to make it okay. Forcing a smile, she took his hand gently. "Henry is okay," she said again, and firmly. "And the doctors will make sure of it." She repeated it several more times. She knew that Nick understood about doctors and had a monolithic faith in them.

Nick looked at her, his eyes showing a small flicker of awareness of what she'd said, and then he looked away. Just a twinkle, a shiny drop of dew on a blade of grass. But she knew he was okay now. Then, as if to verify this, Emmy saw his hand open and close. "Frow-up," she heard him whisper. "Hooom."

While she washed Henry's skin, she realized it had been ages since she'd touched his arms like this, seen them up close, the tight new sinew, the coarse, manly hair sprouting. She put Henry's stringy, dirty head in her lap and tried not to cry, for Nick's sake.

Nick remained at his vigil, watching them both, talking quietly with his mouth and his hands. "Feem, sssh, Mommysad, whoooom. Frow up. Smelll."

The paramedics knocked loudly.

Henry woke up in a hospital bed, but didn't know it at first. He felt strange, like he was in a different room from his own, and he wasn't at all sure how he'd gotten there. It was dark, probably past midnight. He could see a curtain surrounding half the perimeter of the bed. It was a hospital room. Why was he here? He tried to remember what had happened. The sheets felt tight, rough, and different, the way brand-new bedding feels. There was a gross chemical smell.

What had happened?

Oh yeah. He'd been getting high. He'd gotten sick again, and had passed out on the floor. Jesus Christ, but what had happened? Why was he here? He squinted in the darkness, and shapes started to emerge. He found a light. He saw machinery, metal drawers, a laundry bin, a sharps container, a sink. It was a hospital room.

Was he really sick? He patted his arms and legs. No pain there. So why was he here? What was that smell? He sniffed hard. Bacon? Barbecue?

No, it wasn't barbecue. It was old smoke.

A fire. There had been a fire. But how? Did his joint somehow cause a fire?

His head throbbed a little, and his stomach felt empty. One thing he knew: something huge had happened, because he was here. Where was Mom? What happened with his brothers? He'd never felt so scared before in his life. He lay back, eyes wide open, panic suffusing his body. Even though it was dark and very late, he knew he wouldn't fall back asleep.

There was a sharp rap at his door, and he called out, "Yes?"

His mother strode in, a her face a crumpled mess. Her eyes looked glittery, overly bright, and underneath them were deep gray shadows. She was carrying a small black, torn towel, which smelled putrid. She'd grabbed it from the house and had been holding on to it the whole time that Henry had been lying here. Now she dumped it on the floor, next to his bed. The smell hung in the air like a decaying animal carcass. Neither of them spoke. Emmy just stood there opening and closing her hands, like Nick. Tears were streaming down her haggard face. She looked old, really old.

Last night returned to Henry like a light switching on, and he suddenly understood. The joint. A fire. The towel. Mom's face— her awful, old-looking face. And he knew he really could have died.

Not knowing where to look, he glanced back down at the blackened towel on the floor. He imagined, for a moment, the heat of flames, licking at his hair, singeing the ends, reaching his scalp, his clothes. Horrible, searing, unimaginable pain, then black, nothingness.

Now he imagined what it could have been like, what might have happened if Mom hadn't— He saw his house, a pile of steaming rubble. Dan, running, panicked. Nick, fearful, not fully understanding. Maybe resisting Mom as she tried to get them to leave the house because the video wasn't completely over. He shuddered. Tears squeezed out of his eyes, which were strangely dry and tight.

And then Emmy was there sitting next to him on the bed. Henry sniffled and closed his hurting eyes, and she threw her arms around him and pulled him toward her in a rough, wrenching yank, saying, "You're okay. You're okay." He didn't know she was that strong, and he was glad she was, because he felt so tired. He laid his head in her lap as her tears spilled onto him, mixing with his and wetting his shirt. He was exhausted, lost in his sadness and his mother's soft lap, and soon, darkness. He fell into a deep sleep.

Back home, Emmy could no longer stand the silence in her

house, more intense than usual because Henry, quickly released from the hospital, was now asleep upstairs, all the way up on the third floor, in the guest room. She knew she had to call Eric, but she was so angry with herself. She hadn't dealt with anything right. She'd let it all go, and had figured that Henry was fine, with his after-school community service and a small talking-to.

But he wasn't fine. He had problems, because he lied and because he kept smoking pot! *How could I have been that stupid*, she thought, making a fist. She was furious at having missed this. *Oh my God, oh my God*, she whispered to herself, the horror of what might have been still with her, as if it had only just happened. She felt as if she were suffocating. Air wasn't getting to her lungs. She couldn't stop this rapid breathing, this gasping. She realized that if she didn't find a way to calm down, she was heading for an anxiety attack, just like her mother used to get.

But she couldn't calm down, not yet. She just kept playing it over and over in her head: What if she hadn't thought to come upstairs? What if Henry had died from whatever was in the pot, or from a concussion, the smoke, the flames? What would it have felt like to discover his lifeless, burned body? Or if she'd come home later and the fire had spread throughout the house, killing Dan, too? Her baby! Her babies.

And there was something else pressing against her heart: Nick. If it hadn't been for Nick's agitation, and that one word, *smell*, Emmy wouldn't have noticed the smoke until much later. She would have just gone into the kitchen and made dinner, oblivious. Nick had, pretty much, saved Henry's life. No, not pretty much. He *had* saved his brother's life.

This made her want to laugh and cry at the same time. Everything was bursting out of her at once, around her, beyond her control, like the way the garden did on that first really warm day, the way suddenly buds were there and opening, and weeds shot up out of nowhere. She felt crowded, hot, confused, and giddy. Nick. Oh God, Nick.

She had to do something, talk to someone, get it out of her head and process it out loud. This time, talking to herself wouldn't do. Who? Eric? But she couldn't face him again, not yet, even though he'd been so gentle and supportive with her last night. He had come right over to stay with Nick and Dan while she tended to Henry, arriving in record time, just when the ambulance did. He'd asked only the questions he'd needed to, understanding that she couldn't discuss more. He'd made sure the boys were okay, not too scared—he'd seen it for himself—and then he'd let her go to the hospital. They hadn't talked about anything; she'd simply left when Eric showed up, and then he'd gone home when she and Henry had returned from the hospital, after watching Henry crawl into the upstairs bed. There had been a moment that passed between them, however, an understanding, without recrimination. Eric had looked at her as if to say, "Are you okay?" And she'd simply nodded, and smiled weakly. They'd both understood, wordlessly, that they would talk later, when this crisis had passed, but that now, they just had to take care of things.

Eric was so different these days. What must he be thinking of this? Would he blame her for leaving Henry in charge? This worried her. But they'd had no reason to think that a fourteen-year-old couldn't take care of an eight-year-old for an hour. They'd had every reason to believe that Henry's little pot experience was over because of the run-in with the law, Mr. Taylor, and everything that had followed.

But the boy was clearly still deeply troubled. That he would resume smoking, even after that, suggested he might again, too. More than the pot itself, it was what this meant about Henry. Who was he hanging around with? Was he becoming a different kind of person than Emmy had always thought? This idea chilled her. What could she do to get him safe again? How could she get through to him, and help him?

She went over to the phone, brushing aside a note hastily scribbled when she'd been talking to the paramedics. She suddenly thought of something else, a tiny déjà vu. That other piece of paper she'd held in her hand, four months ago: the ripped scrap of paper she'd found in Henry's backpack, which had said something about meeting someone at the play structure. It had seemed a little strange then, thinking that Henry had felt the need to record a meeting with a friend. But Emmy had ignored it, chalking up her weird feeling to guilt over looking through his stuff.

Her scalp prickled. Now she knew. She just knew. That note had to be about meeting that kid for pot. She punched her leg. Why hadn't she done anything about Henry when she'd first learned of this problem? Why had she let it go with a slap on the wrist from the principal? She'd been so busy with her stupid flirtation, her idiotic problems. While she'd been in a fog, her child—her children—could have died.

She lifted Henry's backpack to her face and sniffed deeply. There, just on the very edges of the canvas smell, was the faintest hint of pot smoke. A tiny smell. She would have noticed it only if she'd been searching for it. And she hadn't.

She lay facedown on the couch. Her thoughts slowed and blurred as she pushed her face into the pillow, a comforting action she'd taken as a little girl. She lay like that until her nose became stuffy, then she turned onto her back and stared at the ceiling. She felt the pain burst in her heart, again and again, and knew this would be with her for a while.

But she also knew that she would just have to bear it, this terrible thing that had happened and her role in it. She had to. She was the mother. She had to bear it, and she also had to lead them out of it. The tears receded a little, and Emmy now felt the bright-eyed desperation of a person granted a second chance, a clarity and fervor that made her feel extremely grateful that things had turned out the way they did. She gulped the air and went into the bathroom, splashed water on her face, brushed her hair. She looked at herself in the mirror and said, "Okay. Keep going." But instead of feeling that old burdensome lethargy, she felt a small, humming energy inside, propelling her forward, even through her deep exhaustion.

Part V

June

Blooming

Chapter 32

Several days passed, with Emmy off from work while Henry rested in bed. She had figured she would work from home, finishing paperwork here and there, but it was soon apparent that all of her attention and energy were given over to Henry. He had recovered quickly; the bump on his head where he had fallen backwards had receded, and the scratchiness of his throat from the smoke had subsided. He was quiet, but not moody or withdrawn. Emmy didn't know if this peace would last but she was grateful for it. She had even suffered minimally through a visit from Lucy, who had insisted on bringing a few frozen meals and home-baked cookies.

And suddenly it was real summer. The sun beat in through the living room window, carnival bright, giving Henry a bit of a headache. Dad would be there soon. This would be the first day in nearly a week that Henry would be somewhere other than home. He was ready before his brothers, just like always. He waited by the front door with his overnight bag packed, watching his brothers come down the stairs. Sure enough, Nick did not have a bag packed. One time neither Mom nor Dad had noticed until Nick was walking up Dad's apartment steps. And then the shit hit the fan, because Nick started screaming for his bag. Henry always checked after that, because he didn't that to happen again, and he didn't want to leave it to Mom, who was always so stressed out and distracted. He was about to say something to Mom now, when suddenly she ran upstairs. "Nick, come help me pack you," she called from the upstairs hall.

As soon as Eric had retrieved the boys, Emmy felt the urge to go

outside—for the first time in days. Right now was the moment
in the garden that she waited for all year. June, the best of all
bloom times. The roses were out in abundance, some small and
tight, some open and as big as her hand, loose and sloppy, dropping layer upon layer of curly, fragrant pink petals onto the black
carpet of dirt below. In her rose garden, there was Joseph's coat,
a blazing yellow-orange-red-peach number that popped out at
her when she looked in that general direction. There was also a
fat yellow cabbage tea rose, the new squat fairy roses, and a
climbing blood-red American beauty, with stems as thick as her
thumbs and thorns like tiny hooks up and down. She cut flowers
with abandon, bunching together all colors because she could.
There were so many she couldn't even tell where she'd cut. She
bent to snip the indigo delphinium, which had come back, mi-
raculously—it was really a North Pacific plant and rarely did well
here—and the silvery-green stems of the white cerastium, which
had the lovely and accurate name of snow-in-summer. This she
had planted as a neutral background flower.

Truthfully, however, no flower could fairly be called "neutral."
They were all beautiful to her, like her children. Just some were
more obviously so than others. Everyone knew and loved a rose,
for instance—a Henry-flower, as she thought of it. Tall, strong
when it had to be, outwardly perfect, diverse enough to please
many. But not so with the delphinium. This was the Nick-flower.
It grew in mostly deep blue grapelike clusters on tall stems; stood
head and shoulders above all the other flowers in the garden; was
beautiful in a remote, untouchable, singular way. Difficult to get
any kind of result with, but when you did—it was awe inspiring.
And it was always hard to know exactly why they did well and
why they faltered.

Then there were the Dan-flowers, the very male poppies with
their hairy testicular buds, which would burst open to a vivid
orange, red, pink, or white. But they grew only in full sun, in perfectly alkaline soils, with just the right drainage, or not at all.
They needed to be watched, always. If given the proper attention, the precise mix of lime and sand and just enough water,

they would be fantastic, breathtaking. But only if.

She set her bouquets down on the black table and went to the shed for some leaf bags. A few hours of weeding in the perfect 72-degree sun sounded like a pretty good idea to her just then.

Nick, Henry, and Dan followed their father up the dark stairs, one behind the other, each caught up in his own thoughts. Their silent shuffling was magnified by the quiet building's tall ceilings and narrow hallways.

Nick was thinking the words *quiet noise*, which was what he called the echo in the halls. Of the three boys, Nick in particular did not like Daddy's house. Daddy's house was tight and pulled at him, like a Band-Aid put on wrong. He felt confused by the absence of Mommy, by the bed that was supposed to be his. He also did not like the noise. There was always a siren, and Nick hated sirens more than anything. Especially now.

Nick inhaled, looking for, but hoping he would not find, the smell in Daddy's house. It was a sweet, farty smell that made him feel sick, and it seemed to be near the stove, where they ate, so every time they ate, he felt a little sick mixed in with his food. He sniffed a lot, but it never stopped the smell from getting inside his nose and his mouth. Sometimes when he sniffed a lot, Mommy could make a smell go away. But Daddy never did.

When he first got to Daddy's house, Daddy yelled at them a lot. Nick had wanted to cover his ears whenever he saw Daddy, but he knew that would not work. He had tried that many times, and Daddy only yelled more. Today Daddy did not yell. But he did whistle the same song again and again, always stopping at precisely the same place, but sometimes getting the tune wrong. Nick had to squeeze a lot of air to forget about the wrong tune in Daddy's mouth. And Daddy did not like him to squeeze too much, but today he was letting him do it.

Nick looked down, trying to think of something else. He tried thinking about Cinderella. He thought of the song "Sing, Sweet Nightingale," which she sang as she washed the stairs of the castle. Those stairs were white, these were brown. These needed to be washed, Nick thought. "Washshshshsh," he said. *Sing, Sweet Nightingale*, he thought, and then he said, "High, high, high, high, high," which was part of the song. He wished Daddy had the videos here. But he didn't know how to make that happen.

"Who are you saying 'hi' to?" asked Dan.

"No hi," said Nick.

"You were so!"

"Dan, I think he was just thinking of something else," ventured Daddy.

"Why does he think like a weirdo?"

"Shut up," hissed Henry. "He can hear what you're saying."

"Good, then maybe he'll learn that he's a weirdo!"

"Dan," warned Daddy. Then he stopped. Well, actually, Dan had a point. He couldn't help but agree a tiny bit that he wished that Nick would learn about how he appeared to others. "Dan, you know, it's true that Nick sounds a little weird—"

Dan snapped his head up to look at Eric. Nick had his hands over his ears at the moment, so Eric finished his thought. "But we really have to be kind about how we say things to each other. I know just how you feel, though. I wish he knew how he sounded. I wish he understood that."

"Yeah," said Dan, his tone wary but curling up just around the edges in pleasure.

Eric jingled the keys in the lock and pushed open the door.

"Second home, sweet second home," he said to no one in particular.

Dan pushed his way in and flung himself on the couch. "Hey, what's that?" he asked, looking over at the wooden structure Eric had set up in the corner.

"That is an easel," said Eric, gesturing proudly toward the art corner he'd set up between the breakfast bar and the living room.

"Cool," said Henry. "What are you painting?" Wow, what was with Dad? He lowered his iPod volume.

"I'm not. Nick is."

"Nick!" both Henry and Dan said together.

"Okay, yes," said Nick. He was staring at the three big jars of orange paint on the easel's shelf. He started walking back and forth. "Orange, whooom," he whispered, not taking his eyes off the beautiful, bright paint. A large sheet of white paper hung on the easel over the paint and brushes. Nick felt like he wanted to lick the orange. He knew that if he tipped the jar and poured it out, it would move in a stream and form a puddle. He knew that it would smell a little like paste or pudding: faintly sweet and comforting. He knew how it would be slippery to his fingers—and he shuddered, trying not to imagine that—but that it would whisper on the brush.

Daddy was talking. "DoyouwanttopaintNick?"

He heard only "paint." "Yes, okay, yes," he tried, which usually made people happy.

"Come on, then," Eric said. "Let's do some painting."

"Can I paint, too?" asked Dan, who'd been watching the scene with a great deal of interest. Although all the paint was boring orange, this was something new to do at Daddy's house. But he didn't know what it would be like to do it with Nick.

Eric smiled at the blessed fickleness of his eight-year-old, who'd just finished calling his brother a weirdo. "Sure. There's actually four brushes, one for each of us." He looked over at Henry.

"No thanks," said Henry. "I'm good." But Eric noticed that he did pull out his earbuds. His face looked calm and contented, for once. Eric wouldn't push him to do this or anything, not after what he'd been through.

Eric kept trying to rig the easel so that two sheets of paper could be hung side by side, allowing both Nick and Dan to paint together, at the same time. He thought that this would take care of two things at once, kill the old two birds, so to speak: force togetherness, and avoid the ennui of turn-taking.

He got a few clothespins and large paper clips and clipped the paper at an angle to either side of the easel. The paper curled up around the clips. "Shit," he muttered. He had to make this work. He felt way too eager and excited given the nature of the task at hand.

"You said a bad word," said Dan, not looking up from his pile of LEGOs, which he had brought with him from home. He'd spilled them out on the floor near the front door and was attaching a head with spiky green hair to a little yellow body with outstretched arms and hands shaped like *C*'s.

"Sorry," said Eric. He slid paper clips to the sides of the paper to make them lie flat. Satisfied, he filled a cup with water and stuck the brushes into it. Then he unscrewed the paint jars and smelled them. "Mmm, new paint," he said. "Okay, guys. Grab a shirt and put it on as a smock."

Dan jumped up and did as Eric said. The large, wrinkled shirt flopped over his shins and his hands. He pushed the sleeves back and looked at Eric, waiting to start.

Nick remained where he was, pacing in a small pattern of three steps, turn, three steps, turn, near the bedroom door (as far away from everyone as he could be in Daddy's small house).

"Nickgrabashirt," said Daddy.

Nick looked at him, then quickly looked away. He did not know what Daddy had said to him. He started squeezing air and pacing more rapidly.

"Nick!" shouted Daddy.

Dan was impatient to begin painting. He knew that if Daddy started yelling, nothing else was going to happen, though. And Nick would just get crazier. He sighed. "He doesn't even know what you meant," he said, but not unkindly, and his mellow tone surprised Henry so much that he looked up at Dan. Dan wasn't looking at anyone, just fiddling with the overly long hem of the shirt. "You said it too fast for him," he said, motioning with his head to Nick. He noticed how Nick had stopped pacing and was staring again at the paint. "That's paint, not food, you know," Dan said.

"Paint, yes, paint."

"Yeah."

"Yes, paint, paint. Yes."

"You don't have to keep saying it." Dan narrowed his eyes at

Nick, but didn't say any more, because he knew it would make Daddy yell.

Nick smiled just a wisp because no one yelled. Then he looked away, back to the paint. "Orange, hooooom," he mouthed, not wanting anyone to hear him.

But Dan did. He blinked, stunned. He looked as if he'd been slapped. His eyebrows went up like clouds rising away. And he grinned. "Hey, Dad," he said slowly. "Hey, you know what? I think Nick is saying 'paint' because he *wants to paint!*" Dan announced, proud of his discovery.

Though this had been obvious to Eric and Henry, neither of them dared say anything, for fear of shattering the tiny bubble of camaraderie that seemed to have formed around Nick and Dan. They were all completely quiet for a moment, even Nick.

Henry looked at Dan's small body, dwarfed even further by Dad's big shirt, his head bent so that the soft, pale skin of his neck was showing, and his throat tightened up. "Dan's right, Dad," he said softly. Dan shot him a look, thinking Henry might be up to something, but then he saw that he wasn't.

Nick was squeezing air and whispering, "Sing, Sweet Nightingale."

Dan's words echoed in Eric's head. "*Nick wants to paint!*" Clarifying for his brother! He looked from one boy to the other, his children, so different from one another, so difficult in their own ways. But right now, united. How did they know so well what was what here, and he, the dad, was so clueless? Sighing, he felt like crying, and then laughing, all at once. *Okay, Big Ego,* he thought, which is what Emmy used to call him teasingly. *Get over it!*

"Dan, you're right," he said, picking up a shirt. "You know what else? Nick would never wear this in a million years, because it has labels in it!" He walked over to the kitchen drawer that had all the junk in it, pulled out the shears, and snipped out the label with a flourish. "Now it's Nick-friendly." He smiled and handed it to Nick.

"Put this on to stay clean when you paint, Nick," Eric said

slowly.

Nick took the shirt. He smiled a radiant tiny smile again and turned his head away, tucking his cheek into his shoulder. "Okay, yes."

Chapter 33

Emmy opened her e-mail and was startled to see a message from Will. She wanted to delete it unread, but she was curious.

The e-mail was terse: "I can see that my friendship is not welcome. Just wanted to say I know that. Too bad for us both. — W"

"Jesus!" Emmy shouted.

"Mom, you said a bad word," Dan hollered from the kitchen.

"Why aren't you upstairs?" Emmy yelled, walking in. Dan was wearing his pajamas but was sitting in front of an open container of peanut butter, a gloppy knife, a nearly empty jar of jelly lying on its side, and three slices of bread. "Didn't you eat dinner?"

"It was that stupid junk that Dad makes," Dan said, licking his fingers.

"What stupid junk?" Emmy started gathering up the bread bag and retwisting the tie. There were crumbs spread out over the entire seven-foot counter ending with a river of jelly that trickled out of the empty jar. She looked for the sponge, sniffed it, and started wiping up with it.

"You know, with meat. He gave us corn chips like that's gonna make it better."

"What is it, chili?" Since when did Eric make chili? Wasn't he a vegetarian? That sure didn't last long!

"Yeah, that's what he says, but I had chili in school, and it was way better. This tasted like poop."

"Dan, come on, you don't know what poop tastes like! Do you?"

"Ew, Mom!" Dan burst out laughing.

It was so nice to hear him laugh. She realized that it had been some time since she could recall him laughing at something she said. She felt a ping in her stomach, remembering that she'd just thought the same thing about Henry. She poked Dan under his arm and said, "Eat that bread and go to bed." Emmy put the jar away and slid the knife into the dishwasher.

"A poem, Mom!" They grinned at each other. He had jelly and crumbs on his cheeks. After chewing in silence, he said, "Mom?"

"Mmm?"

"Why can't Daddy live here?"

Emmy stopped, bent in front of the dishwasher. "Oh, Dan, I don't know."

"You don't?"

"No, I mean, I do know. I mean, it's complicated."

"But aren't you guys married?"

Emmy smiled a tiny bit and clicked the smelly dishwasher shut. "Yeah, we are. But we were fighting too much, and that's not good for kids to grow up around."

Dan was quiet for a moment, chewing. Then he said, "Yeah, but now it's like we don't really have a family."

Emmy frowned and put her arm around him. "Dan, you do have a family. Your dad just doesn't live *here*, that's all." She knew it was a weak distinction, too subtle for an eight-year-old like Dan.

He turned his body just a little bit away, shrugging off her arm. She moved over to the sink to get him a paper towel.

"Daddy let us stay up late and paint this time."

Emmy turned around quickly. "Really?"

"Yeah." Dan brushed his curls out of his eyes. Then he wiped his cheeks with his sleeve, pink smears decorating the light gray fabric. "He made this cool easel thing, and me and Nick could paint at the same time."

"Me and Nick" had just rolled off Dan's tongue, as if he'd talked about doing things with his older brother all his life. "You and Nick . . . ," she repeated, but the words caught in her throat. Her nose and eyes quivered, as if she'd just mowed the lawn. She looked away from Dan, not wanting to overwhelm him with her tears.

"Yes, Maternal Unit," he said in a staccato robot voice. "It.

Was. Cool." He started to walk toward the stairs with his arms flat against his sides, beeping like a robot.

Emmy wiped her eyes and headed after him. "Well, what did he paint?"

Dan shrugged stiffly, still in robot mode. "I. Don't. Know."

"Dan, come on. Talk to me."

He rolled his eyes. "Stupid stuff. Houses that looked like a baby's drawings. Well . . ."

"Well, what?"

"Nothing. It. Was. Okay." This last bit he said in his robot voice again. Then he darted from the room, whirring and clicking.

Emmy sighed. Son of a gun, as her mother would say. That Eric. She smiled, warmth spreading inside. She wanted to do something, talk to someone. What could she do now? There was no one. Well, obviously there was Eric. She could talk to Eric about what he'd done. But—that was so complicated. Why did it have to be so complicated?!

She sank down on the white couch to think. Her eye was caught by an old juice stain Henry had made long ago, which never quite got Shouted out. It always reminded her of an embryo. She traced its fetus shape with her finger.

Eric. Always Eric, she thought. *Even when he leaves, he doesn't really go away!* And just now, she suddenly realized that was true. He hadn't actually left her at all, or at least, he had kind of come back. She'd had never thought about it that way, and her elation stunned her, left her feeling light and giddy. He hadn't truly abandoned her. She was just so glad to know this.

And she also knew that Eric was the only one who would truly understand how she was feeling right now, so incredibly happy about the boys, the painting, that she was grinning like Goofy— and he would probably make fun of her.

She even missed that! She was so sick and tired of this arrangement, her living situation. Always just her and the boys, no one to help her, except when Eric took them away on the weekends, and then she was merely alone, which wasn't good, either.

She sank down into the white couch, reveling in its simple, soft comfort.

She was so worn out. She just wanted another adult to take over. "Blah," she said out loud, practically tasting her disgust with herself. Where had she gone wrong? How was it that Eric—whom she now liked again—wasn't here anymore? Well, she knew *how* it had happened, but why? Really, why?

Carelessness. Not taking care of each other. So things had gotten irrevocably bad between them? Forget about the way he'd left. Now she wondered, how had *she* let him go—or, really, kicked him out? How could she have been so unseeing—not only of how much the boys needed Eric but also of how she really felt about him and needed him, too?

Why had she been so careless with him? She felt a huge pressure building up, like a fist to her chest. She burst out in convulsive, little-girl sobs.

"I can't think about that now," she said out loud, in her best Scarlett, adding with a sad laugh, "I'll think of some way to get him back." Get him back? Was that what she wanted? Why? Because of how he'd been so great after the fire? Because of the painting? Dan? Loneliness?

If she were to be totally honest with herself—she sighed hard, flaring her nostrils—it was the whole *Eric* gestalt. His shapes addiction, the stupid jokes, the lack of fashion sense, the sloppiness. The way he knew her like no one else. The way he still took care of her, even when he was so pissed at her. The way he'd tried with the boys the other night. He'd even gone to see Tom. She felt a sweet rush of happiness thinking about it all.

There was no way to know what to do. The whole thing could happen all over again, all the fighting. They could backslide into their old patterns, of Eric demanding more and more of her and at the same time withdrawing from the demands of the kids. All those self-absorbed demands he made on her, to choose him over the kids, his unwillingness to help with Nick. She hated that so much about him. It was so . . . needy. Unattractive. Weak.

Argh, she thought. That is so unfair of me. He's allowed to

have needs! And flaws! God knows I'm not perfect.

She pictured them all painting in his apartment, a tall easel squeezed in among Eric's tables and books. She thought of their endless trips to the science museum, Eric's enthusiasm over *Star Wars* a perfect match for Henry's. She pictured his longer hair, his new confidence. Oh, could she really trust this? Would it be okay if she let him in again? It was all so messy, and she hated mess. But then she looked around the living room, at the boys' shoes clumped here and there, their mouths gaping open like carp. Every table had a gray sheen of dust on it. Mail was still piled near the television, unsorted. A note from Merle sat on top, unopened. Merle was clearly concerned about having heard nothing from Emmy in months, not since their dinner together. She'd also left a phone message last month.

"I could call Merle," she said out loud. Smiling, she imagined Merle's animated voice. But then she tried to imagine telling Merle about how she'd been right all along. That Emmy had done the wrong thing, kicking Eric out. No, she just didn't have the energy for that conversation right now. Soon, though.

But Emmy felt very heavy, and so tired. She noticed that one of the kids had drawn a face in the dust on the telephone table. *Wash me*, it read, in Dan's careful, circular handwriting. "I may hate mess, but I'm sure as hell swimming in it these days," she said out loud, standing up. She wasn't going to call anyone. Too complicated. Instead, she dragged herself up the dark stairs. At the top she noticed a white sheet of light projecting down the stairs of the third floor, from the attic room where Henry had been sleeping since the fire. Since his door was open, Emmy decided to go up and check on him—she couldn't get enough of that these days.

"Hi," she said. Henry was sitting up in bed reading, a phone beside him.

"Been talking to people?"

"A little."

"Mind telling me who?"

"Uh—Sylvie?"

"You like her, huh?"

"She's all right. She had a question about the English."

"Day No Pigs Would Die?"

"Yep."

"She seemed like a sweet girl, the other day, when she called."

Henry looked down. "She is. She has a brother like Nick."

"Really? She told you that?"

"Yeah, but he's little."

"Still. Must be . . . nice to have that in common?" *Poor baby*, she thought, wanting to go over and take Henry in her arms. She took one step closer but felt that she shouldn't. He was so heavily shielded against emotions these days. So alone, too. She hoped that this Sylvie would help somehow.

"Yeah." Henry yawned. "She's kind of sad about it. I told her that it's okay. You know, Nick is just kind of quiet, that's all. It's no big deal."

Only then did Emmy notice three wadded-up tissues at Henry's feet. "Yeah, I know," she said, and bent over to kiss his head, then backed quickly out of the room, swallowing down tears. "Good night, darling. Don't stay up too much longer."

Emmy lay down on her bed, breathing in the baby-sweet detergent smell of the white pillowcase, and was asleep in moments.

Chapter 34

Emmy'd had a long week, buried in work and her boys and nothing else. All she wanted was to hole up with them and make sure nothing else bad happened.

She remembered she had to call Eric and remind him that they had to get Henry a therapist. She wasn't going to let it go. Her fingers flew over the phone buttons.

Of course he was home. Where else would he be? He was, and had always been, passionate about one thing: his work. Except when she'd come into his life, and then he'd been passionate about two things. How could she not have clung to that? The longing was a heavy hand, pressing on her heart. She was so vulnerable right now; maybe this had been the wrong time to call Eric.

"Hey, Em." His voice was friendly, which encouraged her.

She decided to forge ahead and get him to help with her plan for Henry. "Eric, we need to talk; you have a min—"

"How is he?" Eric interrupted.

She realized that "How is he?" was now going to start all their conversations. Used to be that "How is he?" would always imply Nick. In some strange way, this new focus on Henry, prompted by near tragedy, was actually a good thing. "Oh, he's okay. Reading in bed."

"Okay, what, then?" He sounded a little wary.

Emmy exhaled sharply, and then, instead of talking about Henry and therapy, she found herself telling Eric everything that was on her mind—things she didn't even know she'd been thinking about. She lay down as she spoke. She just talked and talked into the phone while it became sweaty in her hand, sometimes not even sure if Eric was still there because of how quiet he was. She told him about how she was always so lonely. She even brought up Will—how giving Will a second thought had been a stupid mistake. But she also wanted Eric to know that the thing with Will had brought her back to life—to wanting happiness again.

She also told him how she felt not just lonely, but alone—so alone. And it never stopped, the feeling that she was in this all by herself, as if she were the only adult around for miles, and was barely enjoying her life at all.

Except when she was out in the garden: that was the only fun she had. Emmy then told Eric about Gardens of Eden, and how she could even imagine a little van and her business cards, cream-colored with sage-green letters and an abstractly drawn delphinium, rose, and poppy. Nick, Henry, Dan. Her three boys. She went on and on about the gardens in her neighborhood, which needed help, the neighbors who always asked her questions, like how she'd gotten that wisteria to grow like that, could she help them with choices for their planters, that kind of thing.

Her words spilled out. She closed her eyes to all the ugliness of the last weeks and just imagined the Gardens of Eden van filled with hydrangea bushes, clematis, ivy. Drawing tiny gardens in small, dark city yards. Calling forth color and sweet scent where everyone else had given up long ago. This was the kind of challenge she loved. She'd learned that about herself by raising Nick.

She stopped all of a sudden. Eric gave a low whistle and said, "Sounds like a plan."

"What?"

"I think you should do it. Gardens of Eden. Good name." Up until this moment, he hadn't really thought about her business proposition except as something frivolous she used to fantasize about when she was having a bad day in the real estate world. It had all seemed vain, sure to fail. But listening to her voice just now, so vulnerable and yet so strong and full of knowledge and passion—a passion that, he could see now, was a lot like his own love of shapes and math—he could not honestly say she shouldn't try.

And the more he thought about it, the more he could envision it. After all, the house was paid for; they had enough money to support two households, in fact. It might actually be a *good* time to start a new venture. It wasn't something he would do, but then again, they were so different. She was—well, she was brave. Braver than he was. She was always the one who'd ended up taking Nick to the tough things, like Special Olympics, speech therapy, and the supermarket or to wait in line with her to pick up medicine at the pharmacy.

But now that he'd had his own successes, or whatever they were, with Nick—surviving the *Star Wars* debacle at the Science Museum, the painting together—he could better understand how it felt for Emmy to venture out there and try something with Nick, and have it work out. How fantastic it felt, as if now he could do anything. Maybe that's how she felt. And if she felt that way, she should definitely try her own business. In fact, he could suddenly imagine the little van and the business cards.

In the odd silence on the other end of the phone line, Emmy waited with trepidation for the other shoe to drop. That always happened with Eric, through either a joke or a jab, and she would slam the phone down. She couldn't handle that, though, not now.

But nothing happened. He'd sounded as if he meant it: her own business was a *good* idea. He wasn't telling her how ridiculous it would be to leave real estate now, during a boom time for Boston. He wasn't interrupting her with questions about her weaknesses and areas of limited expertise in running a business. He wasn't telling her that she couldn't depend on him if she hit any snags, or reminding her that they lived apart and were practically divorced, and that she had sent him there, blah, blah, blah.

Even though Eric had been so kind lately, it still surprised her every time. She realized she'd been waiting for Eric to interrupt with something silly or worse, to point out in his most rational tone of voice—the one Emmy hated—that she was hardly in a position to start a new business now, especially as a single mother.

How she hated being a "single mother"! It conjured up images of poor, beleaguered souls running around in housecoats, asking everyone for understanding and favors, with messy babies clinging to them, their diapers in desperate need of changing.

Her words caught at her throat and came out sounding hoarse. "I don't know why I'm talking about this right now." And then she started to cry. Without Eric pushing back on her with his skepticism, she felt something disintegrate inside her, but it felt nice, a hard, lumpy burden softening. Her whole heart felt fluid, like river water breaking through ice in March.

To her surprise and delight, he said, "I'll be right over."

An hour later, Eric was sitting with Emmy on the couch—the couch that they'd picked out together five years ago. Nick's favorite spot in the whole house. Emmy had a soft pink cashmere afghan wrapped around her, and Eric was rubbing her shoulders.

They were talking about the fire again. She was bleary eyed from crying and wiping her eyes with paper towels. She never remembered to stock tissues downstairs.

"The point is, everyone's okay," Eric was saying. "You did a great job. You rescued Henry. You kept the others safe. You put out the fire with very little damage. You didn't panic. I don't know how many other people could do all that so well."

Emmy shrugged. "I fucked up and you know it."

"We both fucked up. I'm his parent, too, right?"

"Eric, we should have gotten him help as soon as he was busted by Ben Taylor. As soon as he cheated, really. Jeez, all I could see was my own misery. And—well, Nick."

Eric could see she was about to start crying again. Her nose was already looking fat and pink. He laid a hand on her arm. "That's really all either of us has been seeing for a long time."

"Well, we've got to do better than that! We're parents. We're responsible."

Eric gritted his teeth. There she was again, with that martyr crap. He sensed the raw rub of this old annoyance grating at him and felt himself withdrawing, his habitual response.

But no. He shut his eyes, and tried to clear his head. Focus, he told himself. Stay with it, even if it feels shitty. Otherwise, you'll be back on Mass Ave. by yourself going to the Science Museum every other Saturday, eating nothing but bad chili.

"Yeah, we're parents. We're also just people. And we happen to be dealing with a shitload of stuff."

"That's just an excuse." She glared at him, daring him to fight back.

"No," Eric said softly, even though he wanted to scream at her to shut up. He tried something really different. He stroked her hair and said, "Shh." Her eyes went wide in surprise. She looked like a little girl for a moment. He felt a charge go through him, telling him this was the right approach. "It's the truth," he went on, "and all you can do is learn from what happened and try to do better from now on."

She knit her brows together, as if she were trying hard to concentrate on what he was saying.

He continued, while she was still quiet. "Come on, how long are you going to beat yourself up? Yes, we should have gotten him help sooner. We're going to get him help now, right? It's not too late."

She nodded, and snorted back her mucus.

"Nice," he said.

She gave him a tiny smile that pierced his heart. *That* was his girl. Even now, with the smell of stale smoke still lingering in the air and her puffy pink face, he wanted to hold her so badly it was all he could do to keep from wrapping his arms around her and begging her then and there to take him back.

"Ha!" she said, out of the blue.

"'Ha?'" he asked in a puzzled voice.

She rooted around in her pocket and pulled out Sally's phone number. "Actually, I think I've got someone already. A therapist, I mean. Someone Tom knows. As a matter of fact, I know her, too. She's a nice lady. I sold her a house."

"Good," Eric said, biting back a joke. "That's what we'll do. We'll call her in the morning."

Emmy liked the *we*.

Eric stretched and looked at his watch. "It's been a long day. I'm just going to run up there and say goodnight, okay?"

"Sure, I'll come, too." They went upstairs together.

Eric tiptoed into Dan's room first.

"Watch out for all the LEGOs." Emmy whispered.

"You think I don't know?"

They stepped carefully through the center of Dan's room, following a path of bare floor surrounded on both sides by LEGOs, both loose and pressed into creations. There was a clatter as Eric kicked a wayward robot dog by accident, but Dan didn't stir. "Oops," he whispered sheepishly.

"LEGO happens," Emmy said, shrugging and smiling.

They looked down at him asleep, his small ivory face perfectly still, his stuffed robot staring blankly at them from the pillow. Eric bent to kiss him. "Don't tell," he said, smiling.

Emmy kissed Dan, too, breathing him in, noting that his breath was still sweet. *Still kind of a baby*, she thought.

Emmy and Eric walked past Henry's room. Henry was not in there, of course. Emmy figured they would probably make the attic into his room permanently, so that he'd have a lot of space to himself, and fix it up however he wanted to—as the teenager he was. Eric sniffed the air and flared his nostrils. "Wow, that smoke smell is intense," he said.

Emmy started crying again.

"He's going to be okay now," Eric whispered, putting his arm around her shoulders. "Let's go see him."

They took the stairs to the attic, and were a little surprised to find it dark up there. Listening carefully on the landing, they could hear the low tide-like murmur of Henry's breathing. Emmy sighed. *It really is okay*, she thought. But she knew it would be a while before she truly believed it.

"I guess."

Eric grabbed Emmy's hand. "You done good, Emmy."

They walked back down to the second floor. The landing window was open, the sky was indigo, and Emmy could feel summer in the sensuous heaviness of the air from outside. Nick's room was a few steps away from them.

They poked their heads inside. "Yes, okay," said Nick, still awake.

"Hey, Nickster," said Eric, walking in.

"Hi, DaddyMommy." This was what Nick had always called them when they were still living together. Emmy hadn't heard it in a while, and its sweet oddness filled her with a sharp longing that she couldn't quite explain, but it made her reach out and take Eric's hand.

"Sleep well, darling," Emmy said.

"Yes, okay DaddyMommy okay."

Nick could smell DaddyMommy in the air after they left. He felt water in his eyes now, and did not understand why, because his tummy did not hurt. He felt bubbles tickling his throat and he smiled, eager for the laughing noise. Mommy did not like his laughing noise at night, but up came the bubbles anyway.

"Good *night*, Nick," came Mommy's voice through the floor, but it did not hurt his ears because it was softened by being far away. Nick could hear the low rumble of Daddy's voice, and Mommy's higher noises.

"Feeem," he whispered. "Ssssh. DaddyMommy ssssh."

Acknowledgements

I want to thank my agent Barbara Moulton for working so hard to sell this book and for doing some very high-level editing, and for believing in this book so ardently. I'd also like to thank my other agent Diane Gedymin for sticking by me since the day we met, years ago, at the W Hotel in New York, for being an agent even when she was no longer an agent, and for being a friend always. Thanks also to my editor Eden Steinberg for being supportive of my book ideas, and editor Beth Frankl for reading *Dirt* "for fun" and liking it. Thanks to Susan Rothstein, friend and real estate guru. Thanks to Susan Cohan for a terrific job copyediting, and to Ame Mahler Beanland for her gorgeous cover design. Thanks to my friends who were readers for me: Claire LaZebnik, Emily Miles Terry, Kim Stagliano, Nancy Bea Miller, Ed Plunkett, my cousin Jessica Kogut, my parents Mel and Shelly Senator, my sister Laura Senator.

Finally, gratitude and love to my dear sons for inspiring the characters and the story, for putting up with me while I wrote it, and for letting me use their voices to animate Nick, Henry, and Dan. And of course thank you to Ned for talking me through it, letting me read various parts to him, formatting, researching, critiquing the book. And above all, for loving me and telling me that yes, I am still a writer.

About the Author

Susan Senator lives in Massachusetts with her husband and whichever of her three sons are around at the moment. She teaches English at Suffolk University in Boston, and is a freelance journalist for many newspapers and magazines.